The Born Again

The
Born
Again

by John Mullins

T

Troubador Publishing Ltd
Unit E2 Airfield Business Park,
Harrison Road, Market Harborough,
Leicestershire LE16 7UL
Tel: 0116 279 2299
Email: books@troubador.co.uk
Web: www.troubador.co.uk

ISBN 978-1-80514-486-1

British Library Cataloguing in Publication Data.
A catalogue record for this book is available from the British Library.

Printed by Printed and bound in Great Britain by 4edge Limited
Typeset in 11pt Minion Pro by Troubador Publishing Ltd, Leicester, UK

This book is dedicated to *The Prison Phoenix Trust* (UK) who teach life-enhancing yoga and meditation in UK prisons, and who, against impossible odds, redeem broken and hopeless lives.

Contents

Part Two

Part Three: Goodbye

Part Four: The Gift

Prologue

- - - - - - - - - - -

The "Completely Destroyed"

Those were the words of the family of Zara Aleena, a bright, vibrant law graduate who planned to become a solicitor. While walking home from a night out on 26th June, 2022 she was randomly raped and brutally murdered. Forever "stuck in a nightmare," that's what her family said, feeling "constantly tormented" by thoughts of how she died. "We will never have peace", despite Zara's killer, Jordan McSweeney aged 29, being jailed for a life sentence of 38 years. One day, aged 67, he will probably get out.

Justice? McSweeney appealed his life sentence. On 3rd November 2023 his sentence was reduced to 33 years, out when he is 63. See what I mean?

An aunt who described themselves as a 'tight knit family', said "We feel stuck in time, we feel lost, we find it difficult to connect with each other. When a human is murdered, a family is murdered. And when a family is murdered, humanity is murdered. Everything she was, everything she worked so hard for, every dream was destroyed by someone she didn't even know. We feel we can't be hurt anymore – the very worst has happened, nothing more can happen to us."

The court was told by his barrister that McSweeney's life as a child was "far from ideal." Domestic violence was "the norm." His mother was a drug addict, a "very spiteful, vindictive and horribly poisonous person," his defence barrister pleaded. McSweeney's first memory of his father was of him "attempting to drown his mother in the bath." He was taken into care, expelled from school and began drug dealing and "bare knuckle fighting for money," the court was told. The final defence: "He was deprived of love."

Aren't we all to some extent? Most of us not as cruelly as him, thankfully. In court, on the scales of justice 'deprivation of love' carried no weight. But what about the prison sentence that followed?

Zara's family have been tormented by the 'what-ifs', the painful sense that her death was preventable had it not been for a series of devastating state failings. McSweeney had 28 convictions for 69 separate previous offences, including assaults on police and the public. He had a documented history of domestic violence against ex-partners. McSweeney had served nine prison sentences and notched up more than 100 incidents in prison, including violent and threatening behaviour towards prison guards and misogynistic language against female staff.

Yet despite all this, when he was released on probation in June 2022, his risk level was classified as "medium", because his offences and behaviour in prison and wider criminal history were looked at "in isolation" by the inexperienced and overworked Probation staff who had been quietly privatised by the Tory government. Nine days after his release, he raped and murdered Zara.

It begs the obvious question – what's going on inside our prisons? To most of the public, prisons are out of sight, out of mind. But we should take a greater interest. When a rapist is released on parole, the impact upon his victim(s) is haunting, reliving her original experience. Will he try to find me because I gave evidence in court that got him put away? Once a rapist, always a rapist? Does 'good behaviour' in prison translate into 'good behaviour' after release? Reoffending is chronic. On the taxpayers' level of 'value for money', prisons are grossly ineffective, if not a breeding ground for further crime. For some crimes, should they ever be let out at all?

* * *

And then there was David Carrick, the police serial rapist over two decades who started out as a mere "flasher." What schoolgirl or woman hasn't been flashed at? Giggled off by the girls themselves in their immediate shock, then pooh-poohed by their parents and boyfriends, "Well that's men for you, what can you expect?" Even by the police when it is rarely reported, and rarely traceable. So-called low level "flashing' leaves behind its private haunting. Exposing his penis, what will he do next? She doesn't know. How can I get away from him off the tube or in a public park? Will he follow me home? Is he going to rape me? Many schoolgirls, too young to even know what rape is, just run and hide in their bedroom, saying nothing about what they don't fully understand or have the proper words for. Flashing can escalate to rape and murder.

For 49 brutal and humiliating offences Carrick received 38 'life sentences.' Where was the bloody justice in a single life sentence, let alone in thirty-eight? What does a life sentence really mean? What does any court sentence mean? Prisoners routinely serve only half their sentence.

* * *

Although this book is purely fictional, it attempts to reach out to a reality that is incomprehensible to the victims' families. They carry their hidden world of inconsolable pain, numbed to the soul, as they walk along our high streets and we walk past them unknowing. They are like traumatised refugees who speak a foreign language and live a foreign silence. I don't even dare to use the F-word – forgiveness – because that's not what this story is about.

It's about something else, beyond the chance encounter that has condemned them as perpetrator and victim, locked inside the same prison cell together.

This story is about trying to find that "something else."

Part One

- - - - - - - - - - - - - -

"The mind is its own place, and in itself
Can make a Heav'n of Hell, a Hell of Heav'n."

Paradise Lost, by John Milton (1608 – 1674)

One

When Life Means Life

Little did I know on that first day in court for multiple murder where I would eventually end up. Prison, of course. A life sentence, I expected that too. I wasn't dumb. But this? This was something else!

In court my lawyer's first line of defence was the standard tactic. You know, trawling through my abused history and traumas, and then my chaotic teenage run-ins with the police which later escalated to domestic violence and further cruelties. It was the same old story told in countless courts to mitigate my blame and responsibility. "He didn't stand a chance in life," my lawyer pleaded. Yawn, went the judge, and frowns furrowed across the faces of the jury. But his second line of defence, I thought, was pretty slick. My violent and cruel social behaviour was all down to bad genes, some kind of chemical and neurological imbalance, which basically, made me blameless. Like when a kid gets born with some genetic disorder, or cancer. I was simply born with a mental cancer. It wasn't my fault.

Medical experts testified in my defence. Bad genes plus childhood abuse and trauma equals... Well, you get the picture. "He didn't stand a chance in life."

Neither did my victims.

* * *

"What's the worst thing you have ever done in your life?" That's what the prison shrink asked me on the first day of my Life Sentence. That was a long time ago, when I was still full of hatred, rage, blame and bitterness. What you are reading now is what the prison calls, an "exit story" – my last thoughts before there is nothing left of me. I'm told it is very rare for a lifer to get to this stage of telling his full exit story.

The shrink spoke from a video-link screen on the wall across a table in a dull little room where I sat strapped to a chair that was bolted to the floor. The usual stuff, in case I threw my chair at the screen. His face and body were darkened for anonymity. Humph, a real tough guy, I thought.

"You know already. Why I'm in here."

"No," he shook his head. "No, these are only the ones that we know about. Not the others."

I laughed at what I imagined to be his know-it-all face in the shadows, too scared to face me in the same room. "What's the worst thing *you've* ever done in *your life*?" I challenged him, smiling to myself as I thought of Mr. Do-Good, Mr. High and Mighty, his worst thing? Secretly hated his parents? Bully and torment his little brother to the point he needed to see a shrink? Some asshole just like him? In high school, rape a girl when it wasn't called 'rape'? Just boys will be boys? Backstab his colleagues to get a promotion?

His voice remained professionally impassive. "This isn't about me, it's about you."

I had heard it all before. He knew the patter. So did I. "See?" I smirked. "You can't answer your own question, can you? Let alone *dare* to tell a psychopath how human you are." I kept grinning, "Your secret will be safe with me. I'm not going anywhere."

He chuckled, "Human? The likes of you?"

I snorted a laugh, "Human? The likes of you? I'll show you mine if you show me yours."

"No need," he said with a hint of arrogance. "This will be the last time you will see me. In supermax we don't play around with psycho-babble anymore. It's all science now, chemical injections, remote neurological implants, electrodes, the mind-monitor, biofeedback, etc."

He noted my surprise.

"Talking therapy is dead here. Like your victims. You didn't give a damn about their lives, and you never will, so why should we? Victims mean nothing to us. There's no point in getting you to talk about them and fake your remorse with us. No, we do things differently here. It's the reverse of the old 'victim awareness' stuff. It starts with *you*, not them."

He paused to let that sink in. "Not by talking about yourself. Mere words, all bullshit. But with science and the latest technology, you will be given the chance – and the *choice*," he emphasised, "to see what it means *when life really means life*."

On the screen his shadow figure leaned forward from a chair, "*To be alive,*" he half whispered.

He had lost me.

"We call this treatment, *The Born Again.*"

I listened dumbly. His voice seemed to inflect with amusement. "How shall I put it? The Born Again is all about you finding the will to keep on living – with the worst things you have even done in life – or give up and die. You'll see what I mean. A lot of inmates in supermax don't survive The Born Again. Either suicide or they go mad. It's up to you."

Taken aback, I wasn't expecting any of this. I didn't understand what he meant, all this science shit and keep yourself alive? I knew that in prison the worst of the worst got hell from the other inmates, the guards letting rough justice take its course. Is that what he meant by "find the will to keep on living"?

Punishment, I thought. What's it for? Justice? To make someone suffer for doing something bad? To lock them up in their suffering, to make it so painful they will never do it again? Is that how we learn to be good?

The shadow shrink leaned back in his chair, noting my confusion. "That's why my first and final question to you is – What's the worst thing you have ever done in your life? Until you can face that, and find the will to live with that..." His voice trailed away. He left the screen, like a ghost.

Into the room wheeled an automated, mini-forklift made of stainless steel. From its fork ends, two mechanical claws suddenly protruded and delicately untied me, then they retracted into the forks, liquid steel that could change shape. It narrowed its forks for me to sit on face forward. Warehoused for life, I thought. Then the fork ends bent up and a metal rod flowed across to join them, a handle which I could hold as it transported me along a series of long white corridors. No sight or sound of the traditional prison blocks tiered with barred cells. Wherever this was, supermax, it didn't look like a prison at all. I smirked to myself. I bet the shrink gets a kick out of his science toys. Well, let him throw all his science shit at me. I'm tough, I can take it. As the robotic forklift hummed along, the corridors vaguely reminded me of empty test tubes, awaiting a specimen, to solitary confinement.

Ahead of us, as the secure door automatically opened, all I could think of, bizarrely, was that the psychiatrist had never asked me, "What's the best thing you have ever done in your life?"

Two

Life's Too Short

Supermax. Where is it? No one really knows. Who runs it? It's rumoured they are called 'The Project', a clique of retired judges who became frustrated by the injustice of traditional life sentences which have a fixed 'minimum term' set by the trial judge. In the UK the average life sentence which a prisoner serves is around 15 to 20 years before eligible for parole. Murderers, paedophiles, rapists, kidnappers, torturers. Eventually most get out. It's only a matter of time. But their victims cannot be brought back from the dead, or from psychic mutilation. Their families endure a Life Sentence of suffering from which there is no prison release, haunted for decades after the crime, usually into the next generation and after. Poor lass, poor lad, in the wrong place at the wrong time when they met the monster of Evil with eyes of barbed wire and tiger fangs at their throat. Raped and clawed to death. For no reason.

Those sentenced to a Whole Life Order can never be released. The WLO is rarely imposed because the crimes which warrant it are so rare. Amidst the UK total prison population of nearly 83,000, only 70 are subject to a WLO. For crimes such as: murder of two or more persons involving premeditation, abduction of the victim, or sexual or sadistic torture; murder of a child(ren) under the same circumstances; murder of a police or prison officer in the course of their duty; murder committed to advance a political, religious, racial or ideological cause; and murder by an offender previously convicted of murder. Sometimes a trial judge states his personal view that a WLO should be imposed, but he is hampered by sentencing guidelines which constrain him to a traditional life sentence. Conversely, when the criteria for a WLO are clearly evidenced, some judges use their discretion of 'minimum term' to round down the sentence to mere 'life', with possibility of parole.

Hence, the simmering outrage of The Project who formed something like a secret supreme court to covertly review all the traditional life sentences, and, in cases of the worst injustices, intervene.

They employ a network of ghosts to secretly whisk away the selected prisoner to the invisible supermax, which remains unknown to the government, to the public and the working courts. Prison records are falsified. The rare family or friends who might plan to visit him are told he is in solitary confinement, that he is not allowed to receive visitors. They assume he is in the traditional prison. Perpetrators' families, if there are any, are fobbed off in a fog of bureaucracy. Rare persistent ones are bought off or blackmailed, etc. Justice had to be done in secret – because supermax did not employ ordinary methods compatible with so-called human rights. There, the Project imposed a sentence of *When Life (Really) Means Life* for the unforgivable, those who deserve Old Testament hell, never to be let out.

That was the hidden beauty of supermax. That's why life is too short for them, for the unforgivable. The Project deemed that they had to suffer, really suffer, for as long as possible. Supermax really had nothing to do with time and loss of liberty. The demands of justice could be met only by the justice of suffering.

Three
- - - - - - -

The Cube

They called it the Cube – solitary confinement. A room 12 x 12 paces. The Cube floor, ceiling and walls were polka dotted with black circles that varied from pinpricks to about a foot wide against the all-around white room. The round blacks were spaced randomly, from inches apart to several feet. The effect was startling. Along the floor-base of each wall ran long-tubed, dim, fluorescent lights. The same at the ceiling, a square of dim light above. And same again in each of the four corners of the Cube, dim fluorescent tubes that ran vertically from floor to ceiling. The room existed in a dull irritating glow. They were never switched off. No windows. No night and day, no sun, stars and moon. My only refuge into darkness was when I closed my eyes.

A bed. No TV, no desk, no clock, no writing paper, no books, no laptop, no computer games, no limited internet access. No playing cards or trivial items for dreary prison hobbies. No access to an exercise yard. No fresh air. The air in the Cube breathed like recycled airplane air. Temperature lukewarm. Food was a mystery mush, without taste or texture, delivered through a letterbox opening in the secure door. Next to it, to my surprise was an inside door handle. In supermax? What a fucking joke! The mush food seemed to be delivered randomly. Sometimes it came a couple of hours after I had eaten when I didn't want to eat, sometimes it felt like days had passed. Sometimes I couldn't stomach the food, whatever it was. A separate toilet, cold shower and sink. Squares (not circles) of black and white tiles on the floor, walls and ceiling jarred my eyes. Head-height above the sink, there was no mirror. Faceless, I was soon to learn, also nameless. My prison uniform was also polka dotted with blacks and white.

It was forbidden to talk out loud to myself, even a whisper. If I did, a skull implant zapped me. At least I didn't get zapped for thinking. That was my sole freedom.

And torment.

Silence was King.

Of the Cube.

The absence of Time, his Servant.

I did try once to measure a 24-hour period. The Cube was 12 x 12 paces. I'm no good at maths but I figured, one second per measured step equalled twelve seconds from wall to wall. Five back and forths would take one minute; ten – two minutes; twenty-five equalled five minutes; 300 pacings would take an hour, my legs beginning to ache, my panting just below a whisper. When multiplied by twenty-four hours, my pacing involved back and forth 7,200 times until I collapsed to the polka dot floor, my legs a puddle of aching rubber beneath me, as my hand covered my mouth to muffle the sound of loud panting. I did it once, never again. I couldn't keep up this mindless pacing.

So, I let go of time. That was my first choice made in solitary confinement. But looking back, it was a no-choice. I simply had to endure. Sleep was impossible in the early days, whatever a "day" in this nonstop fluorescent light actually was. It might have been two or three normal days without sleep? Cut adrift from time and sounds, colours and stimuli, with no fresh air or window to note the weather or change of seasons, and no human contact, I simply existed. 'Alone' had gained a new and chaotic meaning as my mind wandered frantically, naked, frightened to be awake, frightened to sleep.

I don't know how long I was kept in the Cube before The Born Again started. Weeks, months, years? For a while I did try again to get a measure of time, crudely. Because the sink had a three-blade safety razor and a bar of soap for cold shaves – I guess they weren't bothered by suicide risk here – I remembered that on the outside, I could get away without a shave for about a week. That was pushing it. Not a hairy bloke. Feeling my stubble grow until it felt "time" to shave, I guessed this to be one week. After fifty-two shaves I stopped counting. What was the point? To count the damn number of shaves of my life sentence? I can't remember The Born Again starting during my first fifty-two shaves. After that, well, I lost count.

What baffled me was my unexpected attachment to time. Its absence felt like an amputation, my mind grasping for a phantom limb of me that wasn't there anymore.

Often, I just sat on the floor, my back to a wall, staring

at the polka dotted, fluorescent Cube hour after hour in silence. I became mesmerised. Probably this was to soften me up. Soon the different sized and spaced black circles began to bulge out of the white walls, floor and ceiling, then dimpled back into themselves and bulged out again, not in unison but arrhythmically – the polka dotted Cube wobbling in and out at me. Other times, the blacks gathered close together, circling round another hypnotically, round and round clockwise, and anti-clockwise, before swarming out across the white walls, floor and ceiling like wriggling, black-dotted snakes. Other times, from a tiny central spot, larger black spots radiated out like the spokes of an umbrella, then suddenly collapsed into nothing but timeless white.

Often, I had to close my eyes to regain a sense of the reality of ME, as an observer – of what, God only knows? But the spots even remained before my closed eyes. When I opened them, I tried to blink them away, but the black circles in the Cube had now become black holes which felt like a multitude of secret eyes watching me. Suddenly, I realised I too was simply a black hole – one of them. "Oh my God!" I cried out loud. ZAP! The black eyes laughed as I slumped forward onto the floor. My half-conscious face hung over the brink of a black hole that beckoned me, deep, deeper, falling until I was swallowed into a lost world where I became an invisible watcher, a detached knower…

* * *

From an island tree-perch a sea eagle swooped down, having sighted a large octopus floating in the shallows.

Holding its talons far forward, almost under its arched beak, it struck, raking backwards and hooking the octopus with a single talon as it beat its powerful wings to lift upwards. But octopuses are slippery, quick and super intelligent. Like a Native American Indian jumping astride onto a wild horse bareback, the octopus instantly straddled itself onto the back of the eagle. Its eight tentacles, with as many as two thousand powerful suckers, strangled the lifting eagle wings, plunging them both into the sea.

Prey had become predator. The octopus dragged it underwater in a cloud of ink, while repeatedly biting the eagle on the back of its twisting neck. The mouth parts of an octopus are hard as a parrot's beak, and it can inject toxins that paralyze its smaller prey. The eagle wings soon foundered, waterlogged.

The octopus knew the eagle was drowning. But something made her stop. It was a she. The eagle a he. Abruptly, the octopus pulled the eagle to the surface and propelled it to the water line where it dragged it up onto rocks – and let it go.

Let it live.

Octopuses have nine brains, a central head-mantle brain while each of its eight arm-tentacles have a decentralised brain that can think independently for itself – and feel independently. They have episodic memory, that is, they can recall autobiographical events, and learn from them. And, although predatory creatures, it is believed octopuses are capable of emotional intelligence – empathy.

As the sea eagle floundered catching its breath, the octopus extended several of its tentacles and gently stroked and sucked the water-logged feathers, drying them until the eagle could stand and half-flap its wings wide into the sea breeze. Shaking itself, it turned his head and beak to the octopus, eyeing it fiercely. On land, a quick stab of his talons could have killed her. But something stopped the eagle. This slimy wriggling slush had outwitted him. With a curious gratitude he let the octopus slither back to the shallows.

Over time, they kept an eye out for each other. Eagle eyesight is legendary, but octopuses also have far better vision than humans. Eventually, they began to share their hunting spoils. The eagle built a ground nest amongst rocks close enough to the waterline so that the octopus could crawl along with her prey of crabs, shrimp, and molluscs, to share. In turn the eagle left her a variety of fish he had grabbed from the sea.

She admired his fierce looks – tall, a yellow hooked beak, intense eyes, white headed and white-breasted, black plumage with large fingertipped wings, standing on splayed talons. She had always marvelled at how birds can fly, but the eagle was special, a majestic bird of flight and power. When she had nearly drowned him, her brain tentacles had sensed that an eagle's mate-loyalty is for life. It was an old evolutionary dream of hers which plagued her solitary life underwater – to have a mate for life. That's why she had stopped drowning him.

On his part, the eagle always envied underwater creatures that swam through mysterious depths and darkness. But an octopus, they were something special. So solitary and so physically vulnerable, yet so clever. They can instantly change their entire body colour and camouflage against any background, making themselves invisible. Or, they can mimic the shape and colour of their predators' predators, like a poisonous sea snake, to scare them off and protect themselves. And, so flexible, they can squeeze into the tiniest nook or cranny. But what he most marvelled about this particular octopus, was her super intelligence. Not only had she outsmarted him, he the dragon from the sky and nearly drowned him, but inexplicably, she had saved his life. She was very special, the eagle knew that.

They became, what else can you call it? Friends. Most improbable friends. To her ecstatic delight, the eagle learned to lift her with his talons without hurting her and fly the octopus over the sea in great high circles at a zillion miles per hour, so it seemed. Back on land, he gently used his fierce hooked beak to tickle her head mantle, making her octopus limbs laugh all over the place. She in turn, used her brain-tentacles to give the eagle a head massage which, like a Star Trek mind-meld, became a communion of minds as she fully cuddled him.

They broke the taboo of interspecies mating. Afterward, during a post-coital head message, the octopus told the eagle she would have to submerge into a secret den for several months to lay and hatch her eggs. But she promised she would come back to him, with their offspring. He understood her new-found loyalty. He would fly round on the lookout for her. He told her he would protect their young, that he was her mate for life.

That's when she had to tell him. This was her first and last mating, because mother octopuses die about a month after their eggs hatch. The eagle didn't know this. Taken aback, he half-fluttered his great wings, and blinked. From one fierce eye a tear dripped. That's all a mate-for-life could say, in confused, anticipatory grief.

Their longing separation seemed to never end. Eventually she swam to the surface, guiding a miniature octopus to the waterline where they slithered into a rock pool near the eagle's ground nest. He flapped to the edge and stood domineering but caring over them. Unusually, only one egg had hatched and survived. A freak. A tiny octopus with six limbs and two fledgling eagle wings.

As the invisible watcher and knower, suddenly I realised, "That's ME!" I cried out loud.

ZAP! Stunned, I knew if I opened my eyes immediately, I would be back in the Cube. I scrunched my eyes shut and held my breath for as long as I could until finally, daring to flutter my eyes open, there I was – the little freak in the rock pool. My octopus mother told me to look up at the sea eagle standing over us. "That's your father," she said proudly. Instinctively, I sensed him as a predator and tried to squirm into a rock crevice, but she held me back. "Look, he won't hurt you. He's your father. Look at yourself."

I did. I tried to flutter my fledgling wings but they were too immature. The tall eagle tilted his fierce head and eyed me closely. Can an eagle smile?

From the rock pool my mother stretched a brain-tentacle to the lowered eagle's head, now so curious and eager. She told him, "He's special. Look after him after I'm gone."

I didn't understand. For the past months in our secret den my mother had been constantly caring for her eggs – me – the one who survived. Where was she going now? She held one of my small tentacles, and for a moment her body displayed a rainbow of colours as she told me that all mother octopuses must die soon after her eggs hatch. "It's meant to be."

Then, to my father she urged, "He needs both worlds – water and sky. Promise me you'll teach him how to fly. Our son, a flying octopus. Promise?"

He replied through her outstretched tentacle-tip that kept touching his head lightly, as if kissing him, "I promise. Our son will be a flying octopus. It's meant to be!"

With that, she whispered to us both, "Goodbye," and crawled out of the rock pool, slithered to the waterline, and disappeared into underwater tears. In the depths somewhere, in a secret, dark, hidey-hole, cocooned in all her memories and dreams, she went to die in solitude – knowing it was the best thing she had ever done in her life – me.

Me! A little octopus with six limbs and two fledgling eagle wings that were partly water-resistant. I only had seven brains, not nine, but like all octopuses, three hearts. Also, a single primitive lung. This meant I could breathe out in the air for up to an hour. It would power my wings as they grew bigger.

My father taught me to fly. First, on the island I learned to glide-fly from tree to tree, easily grasping the branches with my tentacles. In fact, like a human Tarzan, I could fling myself from tree to tree with my arm-tentacles. The monkeys didn't know what to make of me! In time, I could hunt from the air, a flying octopus swooping down upon fish that could normally evade an octopus in the water. My father always kept a watchful eye out for sharks. We bonded in the rock pool near his ground nest. Often, I rested in the rock pool while he circled above protectively.

Then one day, some fisherman landed on the island close to our rock pool. Father, high in the sky cried out to me with goose-like calls, but octopuses are deaf. I must have been daydreaming and didn't notice his skydive toward me before it was too late. A net was thrown over me. As I scrambled and flapped helplessly, one of them yelled, "Don't kill it, whatever it is?! We can sell it!" Father's talons raked the back of one of the fishermen, felling him, bleeding profusely. "Get back to the boat!" They dragged me netted and dumped me into a tub of saltwater while father sky-bombed them. "Get the shark gun! Kill it!"

Off they went, out to sea, shooting and shooting. For hours father trailed the boat at thousands of feet, sometimes diving and swooping, talons first, at the ducking heads of the cursing fishermen. "Kill that damn thing!" After endless time out at sea, even from the solitary confinement of my netted tub of water on the boat, I could sense that my father – a mate for life, a protective father for life – had died in the sky.

Not from a bullet.

* * *

Kidnapped, sold, I ended up in a marine aquarium. A scientific zoo, where I was observed and studied by humans with computers and laptops. I could recognise their individual faces, even personalities. Some I liked. The ones that I didn't, when the tank lid was off, I squirted water at them. The breakthrough came when one of them realised, first, that I need to be regularly out of the water because of my hybrid eagle wings. But also, that I was obviously deaf, yet intelligent. To their astonishment, I learned their sign language, and with my delicate tentacle-tips, could sign back to them. Then, with my exceptional eyesight, I learned their alphabet and learned to read. Not only that, with my six limb-tips I learned to type out my messages and communications on a keyboard, rattling them off faster than any human typist. Their scientific journals were aghast.

And, I could fucking fly!

I went on tour round the country, mainly to universities full of scholars and scientists who marvelled at me. Then, I was sent to lots of schools for kids. There, at first I was treated like a therapy dog, or like something in a dentist's aquarium, mesmerising, soothing, fascinating. But soon, I became seen as a teacher, a freak of evolution who could show the human kids that all things were possible in their lives. It could be 'good' to be different.

But not all the kids bought that. "Different" was often seen as weird and ugly, like a pubescent girl, something to be teased and ridiculed. And they resented that I was smarter than all of them. A nerd, a swat, and deaf. One school in particular that I regularly visited, hated me. In the classroom I was allowed to splay my body on a pupil desk along with the others, but one of my limbs had to be tethered to the chair so that I couldn't fly away. I couldn't hear what they called me, but by this time I could read lips, and read their scowling faces. "Smart-ass octy! Freako! Freako! Go back to where you belong!"

One day our teacher had to take a class break and speak with the headteacher in her office. She told the class, "Study your maths. Be good. I'll be right back."

My three hearts sank. One of the bully boys taunted me, "Hey Freako, you wanna have some fun?" It had been building up for some time. A bunch of them grabbed me, wriggling and flapping, and dragged me out the classroom door into the playground and round a corner out of sight. One of them kicked my head-mantle as they laughed all around, "Freako! You Fucko Freako!" Someone shouted, "Give it to him!"

Some kid had smuggled in garden shears and began clipping off my wing tips. Cheered on, he then pressed down extra hard, amputating my wings, while my tentacles thrashed wildly. "Who's got the knife?" A girl passed a short steak knife to an acne-faced teen. He snarled at me squirming on the ground, "You think you're better than us? We'll show what it's like to be human!" And stabbed my head-mantle, killing me instantly. Blue blood splashed everywhere. (Octopuses have blue blood.) But I still remained alive in the six lives of my thrashing tentacle-arms. That's when the chopping began, and their chanting. "You Fucko Freako!" Chop Chop! "Let's see you grow them back! (Octopuses can grow back a mutilated limb. But not instantly!) "Fucko Freako!" Chop Chop! "Grow them back!" Chop Chop! "Grow them back!" Chop Chop! – as they mutilated and amputated my living limbs, each snaking wildly, bleeding blue puddles and smears everywhere, until my last remaining lives squirmed out of life at the blue-bloodied shoes and ankles of the school children.

* * *

Back in the Cube, lying face down on the black-holed floor, my head felt like a cannon ball, shot and dead. I must have been ZAPPED over and over again while screaming my seven octopus brains out.

Four

Deliver Us From Evil

High on a hilltop stood a lone farmhouse built in the 17th century, exquisitely renovated, which overlooked distant city lights sprinkled across the night. Upon entering the study, the first thing that would hit a visitor was the smell and look of old furniture, authentic Victorian, and the smell of old books, law books, a wall of them, floor to beamed ceiling, stacked along walnut bookshelves with a sliding ladder. You couldn't help but admire the intelligence of the room.

A one-armed man sat at his mahogany desk between the wall of bookshelves to his left and on his right a deep recessed inglenook fireplace. His dark eyes looked much older than his seventy-five year old face, a face lined by decades of complex decisions – his final judgements made in court. He ignored his desk computer to watch a wide TV-like screen fixed at the end of the desk. Except it wasn't a TV. It was an untraceable monitor transmission from supermax. Staff had alerted him to watch inmate J

– 00 – 001 in the Cube, screaming his octopus brains out.

The one-armed, white haired old judge nodded with sombre satisfaction at the inmate's suffering, thinking to himself, *Now he knows what amputation feels like.*

He switched off the screen, pushed back his heavy Victorian chair and strode forward to the end of the bookshelves where he studied a stained glass window which depicted Christ crowned with thorns carrying his cross. When the sun was just right in the sky, the stained glass angled shafts of rainbow across the wall of law books.

He was the retired Lord Justice Solomon, the founder of the secret supreme court and supermax. His wall of law books contained the human mathematics of justice, impartial equations according to the law, to balance crime and punishment, law books which bulged with precedents of guidance for sentencing the worst of the worst. But it never seemed to add up. Not to the victims' families, not to him, nor to the select judges of The Project who were prepared to do something about it.

The injustice of justice, what he was permitted to sentence by the law, had made him feel like a Judas judge. It had driven him to drink, a secret alcoholic thirsting after the mirage of justice. Just one more drink at the end of another complex trial. His lone right hand preferred Japanese whiskey in a crystal glass at his desk. Samurai whiskey, he called it, smooth as silk that painlessly severed his conscience from the killers and sadists to be released. It was only a matter of time. There was no barbed wire to the law. The law was a tame wire fence that sheep could wriggle through or under, or wild goats jump over. Always a matter of time before they got out.

Drunk with disillusionment, that's how he got though the Judas years, hanging himself trial after trial, lame sentence after sentence, time and time again.

Only suffering could meet the demands of justice. So, the retired Lord Justice Solomon, the creator of When Life Means Life, looked up at the stained-glass Christ as if it was the unforgivable inmate J-00-001 carrying his deserved cross. *Let there be supermax,* he thought. The judge nodded, and saw that it was good.

Five

The Born Again Begins

I don't know how long I was kept in the Cube before The Born Again started. All I knew was that it was getting harder and harder to tell the difference between sleep and awake, between dreams and hallucinations. A little longer, I knew I would lose my mind. That's what they probably wanted. Confined in this room of fluorescent glow and black holes, the only way out was to lose my mind, become a black hole myself, one of them, an absence, nothing.

Suddenly the secure door opened. In wheeled the automated forklift. From a metallic speaker on the back of it, an electric voice instructed me to sit on its forks. A voice! Any kind of voice. An Other was speaking to ME! I wasn't a black hole.

As I was forklifted along those empty white corridors, it took me several minutes to blink away the polka dots. The novelty of this event set my heart thumping. Desperate to ask, I didn't dare. Suddenly, the machine spoke, "Knock,

knock." I turned my head round. Its speaker was right behind my head. "Knock, knock!" it repeated.

"A talking forklift?! You talking to me?" I scowled. Strangely, I didn't get zapped. It was the first time I had heard my own voice in I don't know how long. It was a no-man-land voice, dull, alien, like hearing your voice on tape recorder for the first time. Maybe talking to a forklift didn't count as breaking silence?

"Who's there?" it asked.

I butted my head back against its speaker, "Fuck off, you brainless machine!" If only that had been a human nose, broken, gushing blood. We carried on.

Ahead of us in the corridor a door automatically opened. The forklift wheeled me into what looked like a hospital operating theatre, all shiny and white. REAL LIGHT! Not my fluorescent gloom. Two doctors, surgically gloved, gowned, capped and masked – REAL EYES! – stood on either side of a central, dentist-like chair. REAL PEOPLE! A bewildering array of stainless medical equipment, some on trolleys, formed a half circle behind the doctors. Two other doctors or nurses (?), also gloved, gowned, capped and masked, stood nearby. From the ceiling, monitors on extendable arms and small round lights could be pulled down for focus. Close to the central lay-back chair a large desk-top style computer screen sat on a wheeled trolley. Along the back wall stood a cluster of God-knows-what-high-tech instrument panels. The room seemed wireless, like everything was computerised, like the forklift.

Except the real people. And me? We must be REAL, I told myself.

The unexpected stimuli overwhelmed me. Real people, the shiny lights, the variety of objects and shapes and shaded colours of white and grey and stainless steel. The mysterious purpose of the place.

The forklift wheeled me forward to the chair and placed me on it, sitting upright. "Lie back," one of the doctors instructed. As I did, my stomach tensed, like it always did in a dentist's chair. What the hell are they going to do to me? A doctor stepped forward and raised a finger to his mask, as if to say, "Shush." He rolled up my polka dotted sleeve. TOUCH! Even if surgically gloved, it was a human touch for God's sake! Only then did I notice – my muscle wastage. I must have been in the Cube longer than I thought. A second doctor handed him a syringe. His masked face leaned down toward me as my throat clenched. I could see his eyes bright with delight. As he injected my thin upper arm, behind his mask I could feel him smiling.

Lights out. Blink. Back in the Cube, a foetus on the bed

* * *

When my eyes fluttered open, I found myself, aged six looking up from the bottom step of a wooden staircase, no light, locked in a derelict cellar of concrete floor and concrete walls, a low beamed ceiling. Behind me a black passage led to several large musty-smelling spaces full of junk, a heap of coal on the floor at the bottom of a coal chute, cobwebs, mice and some scuttling rats. Looking up the stairs, beneath the locked door glowed a thin light of normality – from the family kitchen of our comfortable house in our comfortable neighbourhood. Terrified, I scrambled up the stairs and pounded on the locked door, yelling, "Let me out! Please, let me out! I'll be good! Let me out!"

From the other side of the locked door came my father's stone voice, "Get back down there where you belong. Do your bible time."

My parents, they were good Catholics. Good, and brutal. The parish priest, Father Martin, sanctioned their ascetic slavery of me in the cellar. "Be sure to tell him how bad you've been," my mother used to warn before I went to my childhood confessions. "If you don't, he'll tell us, and then you know what."

For generations the courts and newspapers have all reported the "you know what" of child abuse. Everyone knows. It's almost boring. But what the social services' case conferences and the courts and newspapers can't report is – the sound of abuse. Like the sound of Father's fist gut-punching my child's body and my gurgled retching and blinding pain crumpled on the floor, defecating all hope of "Please let me out! I'll be good" into my pants. Or, his single strong hand gripped round my windpipe, begging, going blind for air, as he choked me unconscious to shut me up. That sort of thing.

As if the black holes were ducts that led up from hidden dungeons, these sickening sounds vented up into the Cube – now a din of horror. In the Cube I knew I should be screaming, but I wasn't. Instead, my little fists sobbed softly against the locked door. I had to go back down the stairs into the musty blackness and feel my way along the blind passage, sweeping against cobwebs, to the only room that had a bare lightbulb. A so-called playroom, damp concrete walls, which had a linoleum floor laced with cracks, exposing the concrete underneath. Wooden blocks and play people lay scattered on the floor.

And a bible. To learn the Fear of the Lord.

Under the harsh lightbulb I used the blocks to build an imaginary prison which had a special cell for solitary confinement. That's where I stuck Father, after I had half choked him to death. Cells. Even then I had heard of monks' cells. Now, I wondered if they were the same as prison cells? One for prayer, the other for punishment. Which was which? Forced to read and recite to him brutal sections in the Old Testament, while flicking the pages back and forth to get to them, even then I realised that the most often saying in the bible was, "Do not be afraid."

That's when I learned to control my heartbeat, to keep it steady, and while even-voiced, I convinced him that I understood the Fear of the Lord. So, Father would let me out, time after time. Even then I realised that if I could convince and manipulate the monster of Him, I could convince and manipulate anyone. My aura of menace came later as I got bigger and stronger. Down in the bare lightbulb dungeon I had discovered the Holy Trinity – Convince, Manipulate and Menace. Yes, I understood the Fear of the Lord alright.

Him.

As a child I vowed to kill him. Well, most kids do, don't they? Kill their parents. When they're little. Growing up is mostly about forgetting.

This and other memories weren't anything new. The

sadistic control and the beatings, I took for granted. What else can a kid do? I had rattled them off to dozens of therapists and psychiatrists. But I "talked about" these experiences as if watching a horror film without any sound. I had forgotten the sounds.

As I reflected on this for the first time, the silence of the Cube became overwhelming. The polka dot ceiling, walls and floor all seemed to be closing in on me, all at once. The Cube was shrinking, compressing the silence into unbearable intensity, like a vice squeezing against my breath and body. Aghast, I wriggled off the bed onto the uplifting floor that would soon crush me against the ceiling and closing walls. Eyes shut, I lay helpless on the floor, a trembling foetus holding its breath, about to be crushed, aborted.

When I started screaming. As the pressure of silence collapsed upon me, it squeezed out all the forgotten *sounds* of my memories – the percussion of punches, kicks, shrieks and sobbing, the wails that howled in the dungeons beneath my "talking therapy." Until my spasms of screaming whimpered into unconsciousness.

Eventually rousing, the Cube was normal size. Had they zapped me into oblivion? The King of the Cube – Silence – had squeezed out all the dungeon sounds. I remembered everything. I mean, EVERYTHING! Strangely, I felt an exhausted relief, almost elation, as if I had been "let out" of the cellar for the first time. The door had finally opened. Dungeon to daylight. Sight and sound, past and present, lived as one, for the first time. What did it all fucking mean?

* * *

I was six then. This was far from my first experience of solitary confinement. Father had, what you might call, a 'world view.' When I was a baby, at crawling stage nearly standing, he used to put me inside a cardboard packing box with a lid, the ones used by moving vans. To his amusement, he would watch the lid and cardboard sides punching out from my frantic head, hands and feet, to see if I could tip the box over. When he got impatient, Father kicked the box over and over across the floor, me bawling inside his world view.

Long before I was six, there were the days of hunger. "Man cannot live by bread alone." Only the fucking bible. Only this, and nothing else. All else was heresy, blasphemy – science, music, other religious, literature, art, history, films, fiction stories, all were serpents in the Garden of Eden.

Father's world view went something like this: In the beginning were the beatings, and the beatings were from God. God had made me in his own image and likeness – Bad. So, his only Son deserved the beatings. And God saw that it was Good.

Purple Pain...Purple Pain...

Father was careful not to leave obvious facial or body bruises which could be seen at school gym class. Sometimes there was a fading grip mark on my upper arm, explained away by wrestling games with my teenage cousin. This went on for ten years. I never dared fight back in the cellar. When I was nearly sixteen locked up in a secure unit, a psychologist finally asked me the question which everyone else had asked themselves, but dared not ask me, "Why didn't you just leave when you had the chance?"

The psychologist sat earnestly behind his desk, across a desert wasteland, a stick shadow of rescue in the distance. I looked up at the wall behind him where, like clouds in the sky, framed certificates of his qualifications tried to convince me that he knew better than me when it would rain in the desert. He leaned forward, "I mean, you had ten years of chances. You were going to school everyday, playing sports, free to come and go right up into your teens. Why not go to school one day and not go back, or simply tell the teachers?"

I smiled, "The nuns? It was a Catholic school. They would've told Father Martin. But neither would have believed me, whether I was six or twelve, because my parents were good Catholics and friends of Father Martin. He would've told my parents of course, and then 'you know what,' as my parents used to say."

"Made things worse for you."

"In the cellar, doing my bible time."

The psychologist picked up a pen from his desk and twirled it in his fingers. "But it's hard to believe that someone at school—"

I smirked sarcastically, "You don't understand, do you? No one has ever asked me this question before because they didn't understand. But you, if you have to actually ask this question, it tells me you don't understand either."

He smiled, "Oh, I think I do. The question is, do you? That's why I'm asking. Do you know, do you understand, why you didn't just leave when you had so many chances, over ten years?"

Checkmate, his eyes glistened smugly.

"Do you know what it's like to be Catholic?"

"Ah, to be honest, I guess not." My knight takes his attacking checkmate queen.

"The Catholic world is claustrophobic, small as a closet or a confessional, but it's big as the world. There's no getting out."

He lined up his rook for the kill. "Then why not pretend to go to school one day and go to the police instead. It would have been that simple to get 'out."

Heaving a heavy sigh at his incomprehension, I moved my unnoticed bishop to checkmate his king dumb fucker, "Because wherever I was outside, at school, at the park, with friends, however free, no matter how old I got, and bigger, my little fists still banged against the walls of reality everywhere outside, crying, 'Let me out! Please! Let me out!'

The psychiatrist shrugged, "You still don't get it. We're all free to choose. It's the fear of change, fear of the unknown that holds us back."

Blinking back my tears, "Where do you think I am now? I was born in checkmate. So were you. You just don't know it."

* * *

A pain throbbed in my upper arm. What the fuck had just happened? Ah yes, the injection. The Born Again. Was that it? A needle? As I rolled up my sleeve to inspect my arm, I noticed my hand had a tiny plaster over one of the veins. An intravenous drip? What else had they done? I bolted upright and ripped off my shirt. Attached to my chest above both nipples were two small round disks – metallic, thin as paper. They didn't hurt. But I couldn't pry them off. I stood up and stripped off. I didn't have a mirror, so I began feeling my body wherever I could. At the base of my spine I found another disk. Then one at the back of my neck, and on each temple, these same paper-thin metallic disks. Were they some kind of remote mind control?

My mind raced with all sorts of horrors and tortures they planned to inflict on me.

Six

Lost

Timeless days seemed to pass in the Cube. Lost in bewilderment, I had to think straight. I had to be careful not to think out loud. Look at your body, I told myself. It's getting thinner, weaker. You're eating less and less. It's that mystery mush. You need some exercise. Pacing the room is no good. Something that will get your heart pumping and out of breath. Maybe that will make you hungry and want to eat that shit? What if I did a full knee-bend, then a squat-jump followed by a push-up? Build it up day by day, whatever a fluorescent "day" was in here? But would they consider my heavy breathing as breaking this damned silence? There was only one way to find out.

When I first began the squat-jumps I used to exhale loudly with the effort – "Ughhhh!" – in the transition to the push-up. ZAP! ZAP! Shock therapy, I bet that's what they fucking called it. So, I trained myself to hold my breath while doing the squat-jump, and then release it in a silent whisper to the polka dot floor as I did the push-up. Gradually, I increased my maximum number of repetitions which could be done with quiet controlled breathing. I didn't want to break their sound barrier. It wasn't easy. I got up to fifteen reps of bend, squat-jump and push-up, followed by a cool-down of room pacing. Then more and more, nearly holding my breath all the time. The physical exercise made me feel better, stronger, hungry. I began eating more of the mush, and slept better. Most of all, the exercise kept the hallucinations at bay. The polka dots stopped moving around. But this better health came at an unexpected price.

What was the fucking point?! Of getting fit? For what? "Fit for purpose," was the common saying. Getting Fit for my Life Sentence?!

So, in time, whatever that was – to simply exist in the Cube of NOW without end, without purpose – I succumbed again to depression and lethargy, staring trance-like at the roaming polka dots, daydreaming, hallucinating in a blur of reality and unreality. Reality and Unreality? I laughed out loud at this thought and got ZAPPED for laughing to myself.

That was my reality. Silence or Pain. For talking or laughing or grunting out loud in my solitude – to myself. I was again becoming a black hole, another one of them on the walls, floor and ceiling, an absence, a nothing.

* * *

There were no indicators of time. When the secure door of the Cube finally opened again, the forklift had changed

38

shape into a crude-looking robot. Stainless steel fac
head, a round mouth-speaker grill, squat neck, and
torso that went to the floor, wheels for feet. Crude and
mechanical looking, it vaguely resembled human shape. I
scowled, "You look ugly. I prefer the forklift-look." Again,
I noticed that I didn't get zapped for talking to this robot
or forklift, whatever it was. The robot torso then shaped
itself into a forward-facing chair for me to ride on. Comfy.
Liquid steel, I thought to myself. It could flow through
keyholes and under doors, it could go anywhere. I'd give
anything to be like him. Then I could get out of here, even
supermax.

Finally blinking away the polka dots as it transported
me along the empty white corridors, it's mouth-grill spoke,
"Why did the chicken cross the road?"

"What?!" I replied incredulously. "Piss off moron!" It
seemed a maze to nowhere. No way out. No way in? Simply
here, somewhere, for eternity, transported by a robot that
was asking me, "Why did the chicken cross the road?"

Once again, the door opened into the high-tech
hospital-like room. The four of them – capped, masked,
gowned and gloved – stood round the central dentist-like
chair. The robot placed me on the chair. "Lie back." *That's
what you told me last time, you fucker*, but I managed to
keep it to myself. One of them, a woman, I could tell from
her voice, bound me with specially adapted straps to the
lay-back chair. "It's for your own protection. Involuntary
movements are not helpful." Another of the masked
doctors, a man, spoke, "Welcome back to The Born Again."

I nearly burst into tears. It was the first kind word I
had heard – "Welcome" – I couldn't remember for how

long. In primary school one of the nuns once remarked about my pencil handwriting, "Good boy." I had forgotten. I went to all the best Catholic schools. I wasn't dumb. Extra smart, they all said, but I got kicked out of most of them. Remembering "good boy" felt like a splinter of broken glass on the floor to be swept away, bringing suppressed tears to my eyes. "I'll be good," echoed through my mind. To my surprise the masked medical team eyed me, not with surprise, but I sensed, with approval. My splinters of glass tears shocked me. I couldn't remember the last time I cried.

A doctor, a man, held what looked like a remote TV control and gestured to the others to take their stations at various equipment and monitors. From the back, one of them wheeled the computer-screen trolly forward, in vision of both the doctor and myself. He pointed to it and pressed a button. The screen remained blank. My stomach tensed. Suddenly panting, my throat went dry. The doctor, *he must be the lead doctor*, I thought, wagged his forefinger at me. "Listen carefully," he instructed. "Don't speak. Reply to me only by your thinking. That's all that is required."

You can't read my fucking mind! None of you shrinks ever could, I thought. Instantly, on the black screen my thoughts appeared in white typing. I felt the doctor smiling behind his mask. They could actually read my mind. And so could I! "It's the mind-monitor," he explained."

Another one of your fucking toys! I thought, which ran along the bottom of the screen for all to see.

"During The Born Again we will need to know, not only what, but *when* you are thinking. It's critical for the treatment."

"I don't—"

ZAP! "Ughhh!" My arms and torso tried to lunge up against the restraining straps, but only my neck could.

"Shut up," the doctor ordered calmy, raising a finger to his mask. "Don't talk, think."

My head fell back, as if it had been splashed underwater, bewildered, gasping up for the surface of words, for the air to protest. *I don't – don't understand what's going on. Tell me. Why this goddamned silence all the time?"*

Flashed up on the screen, the doctor continued to read my mind, and answered, "Speaking is a privilege. You haven't earned the privilege to talk with us, not even to yourself."

The screen went blank again. The King of the Cube was Silence.

Except to that forklift robot, thanks a lot, you bastard! Just get on with it, do what you're going to do to me. Give me your best shot, I can take it.

"Let me first ask you this. What's the one thing you take most for granted in life?"

The screen went blank. *What the hell are you on about? I don't know.*

"Some prized possessions?"

I've got nothing.

"Think."

Blank screen for a while. *I told you, I don't know.*

"When we leave aside possessions and things and money, then we get closer to home, to what we most take for granted. Like your eyesight perhaps? Seeing."

Yeah, I guess so. I never thought of that.

"But some people are blind. What do they take most for granted?"

Hearing, of course.

"But some people are blind and deaf. What do they take most for granted?"

So fucking what? Move around, I guess. What's all this got—"

"With help from others. You left that out. But some people are paralysed. What if someone is blind, deaf, and paralysed? What would they most take for granted?"

Ah, I get you now. Touch, taste and smell. The five senses. Take those away, what's left? Fucking ME in that damned Cube!

One of the team came forward and whispered something to the lead doctor. He nodded. "My assistant has just completed a digital fast-scan of your entire personal history. I see you know your bible, like the story of Job?"

Jesus in a hot air balloon! Don't bring fucking God into your madness. I've had plenty of that shit in my lifetime. What's religion got to do with this anyway?

"It's simple, really. God, your very distorted version of God, is tattooed in your mind, as it is in many psychopaths. With you, as the old saying goes, 'Once a Catholic, always a Catholic,' whether you like it or not."

I fucking don't.

"But it's in your blood and bones. That's why we refer to it, to touch base with your bedrock view of life. If you were a bus driver or architect, we would use the relevant analogies. Everyone has their own personal language, their familiar ways of thinking, unique to each individual. We're simply trying to speak your language, like learning a foreign language. It's our way of linking up with you, that's all."

42

No one has ever linked up with me. Never will.

"That's your choice to be alone. If all your five senses failed, you could still be alive. Isn't that what you most take for granted? You – alive?"

A fucking vegetable, you mean! Better off dead. Not fit for purpose.

"For the purpose of living? There's a thought. When God had taken everything away from Job to test his faith, there is a passage which says, 'Why give life to those bitter of heart? Who long for a death that never comes, who hunt for it more than buried treasure?'*

Believe me, I've thought of it.

"We know. The mind-monitor keeps track. If you had tried anything in the Cube, we would have saved your life."

Saved me? You got to be kidding. Is that what you think you're doing to me in here – saving my life?!

"Yes. In fact, that's exactly what we are about to do. So, let's come back to that most taken for granted thing. If you were a senseless vegetable, what is it that would keep you alive? Even against your will."

Blank screen for a while. *My heart? Vegetable breathing, I guess?*

"Breathing, at last, at first. The heart is merely the servant of the breath. That's what we most take for granted – breathing. It's automatic."

So?

"So, we are giving you the chance – and *the choice*," he emphasised, "to learn how to breathe again, as if for the first time, and maybe for the last – breath after breath of life – even forever, you might say. That's what we are offering you."

But I'm doing it already, breathing all the time. There's nothing to learn. Like you said, it's automatic.

"Not anymore."

Seven

One Breath at a Time

As I lay strapped on the dentist-like chair in the high-tech room, reading my own bloody mind and listening to the doctor's shit, I thought, *Stop playing your mind games with me.*

"No mind games."

As he pressed the remote, my lungs stopped like a machine switched off, shut down. Startled, I looked up at him bug-eyed, lurching up against the restraints. My heart began racing. I waited, and kept on waiting. For AIR! My mouth gasped open like a landed fish. Straining to inhale, my lungs felt collapsed.

The monitor screen flashed up, *Let me out! Please, I'll be good! Let me out!*

The lead doctor noted coldly to his colleagues, "He's panicking. His old childhood stuff."

Breathless time passed. The futile, screaming demand to breathe again overwhelmed me. My heartbeat began slowing, weakening. I felt dizzy as I wriggled weakly against the chair restraints. Calmly, the masked medical team monitored my suffocation. They could tell I was about to black out.

"Enough." He pressed the remote.

A desperate in-rush of AIR glutted my lungs, as if surfacing from underwater at the last second, to breathe – AIR! – my chest heaving it in, heaving out, gulping and coughing. Tears stung my eyes. The monitor screen remained blank for a long time as I lay panting like a dog on a hot summer day. Finally, as I lay there, my breathing subsided to a luxurious restful rate. Too shocked and drained to protest, I simply asked, *What the hell was that for?*

"Restraints off, sit him up," he gestured to an assistant.

Then to me, "We take roughly 20,000 breaths a day, mostly without thinking," said the doctor. "It was to show you that breathing is a privilege."

You mean the torture of my NOT breathing, you bastard!

"I mean, not taking it for granted. Remember?" He continued in an authoritative, clinical tone, "Breathing is more biologically complex than the heartbeat. Involuntary, it can also be voluntary to a limited extent, thus it can be both. But literally, every function in your body and mind depends first and foremost on breathing. See? We just saved your life."

I'm sure you're smiling behind that mask, you bastard. I don't need a science lesson to know how you have just tortured me.

"Breath and speech, they're obviously connected. If and when you learn to breathe anew, then you will earn the privilege to speak again. Then you might have something worthwhile to say."

The screen flashed up. *Privilege, you keep using that word. Earning privileges? That's what they used to do in the secure units when I was a teen. Withdraw everything and make you earn things back, one by one, each as a so-called privilege. So that's what you've been doing to me in the Cube. And now, withdrawing my privilege to breathe and to speak. I get your tactics now.*

"Oh, I hardly think so. The Born Again of Breathing is only getting started. You have to *choose* to be your breathing."

What do you mean?

"You'll soon find out."

Or die trying? Is that what you're telling me?

"Yes. That's your Life Sentence."

The screen went blank.

Abruptly, the doctor added, "Cheer up. Tomorrow, we'll start again with something different." I could hear muffled tittering behind the masks of his colleagues. They had switched off their monitors and other equipment, having duly recorded all my vital signs in reaction to my near suffocation.

When is bloody tomorrow? I've lost track of time.

"Tomorrow is when the Cube door opens."

As I stood up to leave, the doctor instructed the robot, to my surprise, "Tell him one of your jokes to cheer him up."

Can a robot smile? Its electric voice replied, "I've been trying for months. His humour died years ago."

On the way back to the Cube, forward facing in his liquid-shaped chair, I grudgingly turned to his head speaker, "Go on, get it out of your system. Which one is it this time?"

47

"The old one that you have never let me finish."

"The 'why did the chicken' one?' It's so fucking stupid, it's not even funny."

"Try it, something different. Cheer up, the doctor ordered."

"In this bloody place?! But go on, you're dying to tell me. So robot, 'Why *did* the fucking chicken cross the road?'"

"To chat with the zebra on the other side."

I couldn't believe my ears. I looked straight ahead in silence for about ten seconds, then turned my head round to its mouth speaker, grinning broadly, "There, you dumb bastard machine, you've done it, made me smile against my will."

It replied, "That's another thing we take for granted until it's lost – laughter. The funny side of life."

"Of my life sentence? Fuck off!"

Back in the Cube, sat on the floor with my back to a polka dot wall, I didn't know what to make of all this. That doctor seemed to be playing good cop / bad cop rolled up into one. First, he kindly welcomes me, then nearly suffocates me and saves my life. Suddenly, I thrust my face into my hands and began sobbing – sobbing with relief – not because I was alive, but because he told me there was going to be a *tomorrow*. And I would know! Something to look forward to, even if it was the dreaded Born Again. Then I noticed. I didn't get zapped for sobbing out loud. But I dared not speak. I hadn't earned that privilege.

Until now, I had forgotten the psychiatrist's words on the first day of my Life Sentence. Now they haunted me, "You will be given the chance – and the *choice*," he emphasised, "to see what it really means *When Life Means Life*... A lot of inmates in supermax don't survive their Born Again."

I shuddered with dread. His talk of chance and choice, I still didn't get it. That had been my defence in court, "He didn't stand a chance in life." But he seemed to suggest that chance could be converted into a *choice*? No, I didn't know what he was on about. And also, he said I was being '*given*' both a chance and a choice. Well, I felt I had never been 'given' anything in life except a raw deal – bad parents, bad genes, bad shit. None of it made any sense. In the end, all I could think about was tomorrow. "You'll soon find out."

Tomorrow.

Eight

Under the Radar

My letterbox mush came for 'breakfast.' Soon after, the Cube door opened. 'Tomorrow' was today. A door open to a future – whatever that might be. Strangely, I was beginning to feel a fondness for my robot taxi, taking me to a future. Here was this high-tech science toy of liquid steel that kept telling me corny kids' jokes along the way, like "What did one eye say to the other eye? Answer: Between us, something smells." And so on. Its voice was sounding less electronic, more human. Or maybe that was my imagination? Along the corridors I couldn't help but smile or laugh in dismay. "You know, robot, only a 'retard' could have programmed you."

"I'm a bit of a freak, don't you think?"

Suddenly puzzled, "Strange, I've heard that somewhere before, 'freak.' Can't place it."

* * *

To my astonishment the masked team greeted me all together, "Welcome back." Voices of men and women. Before supermax, I couldn't remember being welcomed by anyone, especially not to a new school. Maybe for a drug deal or stolen goods, but this felt different. "Sit down and lie back," said the lead doctor. "No straps needed this time." The mind-monitor was trolleyed forward into our shared vision. "You need to practice something, learn a new skill."

The screen flashed up, *Learn what?*

"To breathe without thinking."

What? Why?

"Because in the days to come – "

More days to come? More tomorrows?

"Yes, that's right. You will need to master the skill of breathing without thinking in order to cope with what's to come. To start off, lie there, relax, and see if you can count up to ten breaths, each in-and-out as one full breath, without any thoughts passing through your mind."

What is this? Some kind of meditation thing?

"Some would label it like that. Go on, give it a try. The mind monitor will tell us what and when you are thinking. Close your eyes." He dimmed the overhead lights. "Breathe normally and *feel* what happens."

I settled back.

One. The screen flashed, *What the hell is this all about?*

"Back to One," the doctor instructed gently.

One, Two. More nonsense-thoughts came on the screen. Each time, I had to go back to One. *Three.* The doctor chuckled and whispered to the others, "He's thinking scrambled eggs, hot buttered toast, bacon and coffee. Keep trying," he encouraged.

Five, Six. An old street brawl, a small winning on the lottery, roast beef, potatoes, veg and gravy.

And so on. After an hour, "Not bad, for a first try. Practice in the Cube and we'll see you tomorrow."

My robot was at its best in the corridors, "What do you get if you cross a fish with an elephant? Answer: Swimming trunks."

"Aw, give it a fucking rest, man."

As I sat in the Cube I felt a surprising shift in their attitude – benign, even encouragement. "Good boy," echoed from nowhere. Well, I had nothing else to do but breathe without thinking. But what the hell for? I had no idea. But it was better than pacing the Cube. Hours of practice in silence. Each 'tomorrow' I was tested. Even though I couldn't get to ten yet, it made me feel surprisingly good, even relaxed. I became less bothered by what passed through my mind. As if scuba diving, although dazzled by beautiful fish, I became less repelled or frightened by strange creatures that swam up out of the deep. I slept well. By day ten, twenty, a month(?), the chaotic nightmares and nonsense of my mind had begun to calm, for what seemed like long periods of time, to a deep stillness. My body felt like I actually lived in it now, at home. I started getting up 'early' before the first letterbox mush in order to do a quiet breathing session before my next visit to The Born Again.

They all continued to greet me and seemed pleased with my daily progress. One day as I sat upright in the central chair, the lead doctor said, "We think you're ready now."

Ready for what?

"To discover the source of your breathing. Where does breathing start, where does it happen?"

The lungs of course.

"No, the brain. And a very particular part of it. At the base of the brain are clustered three small sections, the Cerebellum and the Pons / Medulla which all connect to the spinal cord."

The doctor explained. "Out of the 86 billion brain cells inside our skull, our breathing is regulated by a tiny cluster of only a few thousand cells in the Medulla brainstem known as the preBötzinger Complex. These cells, together with the nearby Pons, are the centre of breathing regulation, sending rhythmic signals down our spinal cord which relays them to our skeletal muscles, like the diaphragm, which expands and contracts our lungs automatically. A sort of breathing pacemaker is embedded at the root of the brain stem."

The screen flashed up, *Stop. What's all this got to do with my breathing without thinking?*

"The brain breathes your lungs without you having to consciously 'think' to breathe. You might say, the brain breathes 'preconsciously', then the lungs breathe. But any emotionally-driven thinking will cause static interference with the electrical signals of the medulla. This will shut down your lungs."

You gotta be kidding me?!

The doctor explained patiently, "That's why you have to breathe without thinking – in harmony with way the brain breathes without thinking – in order for you to experience the primal breathing of the brain itself."

I listened stupefied. The mind-monitor remained blank, until finally, *But people are thinking all the time and their lungs don't get shut down.*

"Of course not. But they don't have to do what you're about to do."

What the hell is that?

A masked assistant brought forward a strange contraption and handed it to the lead doctor. It looked like a motorcycle helmet with a dark face visor. "You've heard of virtual reality. We call this, not virtual, but the 'reality helmet.' When you put it on, it interacts with the disks on your temples, chest and spine. In order for you to be your breathing, you have to merge with the tiny part of the brain that is the source of breathing. The reality helmet will enable you to merge with your medulla brainstem, the preBötzinger Complex, where you will feel and be the brain itself, preconsciously breathing its neural rhythms. Like I said, the brain breathes first, then the lungs. The mind monitor will allow us to see what you see and experience."

I – I still don't understand. What's all this for?

"To help you become fully alive. That's your Life Sentence."

Before I could make a bewildered reply, he added, "All the vital organs and functions of the human body work preconsciously, or unconsciously, under the radar of our conscious awareness. It's important that you understand this – in order to trust your body's unconscious, to overcome your fear of not being in conscious control."

The screen remained blank with my wordless astonishment.

He nodded, "That's where you're about to go – under the radar."

I swallowed hard.

Nine

Hesitation

As I sat looking back at them, my fingers clasped together into a knot, twisting back and forth, feeling suddenly irritated and paranoid. To them, it all seemed done and dusted – my compliance to go 'under the radar', like 'under the knife' in an operation, unconscious, down into the unknown.

Finally, my words came across the bottom of the screen from left to right, *What if – if I don't want to do this? Then what?*

The lead doctor shrugged, "Well, that's your choice. You can rot in here for the rest of your evil life. We'll find another inmate instead. All we're doing is offering you the chance and choice to experience that Life is actually wonderful."

Wonderful? That's a joke.

"It's your choice to find out." He held out the reality helmet in his hand, like a severed head. I could feel him smiling again behind his mask as he said, "See what I mean? Your fear of not being in conscious control?" He paused, and then his voice sounded like a quizzical grin, "You're not going to die, if that's what you're thinking."

But you told me a lot of inmates don't survive The Born Again.

"They die by not trying. No one dies in here by trying."

The doctor let this sink in, and then continued. "If you start thinking for more than three breaths, it will cause static interference with the electrical signals of the medulla. You won't be able to breathe. You already know what that's like. If that happens, you can't 'will' the brain to start breathing again. But, if within the time equivalent of ten breaths you can manage to let go of your thinking again, this will kickstart or reboot automatic breathing. Then you will be fine. But if you get stuck, I'll press the remote and let you out of the reality helmet."

Warily, I protested, *If I stick my head in that thing, will I'll end up with a lobotomy or something?*

He chuckled, "It's more like a 'liberation helmet.' You see, breathing without thinking releases *awareness without thinking*. Awareness without thinking is *pure awareness*, a restful state that is our original nature, the brain's pure awareness of itself – just breathing. It's a pretty special experience."

The mind monitor went blank again. I unclasped my knotted fingers. Then my typed thoughts ran across the screen, *I think I'm beginning to see what you're getting at – if I can trust you?*

"It's about you trusting your brain, so let's make a start."

But – but... This is too weird. It's bizarre. I don't think

I can do this. The mind-monitor went blank. At long last it flashed up, *Can I? Can I go back to the Cube and think about this? I mean, breathe on it. It's a lot to take in. I think I would be better prepared tomorrow, to give it a go.*

"Good choice." The doctor's reply surprised me. He pointed a finger to his face mask, "I'm smiling for you." I noticed his colleagues nodding.

"Food for thought," the doctor added. "Consider the brain as God, and our 'thinking' as his creations."

Hold on, you keep bringing up God and religion with me. Is The Born Again a not-so-subtle name for some kind of Christian conversion thing? Is this what's going on here?

"Far from it. I only use the analogy of God because that's what your core mind-set is, pretty screwed up I must say. If you were a plumber, then I'd be talking about a central heating boiler as if it were God, and its creations the radiators, that's all."

My father was a plumber.

"So anyway, our thinking can't think its way back to its creator. It's impossible because the reality of God is too big for concepts and logic. So too is the reality of the brain, the most complex biological structure on the planet, possibly the universe. In the reality helmet it will be impossible to consciously 'think' your way back to the medulla. But you can breathe your way back to the brain, where all breath begins and ends, sort of like God."

He paused. "This is the special chance and choice we are offering you. Do you understand now?"

On the ride back with my taxi robot, I didn't understand a damn thing. Made worse when the robot chortled stupidly, "Here's one for tomorrow's journey. "How do all the oceans say hello to each other? Answer: They wave!"

Ten

A Word of Warning

Back in the polka dot Cube I sat on the side of my bed and sighed deeply, shaking my head. Whew. It all seemed so unbelievable. Maybe the doc had a point about the religious stuff? Now that he had said it, I realized my mind had always felt stuck in religion, like a shit bog. But the way he compared the brain to God, that was something new to me. Let alone a bloody central heating boiler! Where does he come up with this shit? For a long time I sat just breathing, watching my thoughts come and go...

God and the brain. If God is pure awareness, perhaps the deep brain is also pure awareness? And the manifest creations of both God and the brain are the infinity of our thinking? I asked myself, is the human brain literally the evolution of God on earth, divinely incarnate in us all? "Human and Divine," that's what the dogma says.

But the hell with dogma. Why does our 'thinking' insist that God or Spirit has to be separate from matter, as non-matter? "Creation out of nothing" could be "out of dark energy, dark matter." Perhaps matter *is* actually spirit? This soul / body split? Perhaps the body *is* the soul? The philosopher Wittgenstein said, "The human body is the best picture of the human soul." That's Catholic education for you! And when the body dies? Back to dark energy, the invisible mystery of matter? Life after death? Or simply dead, a one shot at life? Who knows? Neither religion nor science. But what did I care in a place like this? I was going nowhere.

Yeah that doc, he really made me think, alright. Suddenly I reflected, he doesn't talk like a surgical doctor. More like a psychiatrist, or a rare priest who actually knows what he was talking about. Holy shit! Could this doctor be the shadowy psychiatrist I had seen on the video-link screen on my first day? Only a brief encounter, it seemed so long ago. I had been too angry to pay much attention to him, let alone his voice. These face masks largely neutralized their voices, apart from male or female, so I couldn't work out if it was really him, or a ghost fantasy. My mind reeled. So, I returned to breathing, breathing, breathing, which eventually calmed my thoughts into slow motion.

With my back to the wall again, sitting on the floor, I told myself, 'Forget about your thinking and your thinking will forget about *you.*'

* * *

"A word of warning," advised the doctor in the morning, as I strained to recognize the psychiatrist's voice. His colleagues stood at their respective monitoring stations. "You have to target the small cluster of only a few thousand cells at the brain stem amidst eighty-six billion brain cells. A needle in a haystack. Overshoot your breathing trajectory, you will be lost in the vast universe of the brain which has nothing to do with your breathing. We won't be able to let you out. It's all or nothing, do or die."

I shuddered a grin as the screen flashed, *Thanks for that! Die trying, after all? That's my Life Sentence? You told me this on day one, didn't you?*

The doctor raised his eyebrows above his face mask. "Have you heard of the poet Emily Dickinson?"

"What's a bloody poet got to do with this? A psychopath doesn't read poetry!"

"Perhaps a psychopath can be a poet? Who knows? Last night the mind-monitor was following your speculations about God and the brain. As a word of warning, or perhaps encouragement, you might appreciate her little poem.

The Brain
The brain is wider than the sky,
For, put them side by side,
The one the other will include
With ease, and you beside.

The brain is deeper than the sea,
For, hold them, blue to blue,
The one the other will absorb,
As sponges, buckets do.

The brain is just the weight of God,
For, lift them, pound for pound,
And they will differ, if they do,
As syllable from sound.

"Good luck," he added..

As I lay back on the dentist-like chair, I reckoned I had several months of intensive breath-training in the Cube. When I got up to fifty breaths without any stray thoughts, I stopped counting, just carried on breathing. After all, counting was still thinking. Two assistants came forward, one to position the mind-monitor in view of the lead doctor, the other to place the reality helmet over my head, its dark face visor blocking out the bright high-tech room. Even my robot taxi asked to watch the mind-monitor 'live' during my first attempt to merge with the brain's breathing. It was the first time the robot in supermax had made such a request.

The last thing I heard was the doctor's voice, "I'm about to press the remote. Think nothing. Breathe deep."

Deep was an understatement.

With my first intake of breath, I felt engulfed in outer space.

Watching the mind-monitor, the doctor reported to his colleagues, "He's imagined himself in a spacecraft approaching a brain-shaped planet. Yes, that's the only way he can do it, a surveillance mission to locate the brain stem below the colossus of the planet. Although the spacecraft is an imagined idea, it seems to be on the level of subliminal thinking. It's going under the radar of the brain's detection of electrical interference because he's not generating any stray thoughts. Not bad."

After a while he reported again, "He's getting much closer, but I sense, I sense…" The screen began flashing up my gushing thought-exclamations of awe and wonder, of unbelievable beauty! But this triggered the preBötzinger

Complex in the medulla brainstem to shut down my lungs. "Come on," the doctor urged. "It's to be expected. Take your time, let go of your thinking. Your breathing will start up again."

But it didn't. "He's panicking. Well, it's his first time." An assistant came forward to remove the reality helmet as he pressed the remote. Spasms of gulping filled my lungs with grateful life-giving Air! How had I taken it for granted all my life? Just breathing?

The screen flashed up, *Sorry, sorry, sorry! I tried, I tried, but it was too overwhelming!*

"It's to be expected. Life is overwhelming when we let it be as it is."

Who the hell are you?

"It doesn't matter. Get some rest in the Cube. You've made a good start. The key is, trust your breathing, or rather, trust in the brain's unconscious breathing."

My robot remained on foolish form, "Why didn't the skeleton go to the dance? Answer: Because he had no body to go with!"

It took me several more 'tomorrows' to get past my spontaneous outbursts of awe and wonder, and my odd lapse of stray thinking, to manage to kickstart the brain's breathing without a remote rescue. Closer and closer, I breathed ever closer toward the brain planet. I soon realised that my first 'thoughts' of awe and wonder were infinitesimal compared to *pure awe and wonder*. That's what drew me ever closer.

"Look," exclaimed the doctor, pointing to the screen. "The spacecraft has vanished. Also, the brain-planet, gone. He's let go of his subliminal thinking." As if in outer space, but in reality, inner space, the mind-monitor now displayed a vast spiral-shaped galaxy of eighty-six billion brain cells, sparking synoptic flashes of neural communications, limitlessly interacting as a vast collective intelligence. Seen on the screen, as if from a disembodied spacecraft racing toward the galaxy, the view suddenly dived down past myriads of neural-sparking cells like stars being born – down, down, down underneath the galactic brain when, "He's done it!" cried the doctor. A tiny spark, a pinprick impact in the medulla, into the cluster of a mere few thousand breathing cells, twinkled and vanished.

'I' was nowhere, yet I felt Born Again in a sort of baptism where all breath begins and ends. From the brain stem neural messengers, like angels of wisdom, pulsed down my spinal cord to its base and back up again, inhalations and exhalations, radiating the universal breath of Life throughout my body. I felt my whole spinal cord breathing – primordial breathing without thinking – purely breathing its eternal rhythm, its unfathomable mystery of Life.

"Come and see," he waved the others to the mind-monitor. "It's as if he's breathing for the first time."

"He is!" enthused a woman doctor.

"See!" exclaimed the lead doctor. "The neural firework-signals to the thorax and diaphragm, the lungs breathing in and out, exchanging gases between air and blood in the pulmonary capillaries, the alveoli. There's over over 300 million of them in the lungs. See! He's totally immersed. His whole body is breathing. His whole being is breathing."

Full of air. Full of LIFE!

Afterward, laid back in the central chair as they

removed the reality helmet, the masked doctors stood gathered round me. I simply breathed-in the wonder and joy of breathing, my chest gently rising and falling like a soft ocean swell. I felt as if the universe was breathing through my body, and through the breath of every living creature on the planet.

"It's amazing," remarked one of the female doctors. "I never thought he would do it."

"To be honest, neither did I," replied the lead doctor.

"I did," said the robot.

Eleven

I Can't Do This!

What Cube of solitary confinement could contain my cosmic breathing?! I was free! With each simple breath I felt my whole body breathing, intoxicated with the joy of life. I had never felt so ALIVE! The psychiatrist had been so right. They had actually 'given' me something. Given me a chance, and the choice to convert this chance into something completely wonderful. "Breathing anew," he had said, "learn to live again." I sat on the edge of my bed, bewildered in wonder.

I reflected, the brain breathed, not me. I didn't have to think to make it breathe. The body did it for me, like a gift, breath after breath. I remembered the doc had once mentioned a guy who said, "I think, therefore I am." Now I realised, he couldn't have got it more wrong! Instead, it should be, "Breathing, therefore I am." In fact, I AM, therefore I think, not the other way round. Thinking comes from breathing, because of the I AM of breathing. I realised that my little 'me' simply surfed along the surface of the breath, 'thinking' I was autonomous, even independent of the breath and body. So many of us 'think' this way, I thought.

"Us?" I surprised myself. Was I coming round to feeling that I am one of 'us'? Sharing something in common? I never used to think or feel this way before. I was always the outsider, the detached watcher, the invisible 'me', never one of 'us'.

But breathing, *we* all do. Laid on my bed now, I dropped into deep sleep.

In the morning, in the high-tech room the doctors welcomed me with gloved clapping. The central chair was positioned for me to sit upright – like a real person – not a laid out passive body. "Congratulations," the lead doctor said.

Suddenly I felt a lump in my throat as the screen flashed up, *I can't remember the last time I ever thought this, let alone told anyone – but, thank you! I can't believe I've said that. You've shown me that breathing comes before who I am. I mean, before who I think I am. Well, maybe both?*

The masked doctor and his colleagues nodded with approval.

But how did I get to be the 'me' that I am? The sick bastard who can look at things with a fucked up religious slant, and abuse people without mercy? Schizo, that's what you shrinks have diagnosed. Whatever the hell that means?

"Perhaps there will be more 'thank yous' to come? We simply gave you the chance, but it was you who chose to take it. And also, to say, 'thank you.' Schizos don't say thank you."

Suddenly irritated, *Who the hell are you?*

"You, simply breathing same as you."

Stop it. No more mind games.

"It was no mind game that brought you back to your original breathing."

You're no surgeon. You don't talk like one. Apart from the zapper implant and these strange disks, my body shows no signs of incisions or stitches. There's no evidence of any physical operations.

"It's all science now," replied the lead doctor. "Chemical injections, remote neurological implants, electrodes, the mind-monitor, biofeedback, etc."

The mind-monitor ranted across the screen, *That's exactly what the psychiatrist told me on day one! You're him, aren't you? Why all this dress-up farce as medical doctors with masks? Why can't I see your fucking faces?*

"Because you haven't earned that privilege – to see a human face. Even your own. That's why you don't have a mirror. During The Born Again you felt as if your body was the whole universe, didn't you? Well, to see the face of another universe is quite a privilege, don't you think?"

The screen went blank for some time.

Eventually, *You keep mentioning damn privileges, earning them.*

"Like the privilege of breathing." A masked assistant pressed a monitor button which levered the chair flat. "Lie back."

What for?

"Listen. There is more to life than just breathing. You know now, from your own experience, that the brain's electrical rhythms breathe first, then the lungs. But the brain is co-dependent on your heart for the blood and oxygen it needs. Your heart beats 100,000 times a day to produce 20,000 breaths a day. Think of that. The heart's electrical field is sixty times greater than the electrical activity generated by the brain. Of all the bodily organs, the heart plays the key role in your emotional experience. That's what I'm trying to prepare you for."

Prepare me for what?

"It's called 'cardiac neurological memory.'

The mind monitor flashed up, *What does that mean?*

"Cardiac neurological memory' means that experiences become encoded in the body. Like an elephant, the body never forgets, even though you may not remember or recognise their presence. Cardiac neurological memory can unlock the vault of your repressed memories, locked in the basement of the body, so to speak – a habitual twitch, a limp, a back pain, a stutter, revulsion to some food or smell, even a tendency of forgetfulness. In other words, the heart won't let the body forget."

I'm not sure about this. Your going on about what I might find hidden in the fucking cellar of my heart. I don't think I need to know.

"I think you do. To engage with your heart, you have to *be your body, be your heart* – like your pure awareness of breathing. Here, in the heart, stray thinking matters little. But your emotional concerns need to be kept in check, neutral, in order to allow the deep memory of the heart to unlock your body and teach you what you have long forgotten. That's your next chance to take, and choice to make."

Sudden anger surged. *Fucking thanks for that! It's one*

thing after another with you guys, isn't it? So pushy. Why not give me the 'chance' – to use your fucking 'choice' of words – to make sense of what's just happened to me with the breathing? Instead, you want me to dive into the unknown again, straight away. I can't, I can't do this anymore.

The doctor's voice chided me, "Look at your breathing now. It's already way out of kilter from your cosmic breathing. You still have much to learn. Like I said before, in here, it's all about you finding the will to keep on living – or give up and die. A lot of inmates in super-max don't survive their Born Again."

The screen flashed my agitated reply, *I've clocked you. From day one, and you know it, you bastard.*

"This isn't about me, it's about you," he said impassively.

One of the other masked doctors chipped in, "That's what Christ said in Gethsemane – 'I can't do this anymore.' The Gospels simply left out the 'you bastard.'"

Think you're funny, don't you?

"We told you, it's imbedded in your digital history."

My beatings weren't digital, that's for sure.

The other doctor replied again, "Neither was Gethsemane. From his 'I can't', to his betrayal and abandonment, to dungeon torture, to a trumped-up court trial, to his final surrender, Christ said, 'It's not about me, it's about You.' Joe, you can do it, if you choose. Why not go back to the Cube of Gethsemane and breathe on it for while? Listen to your heart," he offered with unexpected sympathy.

Sarcastically, *You're the deep one of the bunch, aren't you?* Then a long silence ended in my resignation, *Yeah, maybe you're bloody right. But maybe you're not?* I protested meekly.

On the way back to the Cube, no dumb jokes. I wasn't in the mood. Neither was my robot.

But as I entered the Cube, I stopped, stunned. The black polka dots were gone. A Cube of white silence. Still enough to drive anyone else mad, it was a profound relief for me – white silence.

On the floor, sat with my back to a white wall, I remembered the doc had told me...HE! In another burst of anger, I determined to get to the bottom of him, whoever he was? Suddenly, a neon road sign flashed in the midnight of my mind – CHANCE! CHOICE! Startled, what the fuck was I thinking? 'I can't, I can't go on,' that's what I had told him. But YES I can! I did in the cellar as a kid. I shouted mentally, 'Do Not Be Afraid!' He told me to keep my emotions in check. But look at me now, I was panting, my heart pounding. All that mystic cosmic breathing had gone out the window.

I had to fall back on what I knew best.

'Neutral thoughts,' that's what the doc said. Yeah, I could do that. I've been doing it all my life. 'Callous,' is what the shrinks called it, my neutral thinking. After all, to be cruel, you have to keep your emotions in check, to think neutral, digital, keep your heart rate even. That's what psychopaths do. They call it – No, *we* call it – Can you guess? *We* call it – *pleasure.* A sort of 'neutral pleasure.' Fucking right I can do this! I WILL keep myself alive!

I slept well. A lot of psychopaths do.

Twelve

- - - - - - - -

One To Watch

On waking the next morning, I was all fired up. I'd show them, the pushy bastards. Come on, bring it on. I was ready to shove back. More than that. I felt like a tiger ready to pounce, crouched for the kill. But after slurping my dismal letterbox mush, the robot didn't come. I waited. Still, it didn't come for me. And waited. What the hell was going on? And waited. Nothing.

In frustrated anger I began pacing back and forth, yes like a caged tiger, hungry to prove that I could eat this Born Again thing alive, panting and prowling back and forth with nowhere to go. Stop, to mentally glower and snarl at them – the zookeepers who must be watching – then pacing and prowling. Stop, snarl. Pacing again. Nothing.

Boredom. A listless tiger in its cage. I lost count of the letterbox gruels that came and went. Maybe they weren't coming back? The robot, I mean. Maybe my stupid corridor talks with a robot was a "privilege" they had withdrawn? As punishment for "What if I don't want to do this?... I can't do this anymore"? Maybe they had given up on me? I remembered the doctor said, "You can rot in here for the rest of your evil life. We'll find another inmate instead."

Well fuck them! They had found me and I resolved they would be stuck with me.

As I languished in the surreal boredom of the Cube, waiting, it was the not-knowing that corkscrewed deep into my thoughts. But finally, like a tiger snuffling in its sleep, then heaving a hot, yawning sigh from its primordial dreams, I began to wonder how I had got to be here in supermax in the first place, the way I am.

I always took myself for granted, the way I am.

Was it the classic Nature versus Nurture argument? Probably both. In court I had played the psychiatric card, mentally incapable of being responsible for my actions. That was my defence. "It wasn't my fault, your Honour." The mannequin jury didn't buy it.

My sleeping tiger dreamt on. Maybe it was God's Plan who had predetermined me to be a natural born killer and sadist? My lawyer had overlooked that one. But I needed a powerful, kick-ass witness, someone like St. Paul, the reformed old Saul, a true serial killer who got his rocks off stoning people to death. He might have swayed that damn jury. But we couldn't trace his email address: etcum@ spiri220. In the Latin Catholic Mass it means, "And with your Spirit." I laughed to myself. *Only a Catholic junkie like me could think of a prayer-petition like that.* Reply: "Address not found." Fucking faith! My lawyer was an atheist. And the judge?

Then, what about invasion of the body snatchers? These mind / body snatchers who had enlisted me in their sinister takeover of the human race? The problem again, was finding witnesses willing to testify in my defence. Witness intimidation by the body snatchers was rife. Even the judge could be one of "them."

Alien abduction? Come to think of it, we should have gone with that. There are tens of thousands of eye-witnesses desperate to give their "evidence," especially in a court of law, which would give them – and me – credibility. Surely one of them might have seen me on their spaceship being operated on, my natural humanity being tortured out of me and replaced by their alien mind control, and then returned to earth with no memory of what had been done to me. Yeah, in court we should have run with that. There would be plenty of potential witnesses to speak out against the conspiracy cover-ups. Getting me off on the murder charges due to alien abduction would not only have validated their own abductions, but opened the eyes of the judge, indeed the eyes of the whole world. If it wasn't their fault, it couldn't be mine. "The defendant is free to go." That damned lawyer of mine. He had no imagination. It made perfect logical sense.

But then, engrossed in my tiger / tiger burning insights, I came full circle back to the Nature defence. I should have thought of this at the time with my lawyer. I had once read a book about the evolutionary origin of humanity. Long preceding the African homo sapiens – modern us – by hundreds of thousands of years and more, were lost hominid tribes of humanity who continued to live in parallel with modern humans until eventually they all died out. European Neanderthals are the best well known, but there are at least three, possibly four others in

Asia and Southeast Asia. And there is DNA evidence of an unknown human tribe in Africa distinct from homo sapiens. But there is no archaeological evidence.

My defence in court should have been that *only the worst has survived!* The most intelligent, but the most aggressive and violent human strand has survived. That wasn't my fault. In other words, ALL of current humanity is to fucking blame for my murders. Why single out me for a few deaths when humans are raping and torturing the entire planet through multinational greed and never-ending wars? Why victimise little me, when on the global scale of violent human behaviour, I've simply done what hundreds of millions of other people are doing all the time, killing each other, condoned as legitimate? The hypocrisy of it sticks in my throat. It makes me want to go out and kill someone just for the fucking fun of it. After all, I'm only human.

But finally, the tiger in me yawned its mouth wide open with the OBVIOUS. The most obvious reason why none of this was my fault? Because the worst crime of all had happened in the court itself. The judge was biased, not impartial, even if he wasn't one of "them," the body snatchers. Inflicting his life sentence on me with all the power of his pride and prejudice, that's what he did. If I could get my hands on him now, I'd strangle him with fucking barbed wire!

* * *

High on the hilltop in his remote law library, the retired Lord Justice smiled at the mind-monitor on his mahogany desk as he watched inmate J-00–001 ranting out his self-knowledge on the other side of sanity. "One to watch"?

This lunatic in the phantom supermax?

Or the one-armed phantom limb of the law?

Thirteen

Confession Time

Waiting, watching, always waiting. Would they ever come for me again? As a child, an innocent changeling, I was force-fed the eggs and larvae of bible texts which I swallowed in the cellar, gagging up against the Fear of the Lord. In the Cube I found myself retching up indigestible memories into the toilet.

Chrysalis time – cannot see beyond the event horizon of the present.

My father was middle aged, a stocky, square-jawed, square-shouldered bruiser, with thick heavy fists. When angry, he had eyes of stone. He punished me according to the Old Testament law, Leviticus 5:17 –19: "If anyone sins without realising, if he does one of the things forbidden by the commandments of Yahweh, he must answer for it and must bear the consequences of his fault...The priest shall perform the rite of atonement over him for the oversight he has committed without realising, and then he will be forgiven. This is a sacrifice of reparation; the man is certainly answerable to Yahweh."

My father did the best he could to beat the sin of out of "the *child* who is certainly answerable to Yahweh" – me – the child who was sinful "without realising." But the beatings could never be enough without a holy priest, someone like Father Martin at the Catholic church, to *perform the rite of atonement over me for the oversights I had committed without realising.*

Our church was called Our Lady of Lourdes. "Five doors down the street from the church," my mother proudly boasted to friends. "Be sure to tell him how bad you've been," she warned me before I went to my childhood confessions. "If you don't, he'll tell us, and then you know what." She was a doormat wife, a doormat mother whose face had no face.

Father Martin was so different from my father. Mid-twenties, dressed in black of course, dog-collared Father Martin stood tall as a beanpole, legs like a stork. Dark, side-parted hair, his smiling, blubbery lips didn't belong to his long, horse-like face, always immaculately shaven. He had kind eyes that welcomed me – to confession, the necessary rite of atonement.

"You'll be fine," he once smiled his blubber lips at me in school before I made my first confession, aged six. This was a year before everyone else in my class, because Father Martin was so impressed at my biblical knowledge and daily attendance at Mass with my faceless mother. We always sat in the front row pew. "Do not be afraid," he assured me. *God,* I thought, *He knows what I have learned in the cellar! DO NOT BE AFRAID OF THE FEAR OF*

THE LORD! I couldn't wait to make my first confession.

Only as a teen in a secure unit did I first come to see how weird the Catholic world of confession seemed from the outside. "Hell, man," exclaimed a tough lad, "confession is like grassin up on yerself! How fuckin dumb is that?!"

In the olden days, a Catholic church confessional consisted of three wooden booths joined together, each with a door or curtain for entry. In the central cubicle sat the priest. Two penitents knelt in the darkened booths on either side of the priest who slides open a little wooden door which exposed a latticed screen through which the sinner confesses, and the priest listens in the dark. The penitent sees merely the side view of the priest's head, a shadowy silhouette looking straight ahead, never directly at you, to preserve anonymity. So intimate, even at warp speed the distance between priest and penitent, between holiness and sin, could never be traversed.

For me, as a child kneeling in the dark, waiting for the little wooden door to slide open, the confessional felt claustrophobic and mysterious. It smelled of old wood, and stale body odours, especially in the heat of the summers, penitents sweating out their sins. The wood smelled like a library of ancient sins.

"Bless me Father for I have sinned," I began anxiously for the first time, to be born again through the priest's forgiveness. Only Father Martin could raise me from the dead. Six years old, kneeling in the dark cubicle, my head barely reached the bottom of the screen through which I looked up at his tall silhouette, his side view, not looking at me. Just listening, his head bent slightly towards the little screen as I confessed, "talking back to my mother"; "not doing as I was told"; "naughty in class": "bad thoughts", those kinds of things. Below the screen my hands trembled together in pious prayer shape, awaiting his verdict after my confession of sins.

Father Martin lowered his horse head to speak, but still looking straight ahead, not at me. He had a soft voice, unlike Father. "My son, by the power of the Holy Spirit invested in me, I can see the secret sins which you have not confessed." Stunned, my breath froze. Then his shadow head slowly turned to face me. I gasped, wide-eyed and startled, through the latticed screen. I could see his accusing eyes, black hole eyes peering down at me as I knelt before him, as if naked. I was. Just a frightened little kid. In the darkness of the priest's cubicle, the black hole eyes simply floated in the air, disembodied from Father Martin's human form. The eyes were attached to bat-like wings, hovering silently in the confined space. I lurched back, tumbling in out-of-body panic to the wood floor of the confessional, my body cowering in a tight ball.

"KNEEL!" the creature's voice suddenly growled.

Cringing, I clambered to the kneeler pad, and clasped my hands together into a knot of terror as I watched the winged black hole eyes of –

What?! What was IT?

Then softly, the creature's voice commanded, "Do not be afraid." My little body quivered. I knelt mesmerised by the winged, black hole eyes hovering in the dark, staring at me through the latticed screen. At first I thought it was a vampire bat. I had seen a couple of vampire films before. (I forgot to confess this.) But no, this was something different. From its head, forked out two long antennae and between them extended a strange long thing. Then I knew. It was a night moth. I had seen a few in the musty cellar winging out of the black recesses into the playroom, around the bare lightbulb while doing my bible time. I had even killed some. (Oh no, I forgot to confess that too. Father Martin knew everything!)

The hovering night-moth priest commanded softly, "Say Amen." I knew what the word meant, "So be it." It was my mother's favourite refrain of resignation when after my cellar beatings, I pleaded to her with my eyes, knotted with uncomprehending tears. Her shrug of shoulders, like the doormat Virgin Mary, seemed to say to God and Life, "Amen. So be it. Do unto me what you fucking will."

To me – to her – to fucking anyone.

By Him.

(Swearing, I hadn't confessed that either.)

From the priest's cubicle the hovering night moth commanded, softly again, "It's time for you to receive your first REAL holy communion, my son. Open your mouth to receive the Body of Christ," the creature instructed, "and say, 'Ah' of the Amen. And hold the 'Ah' open."

Knelt in the dark, I opened my trembling mouth, but my throat clenched tightly, choking off any sound. I swallowed hard and tried again and opened, "Ah…"

"Hold it. Hold the 'Ah' wide open." As I did, shaking with confusion and terror, the night moth began to extend from its head a probiscis (I didn't know the word for it at the time), a flexible, straw-like sucker feeder that delicately snaked through the latticed confessional screen and began to insert itself into my open 'Ah' mouth, which gagged, almost retching. My child's body knelt paralysed as the proboscis snake-wriggled down into my throat, deep into my guts, probing for my secret sins, then sucking them out of me, one by secret one: hatred of my brutal father; hatred of being hurt; hatred of my faceless "so be it" mother; hatred of the bible; hatred of a loving bullshit god who didn't exist; hatred of a hell-on-earth world; hatred for being alive; hatred for all the mannequin people around me. Fuck them all!

Six years old. My secret sins.

The hovering night moth began to slowly retract its elongated proboscis out of my guts, up out of my throat and mouth, retracting like a flickering snake-tongue back through the latticed screen into the tall, shadow silhouette of Father Martin, not looking anymore at me. Straight ahead, just listening.

Kneeling, at the end of my sins, I recited from memory, "Oh my God, I am heartly sorry for having offended Thee, and I detest all my sins because of Thy just punishments, but most of all because they offend Thee, my God, who art all good and deserving of all my love. I firmly resolve with the help of Thy grace to sin no more and to avoid the near occasion of sin. Amen."

"By the power of the Holy Spirit, I absolve you from your sins, my son," as he sliced a single hand through the air in front of his chest to make a sign of the cross. "In nomeni patri et fili et spiritus sancti, Amen." (In the name of the Father and of the Son and of the Holy Spirit.) He liked the Latin. "For your penance, say three Our Fathers and three Hail Marys. Go in peace, my son."

Escaping out the door from this coffin of Sin into the Light of Life, bathed in sweat as if baptised and born again,

I walked on air along the church aisle to my mother's front row pew where I said my three Our Fathers and Hail Mary's in a blur of relief and ecstatic tears.

My first confession – turned inside out, eaten alive.

Now I understood. Father could beat the shit out of me, but only Father Martin, empowered by the hovering night moth of the Holy Spirit, could suck the sin out of me.

My mother loved to confess her sins to Father Martin. She told me he had a way with words that touched her in secret places. (I assumed with his probiscis) But even as a kid I knew her sins had no secret places. After all, I was the face of her sins.

My father never went to confession, nor to Mass. But always, after Sunday Mass at the entrance doors where Father Martin would glad-hand the uplifted parishioners, my father waited to the side until everyone left. Then, for ages the stocky brute and the stork priest talked about what no god knows... What?

Fourteen

Penance

As I knelt over the toilet bowl in the Cube, puking my sins out, I suddenly thought to myself, *What the fuck did I have to be sorry for?* As the years of my childhood sins passed by, I came to recognise that the very wood of the confessional stank of rotting lies, blackened with the mould of dead absolutions.

Catholic doctrine told me I was born in Original Sin. I remembered a nun once told our class that the bible is a 'love letter from God'. I nearly puked. As I see it, Adam and Eve were innocents, two little kids playing in the Garden. The serpent came along and played a new game with them of 'I dare ya.' I dare ya to believe you can become just like God! They didn't know any better. Why not? That'll be so cool! But for their one dumb, daring mistake, what did God do? He inflicted 'collective punishment' upon all humanity yet to be born. God our Father is a genocidal God. Death to all. And for those who don't believe in his 'Only Son' to save us, well, they get damned to hell for all eternity. Where is the love and forgiveness in that? Original Sin seemed to say – simply to be born, to be alive is, 'without realising' it, a sin – even before I could fuck up later on in life. The childhood confessional seemed to enclose this darkness of Original Guilt all around me – guilty as charged for being born – "He didn't stand a chance in life, your Honour." Hey! That should have been my defence in court – Original Fucking Sin! My lawyer should have got some high-powered theologians to argue my case.

Dragging my head out of the toilet and wiping my mouth, I staggered to my bed and flopped on my back, exhausted. I lay curled up inside the fluorescent womb, like a still birth. Did that count as a sin? Born dead? Absently running my fingers against my stubbled face, I noticed I needed a shave. Time. Another week had passed? How many shaves since my last confession? Cube time. Cellar time. Bible time. Confession time. They were uniquely different times, yet all were the same waiting, waiting, waiting – for damnation. Hate thy neighbour as thyself.

Still, they didn't come. The Born Again must have given up on me.

* * *

From aged seven to twelve I served as an altar boy at Mass for Father Martin. It made me feel special. The world beyond the communion rail, the chancel, felt sacred, holy – the elaborate wooden pulpit stood at the congregation's left; the raised altar, draped in pristine white linen with a central golden tabernacle flanked by lit, beeswax candles at both ends of the altar. To the right of the altar space sits the altar boy, sometimes two of us, dressed ceremoniously in a white surplice top and black cassock to the ankles. The abiding smell of the altar chancel was that of ancient cleanness, ever-renewed for each Mass, ever-clean, spotless, sinless, perfect, the air of holiness breathed in amidst the fragrance of beeswax altar candles.

Maybe that's why Father's favourite book in the bible was Leviticus? It was all about the laws for the unclean to become CLEAN, and the just punishments for the UNCLEAN – me in the dungeon cellar.

As an altar boy my most awe-inspiring duty was when Father Martin performed the sacred consecration of the bread and wine, the supernatural transubstantiation by which the unleavened wafer host of bread and the golden chalice of wine were transformed, literally, into the Body and Blood of Christ, here and now. Two thousand years of "Do this in memory of Me." As Father Martin genuflected and raised the host and then the chalice aloft, I jangled the altar bells three times for each.

As a seven-year old, the pounding of my heart felt like the altar bells ringing inside my chest, in an ecstasy of perfect timing with Father Martin's consecration, my whole body shaking under the white surplice and black cassock, as if I too had been transubstantiated, literally, into the Body and Blood of Christ. Pure awe.

* * *

"For your penance..."
As I grew older, aged nine, ten, going on twelve, back

and forth between the cellar and confessional, between the stocky brute and the stork priest, my token three Our Fathers and three Hail Mary's went out the window. "For your penance, my son, wait for me in the front pew. I won't be long."

The first time, maybe I was ten, I knelt bewildered in the pew. *What did he want?*

He came and led me through the central swinging communion rails across the altar chancel to the left and through a purple velvet curtain to the familiar vestry or sacristy room. This was where the priest's colourful vestments of red, white, black, green, and purple, designed in patterns as intricate as a Persian carpet, were hung in a large wardrobe, as well as where sacred objects used in the services were stored in cupboards. It was where the altar boys and choir members also put on their robes. There was a central desk with a phone, computer and lamp. Nearby stood a metal filing cabinet with sliding drawers stuffed with official records and church finances. Mrs. Turnbull, a tubby, sweaty retired secretary, volunteered her typing and filing services twice a week, cheerily greeting Father Martin with "Watcha got for me this week, Father?" Then seeing me, "Oh, it's you again. You're a busy little altar boy, aren't you?" as she ruffled my hair. The pale walls had the usual crucifix and pictures of the saints, inevitably the sickly Sacred Heart of Jesus. Even I couldn't stomach that one. The room had several armchairs in a semicircle which faced a two-seater settee. An electric fire for winter. Cosy, business-like, sacred. The vestry smelled both old and modern.

Looking back, come to think of it, there were no family

photos. Nothing of him. The room was as personal as the Bic pen lying on his desk.

I had been here loads of times over the years, robing up with Father Martin before Mass, sometimes with another altar boy, Kevin. *What did he want me here for? I had never done penance in the vestry before. What kind of penance did he want?*

"Sit down," he invited me as he sat on the two-seater and languorously crossed his stork legs, one hand upon his knee, absently tapping his long piano fingers.

Fifteen

- - - - - - - -

Whale of a Time

Abruptly, the security door of my fluorescent Cube opened. There stood the stainless steel robot. My sleeping tiger twitched awake from its primordial dreams, stretching out its claws. *It's about fucking time,* I thought. I was more than ready. *Bring it on. Bring on The Born Again for the kill!*

The robot did, without a word or dumb joke. I strode from my robot into the high-tech Born Again room and plunked myself on the upright central chair. *I'm pissed off with you guys. Where the hell have you been? Tell me that.*

The lead doctor arched his fading eyebrows above his mask. "The last time you told us, 'I can't do this. You practically said, '*I won't do this anymore.*' Against our better judgment, in fact it was the robot who advised us, we gave you the time and the chance to think about your choice."

You let me stew in that damned Cube without knowing if you were ever coming back? I was just mouthing off, that's all. Tell me you haven't done the same. I don't know what this whole damn thing is about, but I'm not a quitter. See? I can take anything you can throw at me. So come on, I'll show you. Lay it back, I ordered them via the mind monitor, *I'm ready.*

"Finally ready, are you? Confident. Cocky?" An assistant stepped forward to strap me down, meticulously.

What's this for? I didn't need it last time.

"For your own protection," the man's voice replied. Ankles tight, shins, then just above the knees, upper thighs, waist, chest and head band – totally immobile.

Protection from what?

"Convulsions," he replied.

Fat chance, this time. With my mastery of breathing thought-less, I know I can rein in any emotionally charged thinking.

"Then keep them neutral. Good luck."

Good luck, flashed up on the screen. *I can't remember the last time someone wished me good luck.*

"The last time is always now," said the lead doctor with surprising kindness.

Well, I don't need luck this time. It's down to me, and me only. You'll see, I can do this Born Again thing.

Holding his remote control, "Ok, bring the mind monitor forward, now the reality helmet please, and at your stations. Let's begin."

The old idea of "journey to the centre of the earth" flashed into mind. *That's fucking neutral, you bustards* raced across the screen. Immediately, I became disembodied, plunging down a volcanic crater into its hidden vent, down a seemingly bottomless abyss. I felt I was skydiving toward the centre of the earth.

"That's interesting," remarked the lead doctor. "Intuitively, he has chosen an imaginary adventure to the earth's core which is the source of the planet's magnetic field, just like the human heart which generates the most powerful electromagnetic field in the body."

Hurtling down through this ever-deepening blackness, sparks began shooting up past me. Far below I could see a tiny light, like someone had struck a solitary flare inside a deep cave. It was getting hotter, sweltering, unbearable. Suddenly the tiny cave-flare erupted into a vast fountain of fire.

Incinerated immediately, I somehow found myself shot up through another volcanic crater on the other side of the planet, bursting up into the sky like a shooting star where, suddenly, I had a satellite view of planet earth.

"His heart rate's sky high, doctor."

"I know. But it's still within parameters."

The monitor screen showed a satellite view of South America and Africa closing together. "Look," remarked the lead doctor, "He's reversing several hundred million years of continental drift." As it did so, the Atlantic didn't flood back over the continental shores, but seemed to be squeezed out of existence as South America and Africa finally closed together, tight as a vice, in one super landmass. "See, he's reformed the original super continent of Pangea which consisted of South America, Africa, India, Antarctica and Australia. Clever guy."

His female colleague quipped, "We know that already, doctor. But what's this got to do with him getting in touch with his heart? That's the point of this exercise. He's merely created a fantasy adventure for himself. Like he's in the audience at a cinema watching a new Hollywood action thriller. The vicarious thrills and spills are meant to get the heart racing, but of course, it's safe. Fun. That's what he's doing now, having fun inside the reality helmet. Clever guy? He's having fun with us. He's got a reputation for this, playing games. Shall we pull him out of there?"

"No wait, let's see what happens."

Seen from space, at the centre of the supercontinent seemed to be a small lake into which, incredibly, flowed all the major river systems of Africa and South America combined – the Nile, Congo, Niger, and the Amazon and the Paraná, together with all their bewildering systems of remote tributaries. All had lost their distant mountain sources of gravitational descent, yet their vast complexities snaked toward, and eventually flowed into this little lake, which appeared now on the screen to be a violent whirlpool. What generated their incoming flow and their outgoing pulsating river systems?

Inside the small lake swam two humpback whales. "You've got to see this!" exclaimed the lead doctor. They clustered round the mind monitor. With a huge knobbly head and distinctive body shape, adults humpbacks can grow to 56 ft. in length and weigh 44 tons. Most striking are their long pectoral fins, almost like airplane wings that swivel back and forth. Famous for their spectacular breaching, and their use of air bubble nets to catch their prey, and famous for their haunting songs, these two behemoths swam in tight circles side by side, round and round, generating the powerful whirlpool.

From space, I watched mesmerized. The original supercontinent was the heart of the planet, but at the heart of the heart, swam these two giant humpback whales, round and round in unison – singing – blow-holing spray – generating a core whirlpool powerful enough to pull in all the vast river systems of Africa and South America combined, while whirling out, pumping out oxygenated water through other river channels to the vast super-body of the continent. I watched as the circling whale bodies seemed to tangle together, to be mating. Seen now from low space, their copulation appeared as one huge, naked organ, like the rhythmic pulsations of human heart ventricles.

"He's replicated the body's circulatory system!" cried the doctor. "Imagine that."

"Yes, imagine that, doctor," the female colleague critically observed. "That's all he's doing so far, imagining that, playing it safe, keeping his distance from the planetary emotions of the heart, trying to distract us. You're letting yourself get carried away."

Chastened, "You're right," admitted the lead doctor. "That's why I have you three, to keep an eye on me, not him."

They laughed. She replied, "Well, we've been here long enough to know each other inside out. No harm in the odd slip up."

Another colleague reported, "His heart rate's above the ozone hole."

I felt exalted. From my journey to the centre of the earth, to my satellite view of the original heartland of the planet, powered by a lone whirlpool of two humpback whales, I watched the rivers of life returning to their source and flowing back out again.

The screen suddenly flashed up, *Man, this is better than drugs!*

The lead doctor observed, "That's him feeling pleased with himself. Yeah, let's pull him out of there." He pressed the remote. Abruptly, the reality helmet was lifted off me.

Startled, *What? What have you done that for?*

Another colleague carefully unbound me. My body lay perfectly relaxed. The doctor pressed the remote to lift the chair into upright sitting position. *See, I didn't need all that stuff. Why did you pull the plug on me? I wasn't in trouble.*

"Having too much fun?"

Why not? What kind of life do you think I'm living?

"That's why you're in here, to find out. Have you forgotten already? Your privilege of breathing?"

Suddenly the screen went blank for a while. *Yeah, ok you're right, you're right. I guess I'm being bitchy because you pulled the plug on me. I'll never take that for granted again – the amazement of just breathing.*

"You even thanked us for that."

Something I've never said before in my life.

"A first. There might be more to come – if you choose. Don't you think the heart has something special to teach you? Like breathing?"

Blank screen again. Then suddenly, I hung my head with a strange feeling, shoulders slumped. *It's just that, well after the cosmic breathing thing, you seemed so pushy to get on with this heart thing, and so full of warnings about what might happen to me, strapping me in so tight. I – I…*

The lead doctor replied sympathetically, "What you took for 'pushy' was simply our encouragement. You are doing so well. But maybe we were too enthusiastic to press on too soon? I take your point."

I didn't expect that admission. I had misinterpreted their positive encouragement, but also, maybe they too had got it a bit wrong. For the first time since I was a little boy, I made a genuine act of contrition by asking, *Where did I go wrong today?*

I felt him smiling behind his mask. "That feels to me like another 'first' for you."

I shook my head. *Except for my childhood confessions.*

"No, back then you were lying to the priest."

I winced at the memory of my first confession.

"No, not just your first confession, all of them," continued the lead doctor. It was your parents who were wrong, not you. And Father Martin must have known. But you never took the chances in later life to be different from them. You never made that choice."

This is sounding like psycho-babble.

"Well, like I said, we do things differently here. The reality helmet is not a fairground thrill ride. Go back to the Gethsemane of the Cube and ask yourself, 'Where did I go wrong today? Is there something I can choose from today to make tomorrow different, better? Instead of another Groundhog Day making the same old mistakes again."

I never thought of it that way before, but think I see what you mean.

Suddenly, I raised my head, straightened my shoulders upright, and looked at him with eyes dawning with realisation. This felt like a new kind of confession and absolution, with a unique penance – "Ask yourself, 'Where did I go wrong today?" It was the old Catholic examination of conscience that you were supposed to do *before* confession. Now, in supermax, I was being given a new kind of penance, a hindsight reflection of 'Where did I go wrong today?' But I realised this question had to come from me. It couldn't be imposed. I had to choose it, and that choice would be my absolution.

"And by the way," the doctor added, "your 'tomorrows' have been a 'privilege' earned. We don't waste our time on no-hopers in supermax."

I smiled. *I thought you had given up on me. Is that what I think it is, a compliment?*

"Another first?"

It's been a helluva long time since 'good boy.'

"Maybe 'tomorrow' will make it worth the wait to stop hiding from the 'good' in you."

The screen sparked up in capital letters, *ME? A PSYCHOPATH?!*

"Good enough."

Dismissed.

"Go in peace," a priest would have said.

* * *

As the security door in the Cube shut behind me, I asked aloud, "Where in hell is all this going?" Suddenly my hand covered my mouth. I had broken the silence talking to myself but didn't get zapped. Startled at the sound of me, I fell back onto the bed and looked up at the white silence, the Cube of never-ending fluorescent light. My voice, it was a no-man-land voice. It had been so long, so long, enduring the silence of me. Somehow, talking to a robot didn't sound like my voice. But talking to myself felt like I was talking to a real person. That's what startled me – the SOUND of ME.

I wondered to myself, how does the brain spark conscious thinking into words? Words had to be breathed out. Like fledgling satellites, words had to be launched from a 'me' in search of a 'you', even if that was only the silence of 'me.'

The 'privilege' of speech, that's what he called it. Yes, after so much silence, it was a 'privilege" to speak again, to hear the sound of my own voice. Then out of the blue, I reflected, look at how I have used this wondrous privilege throughout my life – to manipulate, exploit, control, create fear, to give me the pleasure of hurting others. My choice of words. That goes back to my choice of thinking. And that goes back to, "Your honour, he didn't stand a chance in life."

Or a *choice* in life?

Is there something I can choose from today to make tomorrow different, better?

"You know," I laughed aloud in the Cube, "Forget all his science shit, this doc is doing my head in."

The sound of my laughter exhilarated me. I had forgotten, laughter is like an umbilical cord.

And fell into a deep sleep, dreaming with a foetal smile.

* * *

"Well?" asked the doctor, as I sat in the central chair 'tomorrow', his masked assistants standing by. The mind monitor had been wheeled into position.

Well what? I can't figure you out. You seem to play good doc, bad doc, and then good doc again.

"Like I said before – "

Yeah, I know. This isn't about me, it's about you.

"Let's make a start. Lie back and we'll strap you in."

The screen flashed up. *Hold on. I think that's where I went wrong yesterday. And maybe you did too? You never strapped me down so carefully before. I think it worried me – what might happen.*

"You didn't show it. In fact, you seemed cocky, overconfident, like a tiger on the hunt."

Maybe that's where I went wrong?

"Do not be afraid. That seems to be your rule of life."

You don't forget a thing.

"Neither do you. That's why you don't show your fear."

Of the Lord, you mean?

"Returning to your source, are you?"

Exasperated, *Are we going to talk all day, or get on with it?*

"He nodded to an assistant. "Just a couple of straps this time. He'll be fine." Then to me, "Your robot will observe 'live' again, on standby."

The mind monitor flashed up, *The knock, knock, who's there bit of a freak? Yeah sure, let him stay.* As I laid back, they fitted the reality helmet over my head, its dark face visor blocking out the high-tech light. As the doctor pressed the remote, I heard one of them say, "Doctor, while he was 'talking' with you just now, his heart rate really jumped."

"I know. He's scared, but trying not to show it. Let's see what happens."

Sixteen

Is Love a Sin?

Ten years old, cautiously I lowered myself down into an armchair, facing the stork of Father Martin in the vestry, and swallowed the lump in my throat. "Is – is this my penance, Father?"

From his mini settee his long thin face with blubber lips smiled kindly, "Not yet, but it will lead to your penance one day, my son."

Fidgeting, "Father, w – will it be bad?"

He shook his stork head. "Your penance yet to come will free you from all your sins, my son."

"Father, why do you always call me 'my son'?"

His blubber lips slit wide open, "Why do you always call me 'Father'?"

I blinked, taken aback. "Fath – Can I get a glass of water?"

"You know where it is."

I felt myself sweating as I stood up and walked to a side door which opened to a kitchenette with an adjoining toilet. Returning, my hands cradled the glass of water in my lap. Father Martin placed both hands upon his knee, interlocking his long fingers, and stared at me with his dark eyes. Dark hair, side-parted, immaculately shaven, he looked so young. "Think of me as your father, my son. Your heavenly Father."

The water wavered in my glass.

Without turning, he reached a long arm behind him to lift a paper from his desk, and then studied it. "Sister Bridget says here you're a smart kid, you know." I nodded. "Tell me your dreams."

I blinked. "Dreams? What do you mean, Father?"

"What you dream about, you know, when you grow up."

At the corners of my mouth a smile quivered. No one had ever asked me that before. I thought for a bit. Hesitantly, I replied, "Well, I like maps and stories. Stories about explorers. I'm good at geography and history." My ten-year old voice began to grow in confidence, "I like reading about North American Indians and European explorers, like Henry Hudson who discovered the Hudson river in later New York state; Hernando de Soto who discovered the Mississippi river and explored the American southwest; the Lewis and Clarke expedition which travelled up the Missouri river to the Pacific coast; the discovery of the source of the Nile by Richard Burton and John Speke," and nearly breathless, "the accidental discovery of the full length of the Amazon by a Spanish conquistador I can't remember his name Father."

His eyes widened in amazement, arching his dark eyebrows, as he uncrossed his stork legs and leaned forward, "Where did you learn this from?"

Still excited, "The school library has maps and picture books and little kids' books about explorers. So I got my mother to sign a public library card for me and then she forgets until the next year. I snee—" I bit off what I was going to say, *sneak the books into the house*, but I think Father Martin knew. "And the search for the Northwest Passage to India, the Dutch East India Company; Francis Drake, Magellan, and Captain Cook, and—"

"Hold on," he laughed incredulously. My face enlightened with a smile. I had made Father Martin laugh. "Look! "I pulled out my public library card to show him. His fingers fondled it delicately as I explained, "You see the name of that boy on the card? *He doesn't sin!* I do, Father, but *he doesn't.*"

A cloud-shadow frowned across his face. He leaned back in his two-seater, holding his stork wings behind his head. "Ex-plor-ers," he said very deliberately. "My son, you're running away from something."

Gutted by the bull's eye of his remark, I spilled my glass of water on my lap. His blubber smile slit across his narrow face. "You've wet yourself."

Ashamed, I jumped up to run for a kitchen towel to dry off my pants as best I could. Hiding in the kitchenette frantically pacing back and forth, my mind scrambled for a reply to his reading my mind. This was worse than confession. But finally, I opened the kitchenette door and sat again in the vestry armchair, my heart thumping, determined to face his mind reading radar. I blurted defiantly, "I'm running away from The Fear of the Lord, Father, as far away as I can get when I grow up. There! I've said it."

What I meant of course was HIM, but didn't dare. But I knew he knew as I sat there with my fingers knotted together on my lap, sweating again.

Sadly shaking his stork head, "You can run, but you can't hide, my son. No river is long enough to explore that far."

Still defiant, "I'll find the source that no one else has found, I'll try even if it kills me."

"Or someone else?"

Shocked, ten years old, I gulped hard. "What do you want, Father?"

"Come next week after confession and show me some of your books. I'd like that."

For the next two years, aged ten to twelve, that's what I did. We sat together on the mini settee, my open book straddling our knees as I keenly pointed out the adventures I had read about. If we were looking at a world map, sometimes his long forefinger would delicately trace the outline body of each continent, sensuously. Father Martin was an avid listener, admiring the growth of my mind. At these times I wished he was my real father, not my heavenly Father of all His children. I wanted to be special, his only son.

By this time I was a near adolescent, but totally innocent and ignorant of my body. Once, I brought home a school biology book with basic diagrams of male and female anatomy. My father found me curiously looking at it and ripped it apart with his bare hands. Then his fist hit me hard as a brick down below. Doubled up on the floor, I couldn't stop vomiting. "Clean it up. The pleasure of SIN! Never touch that thing. Remember your catechism!

'Question: Does God know all things? Answer: God knows all things, even our most secret thoughts, words and actions.'

"That thing." That's what he called it. It had a life of its own. Even peeing, I couldn't control that. It had to pee sometime. But this other "thing"? When it went stiff and throbbing, I didn't know what was happening. What was it for? I didn't dare touch it for fear of the PAIN of HELL.

Maybe Father Martin would know? But I couldn't ask. I felt too ashamed. From my parents I didn't know what love was, just a brutal vacancy that's all. During my weekly talks with Father Martin in the vestry, when we sat together so close to each other, my skin tingled with our fringe contact side by side. Hidden under my enthusiastic book reading my heart yearned for something closer. I couldn't remember my parents ever cuddling me. By now, hormones stirring with sin without "my realising", I wanted to throw my arms around him, but I didn't know why. I think I loved him. Was love a sin? Without realising?

Aged twelve, that's when he first enveloped the stork wing of his arm around my shoulders as I read yet another explorer book to him. His feathers brushed lightly against the back of my neck, electrifying "that thing" down below, which stiffened with a near-eruption of wetness of I don't know what.

He noticed. I hung my head as he reached across my lap with one hand and cocked his thumb and middle finger together, and flicked the innocent bulge in my trousers. He turned his long thin face to me, looking down with his slimy blubbery smile, "You think I want to touch you, don't you?" he teased.

Paralysed, my body locked down, breathless, speechless. My mind locked down, stunned, thoughtless.

"I know you want me to. In fact, I know you want to touch me. As a priest I know everything. But you see, I'm a watcher, not a sinner."

He paused, as if waiting for me to breathe again. "I don't want you to touch me." Father Martin slurped his fat lips at me, "I want you to touch him."

He paused. "Kevin," he called.

From out the kitchenette door hesitantly stepped twelve-year old Kevin, a gawky classmate of mine, robed in a white surplice and black cassock. Strangely, I noticed he was bare footed. A curly, ginger-haired, freckled-face lad, he looked frozen, a ghost of his usual jokey self. He stopped at the semi-circle of armchairs just to the side of me. Below his cassock, which hung like a girl's long skirt to his bare ankles, his toes kept gripping the carpet tightly. He glanced at me with confused brown eyes.

"Kev?! Wha—"

"Shush, my son."

* * *

The mind-monitor screen showed a satellite view of the supercontinent with the whirlpool at its heart.

"It looks like he's up to his old tricks again," remarked a masked woman in the team.

Disembodied, I descended rapidly until my view hovered like a soundless helicopter, perhaps five hundred feet above the two humpback whales as they swam round and round, generating the powerful whirlpool that circulated the vast rivers of life. Round and round, blow-holing spray.

That's when it hit me. These ocean-going giants had nowhere to go.

Neither did I in the vestry, flashed across the monitor screen.

Long ago I remembered seeing a nature documentary about arctic beluga whales trapped in a large breathing hole, an oasis of air amidst a vast desert of frozen ice, swimming round and round with nowhere to go, too far to swim under the ice to open sea, round and round, surfacing for their next breath, and the next, until they starved to death or drowned.

At school during my National Geographic fascination for animal facts, I remembered that humpbacks migrate for up to 10,000 miles. Their haunting songs, because water conducts sound five times more readily than air, means they are exquisitely attuned to long-distance listening. A humpback whale singing in the Caribbean, for example, can be heard by a fellow whale off the west coast of Ireland more than 4,000 miles away. Yet here I had stuck them, jammed into this tiny whirlpool of water, cut off from their social pod, with nothing to do but prowl round and round, like my pacing back and forth in the Cube. Yet humpback brains are chock full of spindle cells, like humans, which are a marker of high intelligence. Spindle cells are responsible for speech, social organisation, and rapid "gut" reactions to a crisis. Spindle cells are also credited with allowing us to feel love, empathy, and to suffer emotionally.

Round and round, I watched them – suffer.

I'm a watcher, not a sinner," flashed across the screen.

My casual cruelty shocked me. I always took it for granted, never noticed it, even in my casual thinking or daydreaming. It was always there – like breathing or gravity – like father like son, I liked hurting people. Then I remembered what the doc had once asked me, "What does a blind, deaf and paralysed man take most for granted?" Now I knew – the cruelty of life.

Suddenly on impulse, (it must have been some of my dormant spindle cells come back to life), I felt an urge to rescue the whales. I sky-dived down to the circling behemoths, and dove through the blow-hole spray of one.

"That's interesting," remarked the lead doctor, "he's actually trying to rescue himself."

Deafened by their songs! Their vocal vibrations felt like earthquakes – powerful grunts, long rumbling groans, shrieks, low guttural roars, amidst soothing, tender squeals, so haunting, hypnotic, majestic. Their songs that could power for thousands of ocean miles were caged and stunted. Then I realised their songs were escaping along the vast rivers of life, calling out into the wilderness of the solitary super-continent as if it were a vast human body moaning and groaning in agony…

Until I realised it was my own body groaning and grunting *Ugh! Ugh! Ugh!*

Monitors began beeping and flickering. "His heart's out of control, doctor!"

"Defib! Quick! Restraint off! Shirt off."

"Clear!"

My body jerked up.

"Again."

"Clear!" It jerked up again, arching violently.

"Again. That's done it."

I could breathe again. "Injection," ordered the lead doctor, "Stabilise his heart."

Confused, the pounding of my heart began slowing. For a long time I just lay there, as if coming back to life. Finally, I asked, *What happened?*

"We'll talk about that when you've had a couple of days rest. You need it." He pressed the remote and raised me to a sitting position. "We'll switch off the fluorescent lights for proper sleep. Give you a table lamp, timed for day and night. You've earned it. You did good."

Bewildered, *Did good?! Another 'good boy' moment? You got to be kidding. I nearly died!*

"We won't let you die."

Shaking my head, *Saved my life again? Well, thank you again.*

"Like I said, we don't waste our – "

On no-hopers?

"Like with the whales, you tried."

That was just my imagination.

"If you can imagine something good, it means you can actually do something good, if you choose."

Choice. You keep driving that home to me.

"Think of it this way. Whether life is a fluke chance or not, it doesn't matter. What really matters is choice, how you choose to live. Go back to your bible. The Genesis myth, it's all about choice, isn't it? The primal abyss of choice. The Garden-of-Eden-choice which eventually led to the choice of Gethsemane and the Cross. Sacrifice."

The screen went blank for a while. *I'm shattered. Too tired to think.*

After a few deep-sleep days, *So, what happened?* I asked the doctor.

"You made a good start. At first, we thought you might still be playing games with us, going back to the heart of the original super-continent – and the whales. But this time you saw something completely new. You were moved to rescue the whales from your cruelty of putting them there."

I've never done anything like that before. As a kid I microwaved my father's cat.

"We tend to forget the good things in life."

That's a laugh, I scoffed.

"What's the best thing that you have ever done in your life?"

Jesus Christ! You really can read my mind. Day one. You didn't have the mind-monitor running before my first day in the Cube. How can you know that was the last thing I asked myself? That YOU should have asked me?

"I'm asking you now. The heart never forgets. You see, sometimes the brain is too clever for its own good. It can block out a lot of things, but the heart can't. The pulse of the heart is primordial, the base drumbeat of the body's deep memory. EVERYTHING," he stressed. "I told you before, it's called 'cardiac neurological memory'. The heart encodes, stores, and can retrieve ALL your emotional memories – even the good things you have forgotten."

Before I had time to think of a flippant rebuff, the doctor abruptly commanded, "You have some unfinished business with the whales." Abruptly, an assistant placed the reality helmet over my head and the doc pressed the remote.

Instantly, I found myself inside a living submarine, one of the two trapped humpbacks, but now swimming together in the open ocean, undulating, glide-flying under the surface, nosing up for air, in unison of blow-hole sprays. Their engine room, their heart, five feet in length and weighing 400 pounds, was pounding and pumping fifty-eight gallons of blood through their vast bodies with each throbbing, deafening beat. Once again, I found myself inside their majestic songs, groaning and squealing hundreds if not thousands of underwater miles to their bereft, ever-listening pod. Suddenly, I felt the longing of parents for their runaway or disappeared teen and adult children, waiting, always on the lookout, hoping, ever-listening for a phone call, a message...

It was all in the whale songs, their longing, haunting songs. Humpbacks can live up to ninety years. A Bowhead was found to be over two hundred years old. Yes, it was all in their songs, their heart of deep, ancient and terrible memories. Three hundred years of their human slaughter, these innocent, child-like behemoths had been butchered, sliced and diced. It was all in their whale songs, in my pounding, hoping heart...

An assistant called out, "Doctor, he's actually crying."

"I didn't think it would be possible."

"I did," said the robot.

"You seem to know him better than we do."

As I listened to their anguished memory-songs, I began to realise the whales were not simply repeating the same old butchery and history of hatred, but they were constantly changing their songs, innovating, improvising, creating new songs, joyful thousand-mile songs. And, like getting an email or a YouTube video from thousands of miles away, they knew of other whale pods who remembered over a century of human annihilation in their local territory, but who now, allowed enthralled whale-watcher tourists to reach out from their little boats, to pat and stroke their calves! In this wake of industrial genocide, their trusting vulnerability made me sob. And their forgiveness – all the more because the ocean-wide whale population knows that hunting still goes on. That's what made it so extraordinary. It wasn't 100% safe – to trust, to be giantly affectionate with these tiny human killers. To me, their songs felt like the Israelis and Palestinians reconciling. Like resolution of the Catholic / Protestant thing in Northern Ireland. The whales could do it better than us humans.

Better than me.

They could change their songs.

I couldn't.

The screen flashed, *Get me out of here. Please! Let me out. Let me out!*

Remote, then helmet off. As I wiped away my acid tears, *Thank you doctor. Thank you. I couldn't stand it anymore!*

He remarked, "Even though some carry within their lifetime a century of their pod's near-extinction, the whales' agony of song-memories have returned them to their source – to their Original Innocence – born again with an impossible trust in life, even us humans."

Seventeen

- - - - - - - - - - - -

Cardiac Neurological Memory

After a few days rest the lead doctor asked me, "You couldn't stand what?"

The screen flashed, *Myself.*

"Don't we all?"

But how can I do it?

"It's the old cliché, face your fears."

The Fear of the Lord? Him.

"No, not him. You."

I don't get you.

"Your fears. The whales do. They remember EVERYTHING. So do you. You need to find your whale song, maybe a new one."

I don't think I can do that.

"He does, your robot. He thinks you can."

Him again? Is he becoming one of the team?

"No, it's you again," replied the doctor. "That's the point, the heart of the matter. You – the same old thousand-mile song – again and again and again. The whales and the courts and the psychiatrists have stopped listening to you. Except him, your robot. So try, find a new song. You never know, there might be someone out there who is listening for you."

Fat chance of that, I scoffed. *But I'll try, for him,* nodding to the robot.

"Let's make a new start." Helmet on, remote. My heart-song visualised a handheld cam-video, like a disembodied peeping Tom, a salacious watcher, only 'them' in view. Fear, that's what I got off on, got my heart pumping. That's what you would think, but no. I remained ice cold. In the other prisons, behind my back they used to call me "dead pulse." Their medical tests confirmed it. My aura of menace created fear in others without raising my heart rate. Even in primary school the wary kids nicknamed me "dead baby." As a child I was so controlled, both in my studies and in my "play fighting" on the school grounds, coolly hurting the other kids.

Rapid strobe-like memories flashed up on the mind monitor screen. When kind-faced school mates complained to me about disrupting their class, I bashed them to the playground floor, then a kick in the balls, and my snarl, "Tell anyone and I'll fuckin' kill ya!" They believed me, my power of menace. No one dared to grass on me. The strobe images came fast and furious depicting different scenarios throughout my life – schoolboys and girls, teen boys and teen girls, their faces, once they had got to know the real me, all looked the same – fear stricken, panicked, humiliated – no one daring to tell. Then my high school vandalism, street brawls and stolen cars and later

on, the single mums with dumb brats that didn't deserve
to live, half choking them for fun as a warning to her, the
bitch! Pain, the king of fear, commanded them – Kneel!
Bow down! – to ME without end.

* * *

Kevin, twelve years old, stood bare foot in his cassock in
Father Martin's vestry, the door locked behind the outer
purple curtain. "You," his slender finger pointed to me,
"Get changed, nothing on underneath." From a wardrobe
I scurried with it into the toilet, fumbling off my clothes,
naked under my Mass surplice and cassock. The toilet
bowl beckoned to me with escape, to flush myself down
through the sewers where even his probiscis couldn't
reach.

After he made Kev and I clear the semi-circle of
armchairs, from behind his desk Father Martin rolled
out a mini wrestling mat. From his two-seater, "For your
penance, wrestle for your salvation," he commanded softly.
"On your hands and knees. See who can pin the other
first." We went down on hands and knees, then looked
back to him through our fog of confusion.

"Wrestle." In a tent, that's what it felt like inside our
cassocks, hesitantly trying to find our way out. That's what
Father Martin wanted – to watch two altar boys kicking
out of their cassocks in order to finally hug and kiss each
other, naked, after so many Masses that they had served
together, dressed up as angelic little girls before the altar of
God. That's all they had ever wanted – to embrace naked
before the altar of God and transubstantiate each other's

body into the Body and Spunk of Christ. That was Father Martin's fantasy. He told us.

That's what he wanted to see. But for the first months of these weekly, after-school sessions, Kev and I remained frozen and deeply confused. We never talked about it, avoiding eye contact in classes. Also, both of us were incredibly naïve and ignorant about our bodies. I suspected Kev had the same kind of father as mine. Father Martin became an increasingly frustrated stage director of his play.

Neither of us had masturbated before. Father Martin could tell. He knew from our confessions. He knew everything.

The OBVIOUS came to us so slowly, hesitantly, clumsily. Our weekly sessions of penance in the vestry continued for some time before we found ourselves *wanting* to urgently grapple off our Mass surplices and cassocks and wrestle naked, two twelve-year old altar boys before Father Martin, the "watcher, not a sinner."

When "that thing" down there of mine and Kev's started getting hard and slippery against each other, that's when Father Martin started bringing the tripod camera to film us, and the altar bells, which he jangled to start us off, pronouncing, "Do this in memory of Me" – the solemn words of the consecration at Mass, the moment of transubstantiation into the Body of Christ. Sweating and panting on each other, when he eyed our slippery dicks, Father Martin called out, "It's the holy water. The holy water comes first. Drink it. Then comes the sin." We had no choice. It was our penance. But before the sin could urgently come, Father Martin jangled the altar bells again, "STOP!" We had to pull away, panting hard, leaning back on our bums from each other, wide-legged, gawping at each other's stiff "thing" which was drooling, pulsing in desperation, but DENIED by the jangling altar bells.

"That's your penance," his blubber lips grinned. "Get dressed." But we couldn't endure it. We had to SIN! Suddenly we lunged together, hugging each other all sweaty, panting, thrusting against each other until we grabbed each other's throbbing prick and spunked to our first orgasms.

Caught on candid camera. Searing humiliation, shame, and confused ecstasy. It felt unbearable. But in the months that followed we found a powerful pain relief. Because it became addictive, the pleasure of spunking onto each other deadened our humiliation. We felt helpless in our addiction. That's what Father Martin wanted to see. He was a watcher, not a pusher.

But when our addiction became predictable, when Kev and I knowingly knew what to do, that's when Father Martin began to lose interest. Boring. It was our butterfly metamorphosis from naïve innocence to sexual corruption, before our bodies and minds were ready for it, that's what got Father Martin's rocks off.

Until something changed and grabbed his interest. Long before I was twelve, I was notorious as the school bully, like father like son. Father Martin knew it, the whole school and neighbourhood knew it, even the police from complaints about my local vandalism and street fights. So gradually, the sadism of my father began to snake itself into the discovery of sex with Kevin. My humiliation, I realised, could only be overcome through power. The power to hurt and control, like Him. So, in the vestry sessions I began to hurt Kevin sexually, keenly caught on film. Father Martin loved this development – the growth of my mind.

He made us watch his final edit called, "The Body and Spunk of Christ." But as I watched, I blocked myself out of the horrible scenes. I could only watch Kevin, the close-up shots of his uncomprehending, blinking eyes as I hurt him. *Why?* His eyes begged me, *Why? Why?*

"Because I like to," I panted onto his freckled, pained face.

I think that's when I too became "a watcher, not a sinner." Invisible, only 'him' or 'them' in the scenes of my memory. Never me doing the sinning.

The final frontier came with kissing. "That thing" down there had a life of its own, a sin of its own. It overwhelmed me, both of us. But kissing? Neither of my parents had ever kissed me before. I had never kissed a girl, let alone a boy. "Kiss him," Father Martin ordered. But I felt kissing was something voluntary, deliberate. You had to *want* to kiss someone. Compared to involuntary penile arousal, kissing felt so personal, intimate, too intimate to be ordered or imposed. Lying naked on top of Kevin, I turned my head back towards Father Martin, "No, I don't want to." Tears of relief sprung from Kevin's grateful eyes. He didn't want too either.

"Kiss him," his voice commanded sternly.

I looked down into Kev's frightened eyes. We touched lips.

"That's not a kiss."

My eyes told Kevin, *I'm sorry. I'm sorry.* I pushed my lips gently against his, then withdrew.

"Tongues!" he commanded.

Neither of us wanted to kiss, that was our shared revulsion. So, a forced mouthful of tongues made me gag and abruptly vomit all over Kevin's freckled face.

Caught on candid camera.

I pulled back in disgust and tears, kneeling above Kevin as his hand and forearm swiped across his vomit-laden face, coughing, jerking onto to his side. "I'm so sorry Kev, I'm sorry! Sorry! Sorry!"

The limit of my degradation had been reached. I sobbed to Father Martin, "I'm never going to forget this."

"I know," his blubber lips smiled, patting the film camera with his delicate fingers, "neither will they."

Catholic priests are addressed always as "Father." When you had a father like mine, calling the priest "Father" blurred the two into one monster. So different in appearance and manner, yet they seemed to breathe as one breath, two halves of one brain, often grinning and backslapping each other after the Sunday Mass together, just the two of them as the congregation trailed away. Growing up, I felt that my father could be in two places at the same time, in the cellar and in the confessional. In fact, three places, the third inside my head all the time where, like a knobbled calf held down and struggling against the branding iron, they seared my brain with the Leviticus laws of sin, and then released me to addictive sexual penance. Cowboys of God.

After the kissing, I stopped going to confession and serving at the altar. Aged twelve, that's when I vowed to kill him. "Do this in memory of Me," he had said. *Yeah, ring the fucking altar bells. When I got through with him, he would never forget this day.*

And Him. The fucking both of them.

✳ ✳ ✳

High up on his remote hill the judge watched his monitor screen. "One to watch," they had said. Had he committed a judicial sin of flawed justice by removing this inmate to supermax? A single tear crawled out of a blinking eye and wriggled along the worn terrain of his cheek, tickling wetly down to his chin, dripping off. He had not cried since he was twelve-years old when he lost his arm, like it was his virginity.

✳ ✳ ✳

The strobe memories sometimes stuttered to a stop, like the Father Martin scene, then flickered onward again until randomly…

On the mind-monitor I saw myself for the first time.

"Look!" exclaimed the doctor.

Me, mid-twenties, a lifetime ago, flashed up on the mind-monitor screen. Tall, slim, strong. Shaven head, a scarred left eyebrow, a hard, raw-boned face that narrowed to a pointy chin. A handsome but hard face. The eyes, ever watchful. I had forgotten. All my memories were of 'them', the people that I hurt, never 'me' in the scene. A disembodied, detached watcher. That's how I liked it, how I lived.

But in a little corner-shop queue, there I stood in work overalls, a part time car mechanic. Picked it up as a teen during a spell in secure. Even by that time, I had got away

118

with a lot of things I shouldn't have. But publicly assaulting a teacher? Well, he had it coming. 'Rehabilitation' it was called, the mechanic stuff. Restoration to the community. I convinced them to "let me out." For a while with a tag. That stopped nothing. No one dared to grass me.

Ahead of me in the shop queue stood what looked like a single mum with a weird looking toddler girl in a push chair who turned to smile at all the shoppers, even me. If only the kid knew, I thought to myself. The woman held a heavy basket stuffed with food and nappies and toddler accessories, when a rough looking man entered the little shop and strode past the queue and whispered to her urgently, "I've got to have some. Now."

"But the bairn, she can't go with—"

"You'll get it back, I promise. Get your purse out," he pressed.

The Pakistani shop owner, serving a customer before her, overheard and frowned with concern. So did the rest of the queue but said nothing. The unkempt man grabbed the purse and lifted out a number of bills, kissed her on the forehead, and walked out quickly. He hadn't taken any notice of the kid. Her father? Not a chance. Stepfather? Maybe. Charmer and hustler? Probably, I thought, the whole neighbourhood knew. Probably her girlfriends had tried to tell her, but she wouldn't believe them. Single mums are suckers for charm, promises and a good time in bed – until the damage is done. I should know. It takes a bad guy to know one.

From behind, I bet she had a nice figure, but the baggy tracksuit bottoms and sweatshirt top didn't do her any favours. A short, braided ponytail hung below her neck. I couldn't see her face. Next at the counter, she emptied her basket. When the bill was totted up the shopkeeper, who was middle-aged and no doubt a family man, furrowed his brown face sympathetically, "You're short by quite a lot this week. I'm so very sorry. You'll have to put some things back. Just leave them here on the counter." Behind me the queue fidgeted.

"But she can't go without—"

"I've subbed you before, Caroline. I can't keep – I've got to make a living too, you know."

At that moment, it was as if a door opened, and I stepped outside myself for the first time. I said from behind her, "Here man, what's she owe you? I'll pay the difference." When she turned round, the first thing I noticed was a funny slogan on her sweatshirt top which declared, "Don't Overthink!" Then her face. She was probably nineteen going on thirty-five, but a pretty face if you looked closely. Her eyes, blue as blue, looked at me.

"Oh, that's very kind, but I can't let you."

I smiled back, "Don't overthink."

"No," she protested, "No I can't – "

"Shut your mouth, girl." The queue was getting restless behind me. I turned to face their impatience. My voice hit them like a gust of winter wind, "If one of you fucking do-gooders has a better idea, then step up to the counter so we can all go fucking home." That did the trick.

I sidled past her to the counter. "How much? I've just had a little winning on the lottery, the first time I've ever been lucky in life." I turned to her and her odd smiling kid, "Let me share the luck. You look down on yours."

Embarrassed, she thanked me profusely, quickly

packed her shopping bags, hung them on the back of the pushchair and hurried past the chastened queue, out the door.

The Pakistani smiled warmly at me, "You're a good man."

"No, I'm not. I'm a bad man. You're the good man. I could tell you meant what you said to her. Thanks for subbing her, for trying."

Outside, she was waiting for me on the dumpy high street. "I can't thank you enough. I'll pay you back, I've seen you round the neighbourhood. I promise, you'll get your money."

"Forget it."

"No, really I will."

"I said, forget it! It was a bit of luck that came my way, that's all."

From the pushchair her weird little kid beamed smiles up at me.

"You're a good man," she said gratefully. "I don't know what I would have done this week with—"

"No, I'm bad. You don't know me. Very bad."

Suddenly, she smiled a cute little smile at me, "Well then, it's been my lucky day to meet you, Mr. Bad Guy!"

"I could see you were down on your luck, not just with the money, but the kid. Bit of a freak, don't you think?"

Her petite face reddened, then a SLAP stung my face. Stunned, then I smiled. "Feisty, huh? The last time someone did that to me, they ended up in hospital."

"A FREAK, that's what you think my girl is?!" She ranted at me on the busy street, "She was born with a disability. It's called Down's Syndrome. During pregnancy, the pressure I've been under has been unbelievable – to get rid of it. 'It,' that's what they called her. The doctors kept telling me, 'She won't be able to do this, she can't do that, your life will be a misery.' I've had to fight to keep her. You know, in this country the abortion laws allow termination of a disabled child right up to the moment of entering the birth canal! Worse, they make no distinction between a foetal disability and a fatal foetal diagnosis. They're all the same. Worthless, unwanted. It's morons like you who are the freaks. Not her! I can tell you right now, Mr. Bad Guy, she will do most of the things the doctors told me she will never do, and then some! She's the best thing I've ever done in my life!"

Passers-by gave us a wide berth round her outburst.

And SLAP! "That's for good measure, YOU'RE THE FREAK!" she raged. Put me in hospital, will you? Try giving birth! There's nothing you can do to hurt me."

Completely taken back, I wanted to smile with admiration at the fact that she wasn't afraid of me, but I didn't dare. She wouldn't understand my smile.

Instead, my bony cheek still stinging, I answered simply, "You're right. I'm the freak. That's why I'm bad."

Suddenly, she reached out and touched the sleave of my work overall. Her angry little face softened, "I'm sorry. Getting that off my chest, I've taken it out on you. You know," she shrugged, "him. Him and his gambling and drinking. But he sticks around and makes me laugh though."

"I don't like the look of him."

"I better go. See you round. Maybe a coffee sometime? To make up?"

"No, I'm no good for you. Stay away from me."

She smiled her cute little smile again, "Well, like I said, it's been my lucky day to meet you, Mr. Bad Guy."

I smiled back, "Mine too. See ya." Her little girl merrily waved back at me.

When I asked round the terraced neighbourhood, I was told that Down's kids are generally smiley and friendly with everyone, even people like me. Good natured, naïvely trusting – like the whales.

* * *

I liked her. Caroline was fearless. She felt an equal to my "Do not be afraid." Though I knew she was scared, and everyone is, she had found a way through her fear, so different from me. Mine was callous and cruel, hers was bold and caring. That's what I admired about her. I didn't want anything from her, not sex or love. I simply liked her, that's all. I had never felt like this about anyone before. So, over the months I kept an eagle eye out for her in the neighbourhood. I noticed, and it wasn't just me, that her little girl was no longer smiling.

There was gossip of her running out of money again. I knew where she lived. It was a short walk. When I knocked at the door it was mister "dead pulse" knocking. He opened the door, a bit bleary eyed from drink and looking smug. The freeloader, the controller, I thought to myself. It takes one to know one. Surprised to see me, he asked, "What do you want?"

I shot a straight-arm jab to his throat, gripping his windpipe in a chokehold. "Fucking you!" I snarled. I like the windpipe. It's so soft and vulnerable. He staggered back, startled, gagging, as I threatened him, "Raise a fist to me and I'll crush your windpipe. I've done it before."

Caroline came rushing to the door, wide-eyed aghast at the scene. No, she was aghast at me. In that moment I could see she realised how dangerous I was, just like I had told her – a bad man – whom she had dared to slap twice in the face. Here I was on her terraced doorstep, half strangling her live-in piece of shit sleaze. Like a lion I growled at her, "You're better than him! Your kid is better than him! Ask yourself, why is she no longer happy and smiling? The whole neighbourhood can see it." Then I glared at him, bug-eyed and gasping as I wobbled his head back and forth, "He knows, don't you? Don't you? I'll tell her. He's touching her, that's what he's up to. That's why he's crawled into your life. He's fucking your mind and fucking your life. You can be better than this – better than this! – for yourself and for your kid."

She stood shocked, ashen faced.

I dragged him out the door onto the pavement and beat him to a pulp, for all to see. I taught him the Fear of the Lord that he would never forget. Then I simply sat on the curb, mister "dead pulse", and waited for the police. Caroline had long shut the door, but I could hear her sobbing inside.

Charged with GBH, I faced a long prison sentence, but the charge was reduced to Common Assault due to "extenuating circumstances." First, Caroline and the neighbours testified that my attack had been provoked by him. They lied, but he didn't dare deny it. Second, he admitted running up debts in the mother's name, putting her child at risk of unintended neglect by her. Third, he confessed, he dared not confess, to fooling around with a little Down's Syndrome girl. Headline news in the local paper. I got off with a fairly light sentence, but it was the start of my prison career, inside with like-minded bully boys, picking up tips and tricks along the way.

She wrote to me in prison, school-kid printing on a notepad sheet of paper. It was short, simple, to thank me, offering to visit. I wrote back: "Never write again or come here. I'm no good for you. But tell the little freak, I don't know? Tell her that she's better than you, because of you. Mr. Bad Guy."

So that was it. My lucky 'doing time' for her and the kid, almost like a baptism. When you have ten thousand strobe-memories of guilt flashing before your eyes, all the same nasty shit, it's easy to miss a fluke of original innocence. I had forgotten.

Baptism is remembering and forgetting…

"Doctor, his heart's going like a kettledrum!"

"Ok, let's get him out of there."

Remote, and helmet off.

"He's done it!" I heard the doctor exclaim to the others. "That's cardiac neurological memory for you. I didn't—" He stopped himself, turned to the attendant robot, and winked. "I know, but you did."

On the central chair I lay stunned. My heart felt like an open pit mine gutted down to the geological strata of memories which I never knew existed, let alone should be hauled up to the surface. What to do with them? How to make sense of this ugly slag heap littered with a few paltry diamonds in my life? The open pit of my heart lay too empty and too full, too numb and too raw, to even ask such questions, let alone for answers.

Eighteen

A Pinprick of No Reason

Exhausted, I simply lay there on the central chair, eyes closed, vaguely listening to their group consultation. "Incredible!" a male doctor marvelled, citing my emotional engagement and memory retrieval.

"He's sick," remarked a female doctor bluntly.

Surprised, the lead doctor protested, "What? How so? He's making good progress. Can't you see?"

"It's obvious. His deep sickness. He—"

"Hold on," protested the lead doctor. "Let's pull up some chairs and talk about this. Clear away the monitor trolly." They shuffled four chairs into a circle beside the laid-back central chair where I lay half conscious. In case I woke up they kept their masks on. I was not deemed ready to see them yet.

"Ok, shoot."

The female doctor had a legal tone to her voice. "We all know this man is smart, very smart. The question is – Is he *choosing* to show us these memories in order to make us feel sorry for him? To impress us? Or are these spontaneous memory retrievals which he had long buried? Either way, what difference does it make? Historic sex abuse and the like are a commonplace defence in court for terrible crimes committed later as an adult. It was part of his defence. What we have just seen is very moving, I admit. But the law is there, like a surgeon, to amputate emotion from the factual evidence. Can these early experiences possibly *justify* his later killings? Let's not forget, it's not only what he did, but the way he killed them. The judge and jury had to weigh up the difference between his past and present – and found no connection."

In his remote, hilltop law library, the judge nodded with relief as he watched his monitor screen at his mahogany desk. The log fire sparked and crackled in its deep Inglenook recess as he sipped another crystal glass of Samurai sedative. *Maybe I didn't get it wrong, after all?*

A burst of animated opinions. "Hold on, hold on," calmed the lead doctor. "One at a time, ok?"

"But there *is* a connection between past and present," urged the other female doctor. "You know my specialty is in child development. There is an early timeline in a baby's and toddler's life necessary for healthy development. It's called 'imprinting,' or attachment bonding with a parent or carer. There is a short window of opportunity for talking, walking, social interactions, playing, empathy, laughing, etc. Miss out, and the child can be emotionally stunted for the rest of his or her life. Look at his horrific childhood. No cuddles, no affection, no bonding, no empathy, no conscience, no laughter, no play with others. His stunted and distorted past was brought into his adult present. We all do this to a certain extent. We don't actually see the present because, 'without realising', we overlay it with our past. That's what the judge should have considered more seriously in a case this extreme. So should we."

A male doctor objected, "But that implies we can never change in later life. That's simply not true. Who has the perfect parents and perfect upbringing? What we are seeing with this inmate just now, is positive change. I think The Born Again is gradually re-imprinting him. Give him a chance, and time."

As I lay there it all sounded like far away mumbling until...

"Notice," said the robot.

"Notice what?" asked the lead doctor.

The robot's chest screen came to life, as if running a high-speed rewind of a film, stop, no, start again, looking for the right scene. All eyes fixed upon the robot which until now, they tended not to notice. "There." He froze an image. "Let's start with this one," it's mouth-speaker said. "He's six years old locked in the cellar, pleading 'let me out.'"

Playback: "Do not be afraid." That's when I learned to control my heartbeat, to keep it steady, and while even-voiced, I convinced him that I understood the Fear of the Lord. So he let me out, time after time. Even then I realised that if I could convince and manipulate him, I could convince and manipulate anyone. My aura of menace came later as I got bigger and stronger. I had discovered the Holy Trinity – Convince, Manipulate and Menace. Yes, I understood the Fear of the Lord, alright. Him.

Stop, freeze, went the robot screen.

"Many of the world's dictators would fit these traits," observed the robot. "To come closer to home, think of Lance Armstrong, seven times winner of the cycling Tour de France. He "convinced, manipulated and menaced" his way to global fame, dope-cheating the cycling world and cancer world, who gave hope to millions of cancer sufferers by his inspirational talks, all lies, telling them what they wanted to hear."

"You don't mean," the lead doctor ventured, "Are you saying he might be conning us right now?"

"See?" nodded the first woman doctor, that's what I was trying to say. He's smart. He knows how to con and manipulate people, even us."

The other male doctor protested, "That's hard to believe. We've got all his bio-data to prove his accelerated vital signs, even when out of control. He couldn't fake that."

"But," said the robot. "It's *when* his heart accelerates, that's what's important." Its chest screen fast forwarded to a frozen stop. "Look. It's the journey to the centre of the earth and humpback whirlpool." Then, Play.

The lead doctor nodded as he watched, "Yes, his joyride thrill. Having fun, having fun with us. That's why we pulled him out."

Stop, freeze.

"But you could be right, it's a worry," reflected the lead doctor. Turning to his female colleague, "You were right when you told me that he's 'trying to distract us. You're letting yourself get carried away."

"No, no!" protested the child development doctor. "That's all he knows. What did you expect? He needs a chance to unlearn his past." Exasperated, "Isn't this what The Born Again is all about? The chance and choice for him to unlearn."

"But remember," added the robot, "Even *after* his cosmic-breath experience, he reverted to his old game-playing with us. For ordinary people, such an experience would be a permanent enlightenment. He's not ordinary. But notice," continued the robot, "what happened to his heart rate after you pulled him out and were talking with him. It skyrocketed." The robot screen flicked fast forward to another stop and freeze. Then, Play.

"Doctor," one of them said, "while he was 'talking' with you right now, his heart rate really jumped."

"I know. He's scared but trying not to show it."

Stop. "Wait," cried the child development doctor. "That's when he dived into the Father Martin abuse. That was genuine, scared but trying not to show it."

"True, but that was a hateful memory," replied the robot. "His mind is full of hatred. And don't forget." Fast-blurred rewind. Stop. Play.

I had to fall back on what I knew best. 'Neutral thoughts,' that's what he said. Yeah, I could do that. I've been doing it all my life. 'Callous,' is what the shrinks called it, my neutral thinking. That's what psychopaths do. *We* call it – *pleasure!* A sort of 'neutral pleasure.'

"Remember," observed the robot, "This is a man who can incite fear in others and inflict violence without a raised heart rate. He likes to see fear in others, that's how he distances himself from his own fear. But his own 'Do not be afraid' is vulnerable. Watch." Its chest screen flicked forward, stop, freeze and Play.

That's when it hit me. These ocean-going giants had nowhere to go. Round and round, I watched them – suffer. I felt an urge to rescue the whales.

"When he realised it was his own body moaning and groaning in agony *Ugh! Ugh! Ugh!*, then we did the de-fib.

Stop and freeze.

"He couldn't fake that!" insisted the other male doctor.

The robot mouth-speaker replied, "Of course not. That was the breakthrough. His body was beginning to unlock its buried pain. His whale-rescue, which you rightly observed, was his attempt to rescue himself from his own cruelty to the whales." Quick fast forward, stop, Play. "Look."

"Doctor, he's actually crying."

Stop.

The robot added, "The whales' agony of memories – and their improbable trust. That's what made him sob."

"Then why are we – you? – questioning the sincerity of his experience?" protested the child development doctor.

"To not let ourselves get carried away. His tears are pinpricks of empathy for their suffering. Yes, that was the breakthrough, which then led to his Caroline-rescue, the retrieval of a long-buried impulse of empathy and goodness. These are real. His flatline heart rate only comes alive when faced with these new, unexpected emotions or impulses that take him outside his callous self. Don't forget, during the assault of Caroline's freeloader, he was 'mister dead pulse'. But the actual retrieval of this memory, which included his physical presence on screen for the first time – that's what got his heart pounding near out of control. Seeing himself for the first time. Feeling someone else's need and acting on it for the first time."

"What would we do without you?" praised the lead doctor, his colleagues nodding. "There's more to you than meets the eye."

"And him."

"So," the lead doctor concluded, he's not conning us? It's real progress?"

"Given his data history, it's exceptional. But – "

"What?"

"Stay on your guard," warned the robot. "Never forget his Holy Trinity of Convince, Manipulate and Menace. Lance Armstrong. That's all he knows, and it will probably come back to sting you. After all, he has retrieved a mere pinprick memory of 'the best thing he has ever done in his life.' But in doing something good for someone, he used violence, the only thing he knows. But what gives hope is that even he recognised the difference between the mother's way of dealing with her own fear – 'bold and caring' – and his own – 'callous and cruel.' A most surprising insight, but he's got a long way to go. So be wary. Don't underestimate the weight of his past. One-off experiences of cosmic breathing and cosmic heart beating, impressive as these are, won't completely erase what he knows best, violence and sadism."

The doctor sighed heavily. "You're right of course." He glanced at his colleagues, "We've been here in supermax far too long. When we come across someone like him who has got this far in The Born Again, who stands a chance to – well… We've got our own unlearning to do. The danger is to get carried away with the slightest progress. You, a robot, have more objectivity. Thanks."

"That's what I'm here for. Yes, he returned to the source of 'cardiac neurological memory', but it's only a mere glimpse, that's all. He's got a long, long road ahead."

"I see. But I'm also curious. Your objectivity comes with so much warning. Yet we thought you believed in him more than we do?"

"I do."

"But why then?"

"Because there is no reason at all. No reason that he 'didn't stand a chance in life.' And there was absolutely no reason for his out-of-the-blue impulse to help that mother and her girl. Where did it come from, this tiny spark in the midnight of his selfishness and cruelty? There was no reason for it. But because this spark of good happened once, it means another spark is possible, so I believe in the possibility that it can happen again. In fact, I do believe in him – although chances are, he will fail. From a robot perspective, doctor, it's the mystery of what it is to be human – that good people can do very bad things while a bad person can do something very good – for absolutely no reason. On the one hand it makes me wary, but on the other, optimistic. To keep trying with the no-hopers."

The doctor laughed, "You mean, like the whales with us human no-hopers?"

"Exactly. For no reason."

"You sound more human than us." Then he shrugged, "Anyway, let's get him sorted."

They all looked at me drowsing on the lay-back chair. I had been listening. I felt the lead doctor's gloved hand gently shake my shoulder. "Wakey, wakey, Mr. Bad Guy."

My eyes fluttered open to see the four gowned figures

and my robot stood circled round me. The doctor pointed to my robot. "You've got a fan, a cheerleader." Then, "Take him back for a rest."

As we sped away, the robot-chair felt shaped in an embrace, a cuddle. Its seamless stainless-steel body and arms felt almost like skin. At the Cube I said, "How did you know about the 'bit of a freak'?"

"It takes one to know one."

"Thanks, cheerleader."

Inside, so tired yet amazed, I flopped backward onto my bed, and breathed cosmic breathing and listened to my cosmic heart, to its eternal rhythm of remembering and forgetting, remembering and forgetting…

Until closing my eyes, I dropped off a cliff into a pinprick of deep sleep.

Nineteen

The Dam is Leaking

Dams are built to control the uncontrollable. In the Victorian room of his law library, the 'pinprick of no reason' felt like a hidden earth tremor in the judge's heart. A pinprick, that's all it took. It sprung a secret leak in the dam of his denial which he had been constructing since he was an innocent twelve-year old boy. It was this precise thought of 'no reason', that anything can happen to us, and does, for no reason, by random chance, that sent fissures radiating out from the pinprick across his concrete dam of containment. Throughout his adult career his dam, engineered by the law, by reason, order, logic and justice, was meant to control the flood-threat of irrational human behaviour and injustice.

But Bam! It had happened to him – for no reason!

As the judge watched the monitor screen, the dam wall in his heart exploded open. His horror came gushing out. When he was three-years old, the judge was a musical child prodigy who played a rare, lefthanded mini-violin.

By aged twelve he was making national appearances, on track for a virtuoso, global career when, out of the blue, he was kidnapped by East European thugs. But his arrogant parents refused to pay the ransom. The kidnappers, to punish the parents, chopped of his left violin arm with a Samsuri sword and delivered the arm, via an unsuspecting courier, to the parents' home, with instructions of where to find their son in an isolated farmhouse.

The judge wept uncontrollably – for himself. He wept for Joe. He wept for 'no reason'.

* * *

In the Cube a strange week passed as I tried to assimilate all that had been happening to me. R&R – rest and reflection, rest and recovery, until I finally returned to The Born Again room. I was warmly greeted by the doctors and gleaming high-tech machinery and monitors, as well as 'my old friend', I had come to think of it, the mind monitor.

Sat upright in the central chair, *I don't know what to say.*

Stunned, a stranger appeared on the monitor screen, along with my printed thoughts below. An aging man, bald but for the snakehead of tuft hair at the crown, with a wide, lined forehead. Metallic disks were attached to each temple. A scarred left eyebrow, an old broken nose. High cheekbones, like outcrop rocks. A thin mouth was crescent-creased on both cheeks. It was a weather-beaten face. Below, a pointy chin, above a thin wrinkled neck. And the eyes, old and haunted by doing bad things worse than bad weather, simply looked back at me, like last week's forgotten weather.

It was me, the freak. Was that what an old psycho looks like? I hadn't seen myself in a mirror for I don't know how long. My little pointy chin, I always hated it. So did Father. Not the square-jawed 'that's-my-boy', like father like son. It looked and felt effeminate. "Pussy chin," that's what he called it. But hell, it sure could take a punch. An old, punched up, bad-life face stared back at me.

As I watched the stranger-face speak, my printed thoughts glided across the bottom of the screen, like a translated interview with a traumatised, third world victim of an earthquake – in the wrong place at the wrong time.

I – I don't know what to say – only, THANK YOU! is not enough! First, for my cosmic breathing, now cosmic heart-beating. I've never felt so alive, Alive!

The lead doctor replied, "The robot here advised us that it's not about your feeling ecstatically 'alive', but being awake, living awake every day," he emphasised. "A world of difference, of choice."

I laughed out loud without getting zapped. *Well, it doesn't feel that way to me! It feels like a whole new world has opened up! Climate change of the heart!*

"It warned us this is just a pinprick start, that's all. A pinprick awakening. Instead of your thinking that a whole new world '*has*' opened up, your experience '*is opening up.*' That's the way of looking at it."

Choice again?

"No, *choices*, plural," he emphasised. "Choosing again and again *is opening up*. The abyss of choices lies hidden in a pinprick choice."

The monitor screen went blank for a while as I reflected.

Choices? I've made a lot of bad choices in life.

"Of course you have," replied the doctor, "Very bad, that's why you're in here."

Last week, you know, after you let me out of the reality helmet, I was listening to what you all said about me, especially my robot.

"Good. The best way to listen is with your eyes closed. So, you will understand, *why you need to understand,*" he stressed, "that you have only made a small start."

I'm, I'm, this is not easy for me to say. I'm sorry for messing you around, playing games with you at the start. I couldn't—

"Help yourself? That's the old playback of 'Your honour, he didn't stand a chance in life.' That's like saying, you didn't stand a *choice in life.*"

Blank, went the monitor screen.

"You're sorry?" the doctor went on. "That feels like another 'first' for you. A 'sorry', but nevertheless it's another choice, to allow yourself to *feel* sorry – for the cruelty you have done to other people."

I think I'm beginning to understand. But if this is only a start, I'm a bit frightened of what's to come.

"You frightened? Is that another 'first'?

Blank screen.

I guess it is. I don't know what's happening to me anymore. Look at that old guy in the screen. Who is he?!

"Good. You're not-knowing is an opening up, even if it's just a pinprick at a time, like a dot that can become a series of dots one after another, a line, perhaps going somewhere."

Where?

"Wherever you *choose*. It doesn't have to be a straight line."

The monitor screen went blank again. I couldn't stand that old face, a rock face.

"Meanwhile," the doctor's voice rose upbeat, "You have earned a new privilege. Already, the polka dot black holes have been removed, the fluorescent lights switched off. The zapper has been deleted. You have been allowed to talk aloud to yourself in the Cube. You have been given back a semblance of time, an auto-timed lamp to indicate night and day. To sum up, few in The Born Again get this far. So now, *you*," he stressed, "not us, *you* can choose a privilege. A window? A Cube with a view? Outside recreation? Fresh air, sun, clouds, rain, snow, wind, night, stars, moon, change of seasons. Natural time. Most people dream of the timeless because they don't fully understand their need for time. I think you do now."

I sure as hell do!

"Or," the doctor added significantly, "perhaps you'd like the privilege of talking to someone, any of us? Like I said before, you may have something worthwhile to say by now, don't you think?"

The doctor waited for a long time. "It's a big choice."

Finally, the screen flashed up, *I'd like some decent food.*

Taken aback, all four burst out laughing. "Food?! Of all things?!" the doctor guffawed incredulously.

Yes, some fucking good food!

Gowned, gloved and masked, they were beside themselves laughing, backslapping each other. I thought the lead doctor was going to rip off his mask to get some air.

What's so funny? I don't think it's funny.

But no one paid attention to the screen. Finally, the doctor answered, "Your choice is my command! Robot!" he laughed, "Take him back for a good fucking meal!"

On the way back, even the robot chuckled through its mouth-speaker, "Food?!"

I thought to myself, *What did he know what it was like to be hungry, to be human?*

As the security door opened, I stood flabbergasted. There, in the middle of the white silence, stood a square kitchen table, with four chairs. "What?" I cried aloud in disbelief. "They're really fucking with me now!"

Slowly, I stepped forward. I had to touch the back of each wooden chair to make sure they were real. The feel of wood at my fingertips was a new, vibrant sensation – simple plain wood, but long forgotten, so taken for granted. Then I pulled out a chair and dared to sit down, spreading both my palms flat along the little wooden table in slow, luxurious semicircles, feeling the grain of wood, the unexpected joy of – I jumped up.

What the hell was going on? Solitary confinement with a little kitchen table and four chairs?! Did the doctors plan to have a meal with me? Eating is such a social thing. Eating good food, talking – yes, the privilege of bloody talking, jokes, laughter, drinks, desert, a fag after, and then a few more drinks and – it was unbearable. I threw myself on the bed, my back to the table and chairs, and wept to sleep.

It was the smell that roused me. I didn't hear the letterbox mush-tray open. It was always the dread of my day. Eat to exist, a tasteless existence. Unbelievably, the smell of roast beef wafted into the Cube! I leapt up like a crazed man and brought a tray to the table. A plate with pink slabs of medium-rare beef, browned and delicately crusted at their edges, lay in a red wine gravy full of drippings; sliced carrots, celery, green beans and onions that had been lightly pan fried in olive oil and herbs, lay piled against a mound of garlic-flavoured, mashed potatoes.

The kaleidoscope of colours confined to this round white plate overwhelmed me. Sensorily deprived for so long, I had forgotten what I had asked for – the colours of "some decent food"! These melt-in-your-mouth smells I sniffed with a vengeance of remembering! I had forgotten so much, taken for granted so much in my life. On the brink of bursting into tears, I greedily knife-and-forked it, wolfed it down.

Hardly tasted a thing.

Gone.

Later, I was sick.

Vomiting tears in the toilet.

Next morning I woke early, dreading my expected punishment of another mush-tray. It didn't come. My robot transported me to The Born Again, on an empty stomach.

They awaited me. "What did you make of your 'decent food'?" the lead doctor asked.

What's with the table and chairs?

"Guess who's coming to dinner?" the doctor teased. "You work it out. So, what did you make of your decent meal?"

Sat on the central chair, I hung my head. *I made myself sick.*

"That's like a man in a desert crazed with thirst who finds a clear spring of water and guzzles it down all at once. It's the same with malnutrition and starvation. Hunger-lust."

My robot added, "The body needs to take it slowly."

Shamed by my stupidity and irritated, *What do you know about eating? You're a fucking robot!*

The doctor remarked, "Learning to live again, you have to learn to eat again. To live, we must all eat."

My robot chuckled and seemed to nod his lump head. "Eat, therefore I am," he quipped.

Funny, aren't you?

"Eating, like breathing and your heart beating, will teach you everything," said the doctor. "Go back and have some breakfast."

Back in the Cube, it was a plate of yellow scrambled eggs, salt / pepper, crispy bacon, hot buttered toast, and real coffee. The smells and colours amazed me. This time I ate very, very slowly, savouring every mouthful and molecule of flavour, feeling ecstatic at the crunchy texture of chewing toast, instead of sucking mush. And slurping percolated coffee. Aw, this is so-o-o fucking good! So forgotten! I vowed never again to take it for granted – "some decent food." What half the world's population didn't have. I stopped chewing mid-mouthful, my eyes blinking at this out-of-the-blue thought for others.

Over the week the letterbox food-tray brought me bubbling lasagna, succulent roast duck, Indian curries, humble cheese on toast, on and on. Not 'master chef' meals, but just some decent food. I noticed a difference in my bowels. Instead of the daily mush in and mush out, slushing dirty fluid out my backside in gasping farts, I began passing solid shits, robust shits which had a robust stink. My innards were working again, doing their sweaty job like a factory labourer.

* * *

But increasingly, I became intrigued by the table and chairs, a magnet of mystery. I tried a different chair each day, imagining I was sharing a meal – but with who?! Oh alright, I'll share this meal with myself, a chicken casserole with dumplings. I'll ask 'him' what he thinks. So, I conjured up 'me' sitting across the table. It was easy. Sensory deprivation, and having developed the concentration to breathe without thinking, had enhanced my visual imagination to startling clarity, virtual reality. There he sat, an old rock face gulping down the last shreds of meat and dregs, smacking his thin lips.

"Well Joe, what do you think?" I asked aloud, startling myself to hear the sound of my own name. I actually had a name – Joe. I had nearly forgotten.

"Fucking good!" he grunted. "Get me some more!" he barked.

"Don't be so greedy."

"Fucking now! More."

What a prick, I thought. Worse than a prick. An infected prick, oozing with badness. It was all over his bad face, in his harsh voice, all poison, especially in his eyes.

"You know," I gently urged, "you don't have to always demand 'fucking this and fucking that'."

"You're one to talk," he snarled.

"Yes, I am one to talk. I've finally got something worthwhile to say."

"Fuck off! That's what I've got to say!"

"You're dead, like Him, our Fear of the Lord."

An empty chair stared back at me.

As days went by, I began to feel energized. Until then my body had felt like a stuttering car engine that couldn't quite get going, limping forward day after day as I paced the Cube back and forth with nowhere to go. Now, beginning to feel beefed up, I returned to my squat-jump routine. My old despair about keeping fit had evaporated. Some decent food, exercise and rest simply made me feel better, think better. I felt more awake.

Stranger still, were my daily visits to The Born Again room. No more reality helmet adventures. Instead, all four sat round me as we 'talked' via the mind monitor. I wondered, *Are they going to come for a meal with me sometime?*

The lead doctor chuckled, "Keep guessing."

Two women's voices and two men, plus the electric voice of my robot. You might have guessed, we 'talked' mainly about food in all its wondrous varieties, even philosophizing about food. For example, I told them, *What a weird world we live in. Life, at every level, has to kill itself and eat itself in order to keep on living. Eat or die. Eat and die.*

The robot piped up, "To eat, or not to eat. That was the question in the Garden of Eden."

But they ate and died.

My robot answered, "They ate their own choice, their choice of illusion, and were swallowed up from their innocence."

Oh, you guys are getting deep now! I laughed.

That's when I first noticed – my old rock face on the monitor screen. It was always there now above the printout of my thoughts. But what I noticed was, when I laughed, I mean I could feel and hear myself laughing – but the rock face on the screen looked mainly impassive, only flickers of a smile. My face barely registered what I was actually feeling inside, the fullness of my laughter merely shadowed across the hard features. Immediately, I 'thought' nothing of this, deliberately, to conceal what I had noticed. But as we continued talking, instead of giving them eye contact, I eyed the face on the screen. When we were comparing cultural tastes in food about surprising and disgusting delicacies, yet again the face didn't register my feelings of surprise, amazement or disgust. By then I couldn't help myself, crying out, *Jeezuz! Nothing's coming out of my face!*

"Congratulations," said the lead doctor. "Your disconnection has been obvious to everyone but you."

What's wrong with me?

"That's the wrong question. You should be asking, 'What's right with me?' Right now?"

Right? Look at that face. It's fucked up weird! That's what's WRONG with me! It's obvious."

The lead doctor answered, "No, it's your disconnect from the obvious – the hidden you – who you fail to see. Each day, for an hour or so, you have engaged us in stimulating conversations about food. But just food? We've been talking about the origins of life and death. Eat or die. Humanity's bewildering diversity of cultural tastes in food simply mirror the world's multitude of religious faiths. Religion is a longing for the sacred, to return to the sacred. So is eating. Eat and live, differently but the same. Our universal need to eat is like a universal religion. Hunger is the call to prayer, to taste, swallow, digest and absorb the sacred, in all its glorious flavours. That's what we have been talking about – prompted by you, Joe."

The doctor continued, "You've been talking to us with direct eye contact; you have asked penetrating questions, replied thoughtfully to our answers and speculations, sometimes joking and laughing with us. Not a hint of your old game-playing, nor cynicism or sarcasm, not a swear word uttered. It almost felt, dare I say, like an after-dinner conversation late into the night amongst friends, putting the world to rights."

Stunned, the screen went blank. Tears, too big for words, gathered from rivers behind my eyes that burst like waterfalls over the edge of my self-control. My head and shoulders hunched forward as I sobbed uncontrollably. It was my worst fear – the uncontrollable.

"See?" the doctor invited gently. "Look at the screen."

As I lifted my head, I looked at a tremoring, old hard face and eyes, from which dripped a few tears.

"The dam is leaking," he said.

* * *

After that, they let me have more time in the Cube. I didn't know what was happening to me. I thought they would come to see me, have a meal, talk it over, like best friends.

"Friends!" I shouted at the empty chairs. "Joe, they're not your friends, don't kid yourself! Who would be a friend of mine? Guess who's coming for dinner?" I asked myself sarcastically. "This is supermax, for God's sake." I plunked myself on one of the chairs, head down on my forearms on the table and began to sob, "For God's sake, for God's sake. Who would be a friend of mine?"

Why was I crying all of a sudden for no reason? Crying was a lifetime ago. I noticed that my forehands felt spotted with a few damp tears, that's all. "The dam is leaking," he had said.

Still leaking.

Suddenly, I sat up and began feeling my face all over. It felt locked. I opened my mouth wide as I could and stuck out my tongue. I hooked my forefingers inside and pulled my cheeks from side to side. Then I widened my eyes again and again, raising my eyebrows, pulling up the forehead skin and scalp, even trying to wiggle my ears. I jiggled my jaw back and forth, and rotated my head clockwise and counter, then forward and back. For more than an hour I contorted and squiggled my face until it ached, trying to unlock it.

That's all I did for several days, squat-jumping my face, push-upping my tears. I didn't know what the hell I was doing or why. Neither did my tears.

Twenty
- - - - - - - - -

Gut Feeling

Next day, "You can talk to us, Joe," invited the lead doctor.

As I sat in the central chair again, surrounded by them, the monitor flashed up, *WHAT?*

"Your tears have earned you the privilege."

I – I don't know –

"I think you probably do. Go on, just say it – aloud. It will feel better than thinking it. Have more power of meaning it."

The screen flashed again. *It's been so long…I used to hate the enforced silence, but over time I've grown fond of it. The silence, how can I tell you, compared to words? It intensifies my passing thoughts, clarifies the worthwhile from the nonsense, yet sees through them all. It's like seeing – no, feeling – a bigger reality, a background behind words, like sky and clouds. Words are the clouds. The sky is Silence. Does that make any sense?*

They all nodded, even my robot.

I'm still not putting it right. The silence is more than a background. It surrounds the words that we say – Oh my God, I said that word, 'we' again. I never used to include myself in a sense of 'we'. It was always I or me, me, me. There's a change for you. What I'm trying to say is, because it's been so long, words have become to me like faraway twinkles of the stars. And now you tell me, 'You can talk, Joe, you can reach out of the silence and touch the stars.' I don't know how to touch them anymore, those faraway words, mere twinkles. Can you understand? The act of speaking is so physical. Silence is, well, spiritual.

The other male doctor interjected, "Maybe they're both the same? In the Beginning was the Word. The spiritual includes the body, especially the gift of words, however futile they may seem at times. Words unlock our solitude, our solitary confinement, so to speak. They enable our unique silences to embrace each other. Come on, Joe, try it. We're all ears!"

Taken aback, the screen went blank for some time. Then the lead doctor repeated, "Go on, just say it – aloud."

I looked them all directly in their eyes and heard myself say aloud, "THANK YOU!" Then I laughed. It felt such a release, like a burp after a bloody good meal!

The other male doctor chuckled, "You know Joe, that's the first thing that Adam and Eve should have said to God – 'thank you.' Thank you for existence, for our life."

The screen flashed, *You're the deep one of the bunch, aren't you?!*

"Say it, "chided the lead doctor.

I chuckled. "I'm so out of the habit. Ok, 'You're the deep one of the bunch!" I repeated aloud.

The masked doctors laughed.

Then abruptly I asked, "You mentioned my tears and privilege. Is crying a choice?"

The lead doctor answered, "There are tiny, almond shaped glands located above the eyes which keep them moist and lubricated. These glands also help clear the eyes of dust and other irritants by producing reflex tears. On this basic level, tears are not a conscious choice. But almost any powerful emotion can trigger our crying – anger, rage, frustration, helplessness and despair, humiliation, loss, grief – mostly painful emotions. But also, so can great pleasure, joy, ecstasy, and, as you have just told us aloud for the first time, Joe, 'thank you'.

My robot interjected, "My data base tells me that one of the greatest mystics in human history, Meister Eckhart (1260–1327) who I call 'the Buddha of Christianity', declared simply: "If the only prayer you ever say in your entire life is thank you, it will be enough."

The lead psychiatrist added, "A spirit of profound thankfulness in life can make us, including you Joe, cry."

My words stumbled out, "Us. We. But I haven't *chosen* to have these feelings. They seem to come out of nowhere, out of my control and choice. They're beginning to overwhelm me. That's what frightens me. I've always been in control."

"And alone," added a female doctor. "Locked in. That's why your face has been locked hard in cynicism, sarcasm, calculation, menace and cruelty. Tears are emotive headlights that others can see in the night. We can see you coming, begin to relate to you, to the new 'Joe' coming out of the dark from the horrible things you have done."

The screen went blank for a while. *You mean* – "Sorry, force of habit," I said aloud. "You mean like the whales? Their memory of near genocide. Can whales cry?"

The female doctor answered, "Through their songs. Your tears are your songs. Old and new. Welcome them."

Suddenly my robot interjected, "When these manifestations of unconscious memories and knowledge come to you suddenly and independently of your free will, they come not from nowhere, but from the source."

"The source of what?" I pleaded.

"From the mystery of you. Your worst fear is the uncontrollable, *the unknowable mystery of you* which is beyond the masks of you, a mystery of silence which surrounds you, and all of us."

Suddenly the lead doctor said, "But hey, look at the face on the screen now. Is that the 'old Joe' face from a couple of a months ago?"

I hadn't noticed. Looking carefully, it didn't seem quite the same. Still old of course, but more filled out, less hard-edged and less lined, but *probably because of the decent food, exercise and rest,* ran my thoughts across the bottom of the screen. But it looked somehow softened.

"Tell me if I'm wrong, robot, his face looks a bit, kinder? Kinder, would you say?"

"To himself," the robot replied.

"Kind to myself?! I've never thought of that before."

My robot smirked. "Yes kinder. But still bit of a pussy face, don't you think, doctor?"

"You know," I laughed, "I'm beginning to not-like you anymore, but like you more at the same time." I blinked back some fugitive tears.

The woman doctor reminded me, "Tears touch other people. Touch the stars. Welcome them. You are not alone in the universe."

"Pussy face!" chortled the robot.

"Come on, pack it in," ordered the lead doctor. "We've got some work to do today. Joe, are you ready?"

I grinned, "What can follow this?"

Twenty-One

- - - - - - - - - - - - - - -

Journey to the Centre

As I sat upright in the central chair the lead doctor said, "There's more to life than just breathing and heart beating, which we take for granted. There's also eating."

"Oh my God, I should have seen this coming."

"After swallowing, food is propelled down through the gullet, like a mine shaft, to the cave of the stomach. From there the digestive tract snakes downward to the small intestine and descends through further convolutions as it enters the large intestine, where the digestive tract snakes its final descent to the anus and defecation.

"Remember, hunger is like a call to prayer. Eating is a return to the sacred. Everything in life is a matter of something coming in and going out, or going round and round. Call it the circle of food, of life."

Smiling incredulously, "I'm not sure I understand where you're going with this."

"Let me explain. Be patient. It's simple ABC stuff that

we all take for granted. The digestive tract begins at the mouth and ends at the anus.

"Mechanical and chemical digestion are the two methods your body uses to break down foods into smaller substances. Mechanical digestion begins of course with chewing and swallowing, and continues into the stomach where the chewed-up food is mixed and churned and where chemical digestion begins, using enzymes to further break down carbohydrates, proteins and fats. Propulsion continues into the small intestine where further disintegration of food particles occurs, together with more chemical digestion." He stopped.

"But here!" the doctor suddenly enthused, "Here in the small intestine is where the miracle of digestion really happens – it's call 'absorption'! *Absorption* occurs when nutrients, water and electrolytes traverse the cell lining of the small intestine, to be absorbed into the blood system and into countless cells throughout the body. Absorption is akin to plant photosynthesis, a transfiguration of external food substances into the life of the human body!

"Meanwhile, waste matter of faeces is stored in the large intestine and expelled through the backside."

The doctor concluded his mini lecture, almost like a tour guide. But instead of asking those on tour – me! – 'any questions?', he looked me in the eyes and said, "That's your journey, eating. From the mouth to the anus."

I guffawed in disbelief, shaking my head, "You've got to be kidding?"

My robot quipped, "Your gut will teach you everything."

"I don't know. I'm not sure."

"Squeamish?" the doctor asked.

"Can I have some time to breathe on this? To prepare? I mean, I'll do it," I said reluctantly.

"Ok, timeout in the Cube, half an hour."

There I sat at the table, staring at the empty chairs, pondering the unknown. "Come on Joe," I said aloud to myself. "Why are you shying from this? A journey through shit? That's been the story of your life. This will be nothing new. Talk to me Joe," I said to myself.

Immediately across the table, an empty chair flashed up with the image of 'old Joe', the old rock hard 'me' who grinned and sneered, "Don't kid yourself. You'll never change. You're the same as me." Then he vanished.

I slammed my palm on the table. "Right, that's it!" I shouted and jumped up, but then stopped, and looked back at the table. It was empty. That's odd, I thought. In the past I would have hit the table with my fist.

As the robot took me back, I fingered the metal disks at my temples. They must be able to read my thoughts and feelings all the time. Well, maybe it's not a bad thing?

In The Born Again the lay-back chair was up in sitting position. "You'll be able to sit through this," reassured the masked doctor.

"I quipped, "You mean 'shit' through this."

"A sense of humour." His colleagues nodded with approval.

Then I pointed to the other male doctor, 'the deep one of the bunch.' "Don't tell me that's what was missing in the Garden of Eden – a sense of humour?"

All laughed. The lead doctor said, "Hand me the reality helmet, please." Then to me, "Remember, hunger is the call to prayer. Eating is a return to the sacred. Today, you will learn how to eat again – as if for the first time."

The lead doctor placed the reality helmet over my head. "A final word, Joe. Be your breathing, be your heart beating. Be your eating." Then he pulled down the dark face visor and pressed the remote. He turned to the robot and asked, "What do you think? He seems off to a happy-go-lucky start. More game-playing to come?"

Strangely, the robot remained silent.

The lead doctor beckoned the others to sit round the monitor. "He'll be ok, his vitals are quite robust. Well," he said eagerly, "Game playing or not, there's only one way to find out."

* * *

The monitor screen flashed up a running film-scene of what seemed to be a busy mining site. But as they watched, they realised it was a rock quarry. Bulldozers, dumper trucks, huge, cleated excavators, and tread-wheeled front-loaders bustled round what looked like a large construction site, backed by a gouged cliff. Hardhat drivers and machine operators worked at their specific tasks. Noisy. The scene went on for some time. No thoughts glided across the bottom of the monitor.

"There's no Joe," observed the lead doctor. "He's gone back to keeping himself out of the picture."

"Not a good sign," a woman doctor said, shaking her head.

Meanwhile, a front loader climbed a long dirt ramp to just above a giant rock-pulveriser and dumped its load of boulders into a wide chute, which funnelled down to the mouth of a machine that shuddered, crunched, split and crushed the boulders into rocks and then smaller stones, which then dropped through an opening below, onto a conveyor belt which angled up to a waiting dumper truck which, like a waterfall of stones, filled it.

"Still no sign of him," worried the woman doctor. "This has nothing to do with 'be your eating.'"

"Sad to say," sighed the lead doctor, "I think you might—"

"Be patient," advised the robot.

The deep one of the bunch sounded frustrated, "You're the one who warned us to be wary, now you're telling us to be patient?"

On screen, the view closed in on a small pulveriser, only about fifteen feet high. Adjacent, stood a free-standing jib crane which had a pivoting 360 degree 'swing arm' which can hoist up to five tonne boulders one at a time. These are usually too big for the mass pulverisers. Something could be seen dangling from the hoist, not a boulder. When it finally swung round into close-up view, ready to be lowered into the crusher, only then did the doctors realise, in shock and horror, "It's him! It's Joe!"

Dangling upside down from the hoist, headfirst, his body lurched and twisted frantically, about to be lowered into the crusher.

They leapt up pointing at the screen, clamouring all at once. "This is sick!" exclaimed one. "He's gone back to his old cruel ways!" Another, "He's got the nerve to turn himself into a VICTIM?!" Yet another, "Maybe he's feeling suicidal?" The lead doctor ordered, "Check his vitals." No, we've got to see this!" Another, "I can't watch!"

"Look!" cried the robot. "See the crane operator. Look closely. It's Joe."

"Two Joes?!" exclaimed the lead doctor. "How can that be?" All went quiet.

"Look closely," repeated the robot. "The dangling Joe is rock hard Joe, the 'old Joe.' See? Look at his wild face, you can tell. While the other, the crane operator about to calmly lower him into the crusher, is 'our Joe.' Look at his face, the Joe whom we have come to like and believe in. Yes, admit it."

But—"

Lower, he did. Crane operator Joe pulled the levers, and down lowered the lurching body headfirst. As the skull hit the shuddering machine-cavity, it bounced violently back and forth, head and face splitting open. No blood and brains. Just broken rocks that vibrated down a chute as the rest of the body was force-fed into the gulping mouth of the machine, arms and legs spasming at first, then chewed off, broken up, the torso crumbling, the whole rock hard 'old Joe' pulverised into a rubble of stones and bones that rattled down a chute into the gullet of a mine shaft, where they tumbled down banging and echoing against the walls until finally, soft plunkety-plunkety-plunks could be heard at the distant bottom.

The deep one of the bunch slipped his mask down to wipe away his tears. "I so hoped…Once a psychopath, always a psychopath. I can't believe he's done this to himself. So much self-hatred."

"Look again," commanded the robot as they sat in front of the screen. "Look at the crusher. My databank has recognised it. Guess what it's called?"

"Who cares about a bloody machine," exclaimed the Deep One.

"Go on, tell us," waved the lead doctor impatiently.

"A 'jaw crusher.' Mechanical jaw crushers crush large-sized rocks by compression – chewed up, so to speak," the robot explained. "The rock remains in the jaws until it is small enough to pass through the gap at the bottom, into the gullet, so to speak. Don't you see what he has done?" the robot enthused with admiration.

"You've said it yourself, doctor, 'The digestive tract begins at the mouth and ends at the anus.' He's imagined a mechanical mouth, literally a 'jaw crusher', chewing up his old self, eating and swallowing his 'old Joe', to digest him. 'Our Joe' is eating his 'old Joe.'

"Whatever for?"

"It's extraordinary. Remember? In his 'time out' in the Cube his 'old Joe' appeared to him and sneered, "You'll never change. You're the same as me.' So, he's just chewed him up and swallowed him. This is real. He's on his journey through the digestive tract. This is no happy-go-lucky thrill ride."

They listened, astonished.

The lead doctor replied, "But eating himself. Isn't this an act of aggression, revenge against his old self? It looks like self-hatred."

"Let's see what happens," encouraged the robot. "We can also track his centre of awareness, even if he's not in view. Those soft plunkety-plunket sounds we heard? They were the broken stones of his old self hitting the sphincter muscle at the bottom of the oesophagus which opens into the stomach. That's where he is, well, where the rubble of 'old Joe' is – passing into the stomach. See, the stomach is like a cave, its walls dripping wet with enzymes and secretions of hydrochloric acid, which is the main component of stomach acid. The powerful muscle walls wobble in and out, churning and mixing the pebbles into smaller and smaller fragments of 'old Joe' to form a murky, semifluid paste. Rock hard 'old Joe' is almost completely dissolved, a mush of mince, there's almost nothing left of him now."

As they sat round the monitor screen mesmerised, one of them queried, "I still don't get it. Eating and digesting his old self? What's he got to gain by it? Whatever for?"

Suddenly, the robot's chest-screen flashed like a lightning bolt – a eureka moment. "I should have foreseen this!"

What?" they all cried.

Suddenly the lead doctor cried out, "Yes, I know now, the small intestine is where the miracle of digestion takes place – *Absorption*!"

"Exactly," chuckled the robot.

At that moment the monitor screen flickered and went blank. If the robot's mouth-speaker could smile, it would have been grinning from ear to ear, if it had ears. "Absorption. He's gone mystic, off grid. We'll just have to wait.

Twenty-Two

Gutted!

As if floating along a dark, meandering river-swamp, I could feel the last, slushing remains of the badness of 'old Joe' transforming into nutrients, life-giving nutrients. One after another, countless acts of unnoticed good in 'old Joe's' bad life sprang to life like fireflies in the night. Memories of mostly passive incidents; like when he could have put the boot to someone, but couldn't be bothered, let him off, that sort of thing. And forgotten 'good boy' moments like studying hard, a quick learner, sporty; or when he once stopped the robbery of a bus driver because it was fun to shock the robber. He could do things that other people were afraid to do. Their tiny, firefly gratitudes began lighting up all over my mind and body, usually moments of showing off 'his' arrogant power. But nevertheless, people were grateful.

Other things began popping up. Unexpected, fleeting. Things that 'he' would never do, but which 'I' could remember. Like as a young adult, I sat on a park bench one day half-watching a bunch of kids squabble about setting up a five-a-side football game. Suddenly a scruffy ten-year old boy came running up to me, "Hey mister, help us make up the team, we're one short. Come on, it'll be fun!" Mister Bad Guy would have told him to piss off, but I smiled and joined in. I found myself holding back the old domineering Joe, playing to their level, passing the ball and letting the kids score. It *was* fun. A forgotten memory called out to me, "You're pretty good. Thanks mister. See ya round."

And, at the gym, I gave some impromptu boxing lessons to a few teens for a while. I held back old Joe's brutal punches with them. To my surprise, I liked teaching them. I liked seeing them learn. After a few weeks one of them told me, "The bullies at school don't bother me anymore, thanks to you, Joe."

Or, one Friday evening a group of teens were hanging round a corner shop, forcing customers to run their gauntlet of ridicule. When I came along, I snarled, "Shut it! Fuck off!" They knew who I was. The shop keeper hurried out to shake my hand and thank me. Or, a grudging favour at the garage. I did a bit of overtime so a workmate could leave early for a hot date. And, sat in a crowded bus, with my arms spread across the back railing of both seats, legs akimbo. Everyone shied away as usual. But an old lady with shopping struggled down the aisle and spotted the last seat, next to me. "Sonny, you're not so tough," she quipped. "Move your backside." She wasn't intimidated. I let her sit beside me.

And so on…

Little things, bottom-up revelations bubbled up, more

than I had forgotten. They began to come out and twinkle like stars in the night sky, pinpricks of good.

And rare acts of kindness, like with that mother and her freak kid. All were being leached out of the bad shit of old Joe's life and transfigured into life-giving 'nutrients' to be shared with the rest of my body and mind. Pinprick nutrient memories, long unnoticed or long forgotten, began traversing the cell lining of the small intestine to reach out to the vast blood system, transferring their countless infinitesimal *goodness* from cell to cell, to be absorbed by the galaxies of cells throughout my body and soul. Weeping with joy, I could feel my tears passing through millions of cell membranes, radiating out, everywhere filling my body and mind with life-giving thankfulness! For the sheer wonder and joy of being alive!

And God saw that I was Good. A Good Boy! Transfigured from bad to good, I felt both exalted and humbled, engulfed in an ecstasy of physical and spiritual communion…

* * *

The monitor screen flickered back to life. "Look!" cried the lead doctor. "He's back."

Across the bottom of the screen glided…*want… forever*…But the images were shadowy and indistinct. I felt overwhelmed by the power of the digestive system. It has to keep moving all the time, like a conveyor belt below the conscious mind, as it sluiced the rubble and slush of 'old Joe' down into the dungeon of the large intestine where the indigestible waste of what was once 'old Joe' crammed up against the rectal walls, pressing for release.

Abruptly, a clear image intruded.

"Let me out! Let me out!" I pleaded at the top of the cellar stairs. The pressure of terror and darkness below me felt like it was my future behind me, pushing me up the stairs to the future that awaited me beyond the locked door. "Please, let me out!" I pounded against the sphincter-kitchen door. "I'll be good!" I sobbed. Suddenly the door opened, and I fell forward onto the kitchen floor – a wet turd, stinking of sin and the Fear of the Lord.

The indigestible future of 'old Joe' lay dead on the kitchen floor, a stinking, steaming crap of a life.

"He's had enough," the lead doctor declared. He pressed the remote. "Helmet off. Let him recover."

Dazed and confused, I blinked my eyes at the overhead lights, then at the four of them and my robot standing round me, looking eager with questions. "Hold on," the doctor said to the others. "Give him time to come round."

I lay speechless.

Finally, he asked, "What happened? You went off grid for a long time."

"I – I don't know… There are no words… I mean, molecules of good can come from bad things. I saw – I saw – I'm NOT all bad, not all bad…"

I whispered in amazement. "Our little self just surfs along the surface of breathing, the surface of heart beating, eating, absorbing…We don't know how ALIVE we really are, do we?" My voice choked up, blinking back tears. "To be born again, breath by breath, heartbeat by heartbeat, mouthful by mouthful, shit by shit, piss by piss... I've just come from a world of ecstasy and wonder."

The lead doctor stepped forward with an explanation that I could have done without at that moment. I knew his timing was deliberate and well meant. "Your awe and wonder arise from the holistic right hemisphere of the brain, while the left side is busy trying to figure out the pieces of a picture-puzzle scattered on the floor, a jumble of contradictory images and thoughts. Intuition vs logic / reason? The brain is constructed for both, so we need both, like a checks and balances to see reality as it is. I tell you this Joe, to help you understand what will be happening to you next, so you won't let yourself be deceived by your ecstasies or hells. Your robot keeps reminding us, there is a world of difference between your ecstatic sense of being alive, even being good – and being awake."

"I need some sleep."

Twenty-Three

Strong As I Am!

When I returned to the Cube I forgot the doctor's warning. I flopped onto the bed intending to bask in the revelation of my mystic ABSORPTION when a pinprick memory yawned open and swallowed me.

It was the end-of-year high school assembly, an awards ceremony. On stage, to the side sat the elect few, chosen for recognition in front of the whole school. At special request of a teacher, I sat in the front row. My fellow altar boy Kevin was out there somewhere in the assembly. He was in my same year. We never spoke. After Kevin, I never had sex with another boy or man again. But rumour had it that he was wild for it.

That year, I was on a good run of attendance at our high school, St. Ignatius, thanks to Mr. Johnson my year head. I wasn't in any of his classes because he taught only the top sets. He had a reputation for high standards and didn't suffer laziness. Mr. Johnson dressed in suits and tie, immaculate. He would have had a pleasant face, but his eyes were too intense. In fact, his whole presence felt nervy as a sparrow, restless, ready for flight to any insect task or project – or to peck at a failing student with his harsh criticism.

I first came across Mr. Johnson in detention. Not his role, he was filling in for one of the usual disciplinarians assigned to after-school detentions. These consisted of one hour in the sin bin, sometimes an empty classroom, but often joined by the usual suspects of school troublemakers. Detention consisted of having to memorise fifty lines of Shakespeare from an unspecified play within a single hour, and recite it before you could go home. No one could do this, so they had to return the following week to try again with a new set of lines. The impossible task perpetuated needless ongoing detentions throughout the whole term, when the slate was finally wiped clean. But imagine. What high school could come up with the idea of using Shakespeare as a punishment?! I mean, someone had to first pitch this idea to a head teacher and his senior staff and convince them to nod with approval, "Oh yeah, that's a great idea."

We sat in silence, just Mr. Johnson marking homework at the front desk, and me head down. At the end of the hour, he gathered up his papers and said, "Time's up. See you next week. Well, I won't, but Mr. Evans will."

"I'm ready."

His eyes widened. He put his papers down and strode down the aisle and removed my copy of the Shakespeare lines. "Stand up and recite."

I began at the beginning: "If by your art, my dearest father, you have put the wild waters in this roar—"

"No, stop." He perused down the sheet and then read out a random line to me, "Art ignorant of what thou art, nought knowing'. Now, take it from there."

I followed up, "Of whence I am, nor that I am more better than Prospero, master of a full poor cell, and thy no greater father—"

"Stop." Mr. Johnson raised his eyebrows. Then he read out another random line, "So safely ordered that there is no soul — No, not so much perdition as an hair."

Again, I followed up, "Betide to any creature in the vessel which thou heard'st cry, which thou saw'st sink. Sit down; For thou must now know farther..."

"Impressive, Joe, you can stop."

But smugly, I rattled off the remaining ten lines.

"Come with me, Joe." Mr. Johnson briskly led me along the corridor to his office. Stepping inside, it was cramped and windowless. It looked almost looked like a storage room, but it smelled like an office: a paper-strewn desk with a desktop computer; metal filing cabinets; wall shelves laden with ring binders bulging with school regulations, health and safety, various policies, etc. "Sit down."

His eyes bore into mine, his suit-and-tie body bristling with energy. "You know, Joe, to memorise fifty lines of Shakespeare in one hour is unprecedented in the school history. Yet you're in the lower sets. Your teachers tell me your written home projects are lackadaisical, that's what lets you down. If you applied the same level of concentration to your written work as you did just now in detention, you would get top grades. However, they tell me in class you are quite outspoken, and you often challenge accepted ideas which then prompt stimulating class debates."

Instead of getting the telling off I expected for getting detention in the first place, here I sat listening to my head of year enthuse about my 'potential'. I was almost sixteen and floundering academically. My written work? Well, the cellar didn't help, did it? Even in my teens it still went on. And books, I had to sneak them into the house because to Father, all knowledge outside the bible was heresy and blasphemy. Earth was six thousand years old and still flat. Women were whores and slaves. Father's 'world view'.

"Do you hear what I'm saying, Joe?"

His offer was on the table. We would meet every Friday after school in his office for half an hour tutoring and mentoring. "Stay out of trouble, keep your head down and work hard, get your grades up. You could get a scholarship, Joe."

In a kind of daze, I looked at him behind his overworked desk cramped into this little windowless room, so full of energy and commitment. "Mr. Johnson, why are you doing this? I know you don't even like me."

He shot back, "Well, you don't give people much to like, do you?"

Under different circumstances, I would have spat in his face.

"Admit it, Joe." Then he implored me, "Look, I don't have to like you, nor you me. Ok? For me, this is purely professional. It's my JOB," he emphasised, "to recognise 'potential', and to bring it out in my students. You've got it in spades, Joe. You can do this, not for me, but for yourself, to build your future now. It's not too late."

Mr. Johnson made me believe, in a completely different way from Father Martin, that I was 'special.' Our half hour Friday sessions felt intense as three-minute boxing rounds, on high alert second by second. Not as a fight, as such, but intellectual combat. Each jab, duck, counter punch, body blow and hooked head-shot were a fierce exchange of intellectual boxing. Challenging me, Mr. Johnson was actually teaching me professional debating skills without my realising. Finally, he told me he was head of the school debating society. "You've got to join, Joe, you'll knock em dead."

Quick witted and quick-wordy, I used my bully instincts to bully debating opponents into submission with the power of my arguments, not my fists. I KO'ed their stale jabbing arguments every time. No one could go the distance with me. Our school was entered in the county debating championships. Soon, the team came to depend on me as we worked our way through the preliminary rounds to the quarters and semis, debating such topics as: Is the concept of 'war' on poverty, 'war' on drugs' or the 'war' on terrorism an effective approach for change?

Boy, did I feel special alright. Not for Mr. Johnson, but for me. I had become star of our school debating team in the county wide championships. For the first time in my life, I could see a new stairway out of the cellar, out of the bible, away from the Fear of the Lord, and out of the confessional world of Original Guilt. A scholarship. I could see a future OUTSIDE. A new world beckoned.

We had got to the end-of-year final, an expected slam-dunk win for us – for me – and for Mr. Johnson.

The Cube was relentless…

Something about the little kitchen table and chairs caught my eye. They seemed familiar, from before super-max, but I couldn't place them, just a plain wooden set, cheap. So, I pulled up a chair and sat down, feeling my way into…

Instantly, across the table, Father materialised. A big brawny man, he had a head big as a football, with thin hair swept back, black eyebrows, mean eyes, a strong nose, square-jawed, and a mouth that was always grinning, leering, sneering or snarling. His big, rock-hard hands rested on the edge of the table. Powerfully built, he used to be a very good amateur rugby player. He tried out for a couple of pro teams but didn't make the grade. His failure poisoned him. I guess that's why he always tried to toughen me up, you know, with the beatings. Although slim, I was strong, I could take it. But in comparison to his rugby brawn, my body was fragile. I took after my mother's slight frame, to his disgust. He worked as a plumber. Maybe that's where I got my calculating mind from? My social interactions and so-called friendships were like plumbing systems to be figured out – at their expense. They had to pay the price – me – in their lives. I was never out of work, raking in their fear and submission.

In the chair, that was Him, who lay dead on the kitchen floor, a smelly, steaming crap of a life – come back to life.

"Look at yourself," he grinned, "in a place like this."

"Look at yourself," I replied calmly. "in a place like this. No better than the cellar, solitary confinement."

"You always deserved it."

"Did I? You've bible-bashed the Fear of the Lord into me for so long, you've forgotten what it's like to feel afraid," I smiled.

His cruel eyes menaced, "Don't get smart. I AM the Fucking Fear of the Lord, don't you forget it. Give me any more lip, and you know what."

I went out on a limb, calmly. "That's your problem. You don't know what's what. You never did. Your version of the bible is, 'Kill thy neighbour as thyself.' But do you know what the most often saying in the bible is? Of course you don't. It's 'Do not be afraid.'"

He growled, "I'll soon show you some Fear. That's why I've come back to haunt you. To kick you back down the stairs to the cellar where you belong. You'll never get out this time."

Grinning confidently, "I'm not afraid of you anymore. That's why I've come back home."

"I won't hold back this time because you're no fucking son of mine anymore."

"You're right. And you're no father of mine. My mother was an octopus, my father was an eagle. They are my real parents. I'm their freak. I may be in a place like this, but I'm not all bad."

He sneered incredulously. "They giving you drugs in here?!"

"No, they're giving me a chance to be Born Again. I'm taking it."

"Well take this," he sneered. Lunging forward, he slapped me across the face. "Pussy face!" he taunted, laughing maliciously. "That's what you are. No son of mine."

"My mother was an octopus and my father was an eagle."

Another hard slap.

"My mother was an octopus and my father—"

SLAP! It rocked my head back.

"An eagle. Go on, hit me," I challenged. "My mother—"

Clenching his hands into big fists on the table, he snarled, "Don't you dare turn the other cheek to me, you pussy face cunt!"

"An octopus, my fa—"

A rock-hard fist straight-armed into my face, breaking my nose, blood gushing out all over my shirt and on the table.

"Ea – eagle…died for me… how to fly," I spluttered, wiping blood across my face.

Enraged, he jumped up, ripped away the kitchen table, roaring, "Turn the other cheek on the Fear of the Lord, will you?! Take THAT, and THAT, and THAT! You Fucko Freako!"

Absorbing an avalanche of rock-fists, I was pulverised unconscious…

When I finally roused in the Cube, there he lay on our old kitchen floor, next to the upturned table and chairs, blood everywhere. That's where it happened. As an adult, I had come home, the prodigal son. The old song *STRONG AS I AM!* blasted through my brain while I did it. It was an old soundtrack by the *Prime Movers* from the chilling Michael Mann film, *Manhunter,* singing powerfully as I bludgeoned Father unconscious with a rolling pin. Then for good measure, a frenzied knife dismemberment. Heartrate normal. Do Not Be Afraid.

STRONG AS I AM!

It was my last killing of the day. National news, blanket coverage. TRIPPLE MURDER RAMPAGE. TEACHER SLASHED TO DEATH. PRIEST FOUND CASTRATED. PATRICIDE – FATHER DISMEMBERED.

* * *

It should have been four. That fucking rat Kevin. But I let him off. In the end, I felt kinda sorry for him.

The county debating final had been hotly anticipated, a packed crowd full of ambitious parents to watch their sons shine towards Oxbridge. A debate on euthanasia. But proceedings were delayed as Mr. Johnson frantically paced back and forth, waiting for me to arrive.

I never showed up.

Disaster for our school. And for Mr. Johnson, disgrace. Fellow teachers used to backslap him, "You sure have turned that bully boy round." Crippled by my absence, our team lost.

Mr. Johnson had believed in me, but maybe too much? In the build up to the final, at first I thought it was this pressure of expectation on me, the foregone slam-dunk win and glory. But as we neared the final date, I came to feel a more subtle but forceful pressure. It was not that Mr. Johnson believed in me too much, but rather, I felt he believed in himself too much. The miracle worker who had "sure turned that bully boy round."

Added to this, someone had dared put out a rumour that I was a "cocksucker" behind the scenes, you know, with the judges, and that's why our team always won. "He's good with his mouth," the school kids whispered behind my back. Suspecting who the likely culprit was, I wanted to bash his brains in for all the kids to see, but I didn't want to blow it again at school.

To relieve my mounting tension, on the night before the final I went along on a joy ride with some twenty-year olds, not as the driver, but got arrested, locked in a custody cell overnight trying to debate my way out.

So, a month later, why the hell was I sitting front row to the elite school achievers on stage as Mr. Johnson doled out their awards to admiring applause? After the last presentation, he spoke through the microphone, "Now, for special mention," his eyes smiled down at me, "I'd like one of our students to come forward on stage." He gestured to my hesitant surprise. "Come up, Joe." No applause as I stood awkwardly next to the podium. Mr. Johnson, suit and tie, bristling with energy, cleared his throat, then spoke through the microphone to the assembly.

"Mr. Joe Pagini, as you know of Italian descent, is our well known mafioso at St. Ignatius – (taken-aback smatterings of laughter) – has been generous enough to grace our school with his special failure on our behalf. My debating team lost." Next to the podium I stood shocked to the core. He had given me so much of his personal time over the past year. He turned to smile at me. "I suspect his long-suffering parents and his parish priest Father Martin are not surprised at his sin of failure." He paused. "But I am. I believed he could do it, for me, for all of us. But we lost. He's not only let himself down, me and his year group down, but he's let the whole school down."

The assembly sat stunned.

"I have nothing more to say." Then, cupping his hand over his mouth away from the microphone, he whispered to me, "You COCKSUCKER."

I broke his jaw.

He lost his job for this bitter little speech. He didn't care. But I cared. I lost my 'potential' to get out of the cellar. I lost my future, lost my way out. Got expelled, then locked up in secure. I vowed to kill him some day.

And Kevin? All those years ago his frightened eyes pleading up to me, 'Why? Why?' He had chosen his moment to hurt me back. It should have been four that day. But like I said, in the end, I felt kinda sorry for him. He was still wild for it. He had assumed that as Mr. Johnson's teacher's pet, I was his 'bum chum,' thanks to Father Martin from years ago. Kevin intended to get back at me, but the school rumour had devastated Mr. Johnson, who blamed me. How many other Kevins were out there, cast away by Father Martin like roadside litter?

I didn't turn up that day to prove to the school that I wasn't Mr. Johnson's 'bum chum.'

* * *

Judge Solomon, drinking his Samurai whiskey, sat riveted to his monitor screen. Suddenly, the beast within him began charging around on all fours like a frenzied mountain gorilla screaming and thrashing at his law books all over the planked wooden floor and oriental rug. Then he jerked upright to pound his chest in one-armed triumph, roaring *STRONG AS I AM!* His dam of denial had burst open like a rape-spawned birth spurting out a bloody foetus of RAGE, squalling for REVENGE!

Eye for an eye, limb for a limb, pain for a pain, life for a stolen life. "He's done it! He's done it!" Every stab and slash and spray of blood, "THEY FUCKING DESERVED IT!" (The judge never swore.) He looked with horror at his crystal glass of Samurai on his mahogany desk, and threw it at the stained-glass Christ, shattering it. He stood panting in the middle of his wrecked law library, listening to the powerful song over and over again at full blast – *STRONG AS I AM!* Since the age of twelve when he was kidnapped and the kidnappers amputated his violin arm with a Samurai sword because his arrogant parents refused to pay the ransom, he had never allowed himself to listen to music or sing. Only now did he realise, shocked to the core, that for decades he had been drinking what he called his "Samurai whiskey" to dam and deaden his pain. How could he?! How could his denial be so dumb, so deep and profound?! But now he bellowed out *STRONG AS I AM!* His long dead voice erupted like a volcano of venom and vengeance, ecstatically howling the chorus *STRONG AS I AM!* He couldn't stop weeping. Fiery lava rivers of tears poured out of his eyes, incinerating his old face of DENIAL as the lava-hatred crawled down over the edges of his jaw, and dropped steaming into a sea of oblivion.

Twenty-Four

God of the Ants

Desperate for sleep, I collapsed on the bed, falling off a cliff to the rock bottom of yet another nightmare. All too familiar, it was an old memory told blandly to my 'talking therapists.' After the dungeon beatings, the ones which I could remember, maybe from age four onwards, I used to retreat alone into our back garden and climb a middling-size tree next to tall shrubbery and hedges that formed the boundary of the back garden behind us. In this tree was a sturdy branch-fork where I could sit easily, shrouded by leaves. Here I became invisible from the back of our house, and unseen from the neighbours behind. It felt like a cocoon of leaves, where I disappeared as the green leaves themselves.

Or, in the summer heat, in my T-shirt and shorts and sandals, I would squat on my haunches over a small sand ant hill amidst the uncut grass.

Red ants. And watch.

Watch with a child's god-like view of their tiny comings

and goings below me, in and out of their little nest-hole, scrambling to and from the surrounding jungle grass. I would single out a particular ant and watch it for ages on its bewildering travels. Then, with god-like power, I used a small twig to crush a single leg of this ant, as if struck by lightning from the sky. Watching it struggle, I crippled another leg, then another, watching it struggle and suffer (I hoped it did), but still it remained driven by its need to do whatever it was doing until…

STRONG AS I AM!

I pressed the twig onto its head, and crushed it.

But now laid on my bed, in contrast to my bland 'talking therapy' sessions, I could hear the ants' soundless suffering, like a broken-armed baby screaming or a harpooned whale shrieking and groaning. I watched myself playing this game of life, torture and death for timeless hours, mutilating scores of ants, letting most survive crippled, letting some whom I had watched for ages, roam freely, while killing many others – slowly, crippling and cruelly.

STRONG AS I AM!

The screaming of the tiny ants' suffering shocked me. I had 'talked about' these memories as if watching a horror film without any sound. This is when I must have learned to go deaf to the sound of suffering, to my own and to others. That's the kind of kid I was. Grown up, I still treated people like ants, without feeling or remorse.

STRONG AS I AM!

That's when it hit me, my rock bottom was a new cruelty of realisation. I felt engulfed in a fiery holocaust of shame, guilt, remorse, self-hatred – hopeless and helpless to reach out of the flames with my charred hand-stumps to those who needed me most – to undo my cruelty to them. For God's sake, never to have been done! Then came my tears, like barbed wire, shredding down my face, bleeding what could never be undone. Naked, nowhere to be, I bowed down, no longer deaf to THEIR PAIN WITHOUT END – as if I was stubbing a burning cigarette into their eyes and feeling their PAIN for the first time.

STRONG AS I AM!

For all my life, deaf silence had been my bedtime blanket under which my atrocities could not penetrate. No wonder psychopaths sleep so soundly. But now? As I was about to scream out of my tortured sleep, I remembered the prison psychiatrist telling me on 'day one', "In here, it's all about you finding the will to keep on living – with the worst things you have ever done in your life – or give up and die. You'll see what I mean. A lot of inmates in supermax don't survive their Born Again."

…as I am…

Part Two

- - - - - - - - - - - - - -

"Ride My See-Saw!"

Song by *Moody Blues*

Twenty-Five
- - - - - - - - - - - - - -

It Takes One to Know One

Next morning, I had to be woken, missing breakfast. Shattered by my experiences, I dreaded what the doctors would say. But to my surprise, it was a different robot which came to taxi me to The Born Again, a black lump of a thing like a wheely bin with a football head on top. "Where's *my* robot?" I demanded.

An electric whir replied, "It's waiting for you. It asked me to come instead. Climb in." The head-lid lifted up. Confused and alarmed, I scrambled inside onto a seat which faced two peep holes to look out through. Inside, I fumed with a barrage of complaints for when I got there.

When I entered the room, I stopped, stunned. All the high-tech apparatus, the mind monitor screen and central lay-back chair were gone. It was transformed into a carpeted sitting room, a few table lamps, with five comfy armchairs positioned in a circle where the four of them sat, but still masked and gowned. The only thing missing, had it been afternoon, was a cheery little fireplace and glasses of port. Next to the circle *my robot*, thank God, stood on standby. Stainless steel faceless head, a round mouth-speaker grill, squat neck, and a small chest screen on its torso that went to the floor, wheels for feet. For some time now it seemed to me, its electronic voice was sounding almost human. But it stood in 'sleep' mode. That was strange.

"Sit down," invited the lead doctor amiably.

I blurted out, "Why didn't my robot come for me? What's going on? How come it's in sleep mode? Is it sick or something?"

Behind his mask the doctor sighed, "It's doing research. He'll come back when the time is right." He paused, "Your R & R, you finally worked it out?"

"Humph," I snorted. "Rest and Reflection? You mean descent into hell." I looked around. "Why is this all changed?"

"You have progressed beyond the need for the reality helmet. Coffee?" he invited. "You missed your breakfast." The other male doctor handed me percolated coffee in a cup and saucer, its aroma wafting up. "Enjoy."

Sipping, "The table and chairs, you were never going to come, were you? Only Him. That's why I'm in here."

"No, it never has been about Him, nor the other two you killed. Nor even the ones the police and courts don't know about."

My head sank, spilling some coffee into the saucer.

"It's always been about you."

My body suddenly felt hollow, trying to put words into a voice that could only gasp out, "There's just so much pain," as I blinked back futile tears. "Like a thunderstorm of pain that won't stop."

"Feeling sorry for yourself, Joe?" one of the women doctors asked.

Nodding my head, "Sorry for everyone."

Abruptly, my robot woke up, its chest screen lighting up with columns of numbers. It asked me, "What sentence did the judge give to the painkillers?"

"What?!"

In their armchairs the doctors leaned forward eagerly, no doubt smiling behind their masks.

I felt affronted. "This is no time –"

"What sentence did the judge give to the painkillers? Answer: I could use some too."

The doctors guffawed behind their masks, their eyes alight with laughter.

Against my will, I couldn't help but let out a smile of disbelief.

"Let me explain," the robot added, its mouth grill almost smiling. "I've been doing some research on your behalf, Joe. My database has found some useful therapy for your burden of 'there's so much pain.'

"Suffering," he said pointedly, "How can we measure it?

"Well, only the Americans, turning a blind eye of denial to two hundred years of near-genocide of native American peoples, not to mention the slave trade, could figure out how to measure the Buddha's 'First Truth of Suffering.' Comparable to landing a man on the moon, it took their 'can do' initiative to finally nail down the science – of suffering.

"Admittedly, there was an element of multiple-choice

serendipity in their discovery, as is often the case with great scientific discoveries throughout history. But 'peer reviewed' evidence has confirmed their momentous breakthrough, gathered by TV audiences of a 1950s daytime programme called, *Queen For A Day,* in which four contestants, all women of course, 'share' their private stories of suffering with the nation."

I listened, bewildered.

"For example, the first, whose husband had tripped over a street curb and reaching out instinctively to break his fall, grabbed the breasts of a passing twelve-year old girl. A brazen assault in broad daylight! He was convicted of child sexual molestation. Sentenced to thirty years in prison. The shame of it! She needed the prize money to mount an appeal in court. Plus, her husband desperately needed a ten-hour surgical operation to anatomically correct his erectile dysfunction. She could never afford this. What could be worse, she sobbed? Her marriage had never been consummated, yet he was in prison for sexual assault. She was only twenty-one. He was seventy-six and not worth a penny. She had married him for love. Copious tissues at the ready.

"After each contestant spoke, the live audience responded, measured 'scientifically' by the clap-o-meter, accurate, some claimed, as a lie detector test (but its accuracy still hotly debated). The louder the applause, well you get the scientific picture. The other contestants needed money to pay for her son's iron lung, or treatment for her daughter's brain tumour, or for a last-ditch voodoo remedy to cure her husband's snoring. Like a mirror, the audience clap-o-meter doesn't lie."

The robot paused, indulging itself in an added thought, "Joe, the Catholic church should have had it installed in their confessionals. After all, the baying crowds at public tortures during the Spanish Inquisition were like a clap-o-meter to discern the Truth."

I could hardly believe what I was hearing. The shoulders of the masked doctors were shuddering up and down with laughter.

"Anyway," it continued, "the clap-o-meter winner was then brought forward and regally caped. A crown was ceremoniously placed on her head, accompanied by gushing background music as she wept with uncontrollable joy to the black and white TV camera into millions of homes of forgotten wives and women who sobbed their hearts out for their empty, unappreciated and abused lives."

The robot stopped.

Dumbfounded, I simply gawped at him.

Then it continued, "We can see and feel how badly you have been hurt by your parents and the priest in your childhood. I know it's a cliché, but many have suffered far worse than you."

Shocked, I blurted out, "Wha – what are you saying?"

"Don't you see, Joe, for all your remorse and feeling the pain of your victims, you're still seeing yourself as a VICTIM of life."

"I never felt like I had a choice in life."

"Some evil adults have had good, loving parents and families, but after leaving home, through chance circumstances and bad choices, well, a loving childhood is later corrupted. Or an abused childhood can later become self-redeemed. It works both ways. There's no rhyme or reason. Only chance and choice. You can convert bad chances in life into choices for the good. You've had the chances to change in later life, but chose not to take them. Wake up, Joe."

"Why are you being so hard on me?" I pleaded, "I'm trying, I really am."

The woman doctor intervened, "To jerk you out of any self-pity. Because if you let all this newly realised pain and suffering overwhelm you, it will cripple you, instead of liberating you."

"How? Where does this awakening come from?"

The robot replied, "From the wisdom of your past sins, and from the mystery that is 'you.' It's like waking up from a coma, born again, you could say. Who can say how or why it happens? Waking is the discovery of what to do with all the pain and suffering you have absorbed – your own pain, the pain you have inflicted on your victims, and the suffering of the world – the "First Truth" of the Buddha. Especially the self-torment of your hindsight guilt, remorse and grief. Like an alchemist, you have to turn this suffering into something else."

"What?"

"That's for you to find out."

I shook my head incredulously at my robot. "What were you, a priest or something in your former life?"

"My former life *is* my life," it chuckled. "This is my life sentence. I'm just like you inside, Joe. It takes one to know one."

Twenty-Six

- - - - - - - - - - - - -

Who Are You?

A week later, after mindboggling reflections in the Cube, I came back with a different agenda. "Here," said the lead doctor, "have another cup of coffee."

"You're not drinking any," I suddenly accused them. "Take off your masks. This charade has gone on long enough. I know who you are."

"Do you?" replied the doctor with surprise.

"You're the psychiatrist on 'day one'.

"I'm not."

"Yes you are, I know it."

"I'm not a psychiatrist. You simply assumed. And I'm not the 'lead doctor' as you have also assumed."

"Then who the hell are you?"

He removed his mask and head cap. "I'm not a doctor, I'm one of you, Joe, an inmate," he smiled, gesturing to the others to slip theirs off too. "We all are." They removed their masks and caps so casually and unexpectedly that it shocked me. What also shocked me more, I hadn't seen a real face in years! Let alone talked to a real face.

Transfixed, I stared speechless from face to face. First of course, the lead 'doctor' or 'lead inmate'. To my surprise, after all my long confusions of whether he was 'good doc or bad doc', he was older than I thought, with thin grey hair, fading eyebrows. Maybe seventy? But a young seventy. He had a kind face, hardly lined, with a direct smiling gaze. An intelligent face finely featured.

In the armchair to his left sat a woman, much younger, 40s? She had fading red hair cut boyishly short, with green smiling eyes, a nose too blunt for her petite face, but a face that smiled at me with warmth, nodding approval, seeming delighted with her mask off.

To her left, sitting one leg crossed over his knee, foot jittering slightly, a bald-headed man with a big round face, his chin sprinkled with stubble, sat grinning at me. Late 50s, early 60s? His face had an aura of shyness but his blue eyes extreme intelligence. He winked at me. I smiled. I knew this must be 'the deep one of the bunch.'

And finally, to his left, coming full circle next to me, sat the other woman 'doctor'. It was still hard to get this belief out of my head. She looked 60+, short, side-parted wavy white hair, plain faced but for a scar across her left cheek (a knife scar?), and thin lips. What leapt out from her face was her piercing grey eyes. A serious but sensitive face.

I took another slow, flabbergasted look round from face to face. Contrary to my expectations, each welcomed me in silence with a smiling, kind face. I stammered, "Some – somehow, I thought you would have hard faces."

Then it hit me. "No, no, no," I chuckled incredulously, shaking my head at them. "No, it's not possible. What are you telling me? This is like some old horror film where the insane asylum is run by the patients?!"

All laughed. The redhead woman blurted, "You've got to admit, Joe, it does seem very funny."

"It's NOT to me! Is this whole thing – this place, supermax, the Cube, The Born Again, the reality helmet, the mind monitor, sitting here talking with you – is this some drug-induced hallucination? All in my mind? Some twisted manipulation to drive me out of my mind? Is any of this REAL? Stop playing games. For once be straight with me. I have been with you."

"Take it easy, ask your questions, let me try to explain," reassured the lead inmate. The others leaned forward sympathetically.

"Is this place real?"

"All too real."

The deep one, the big round face with the wispy chin, added, "The illusion of the world, Joe, is not that it's unreal, but rather, it is far more real than it seems."

"That's what The Born again is," added the lead inmate, "more real than it seems."

"Supermax, where is it?"

"We don't know. No one does."

"Who runs it?"

"We don't know who they are, except one, but only anonymously. They're called 'The Project.' It's rumoured they are a clique of retired judges who were frustrated by the traditional 'life sentences.' So they formed, for want of a better way of putting it, something like a secret supreme court to implement a sentence of When Life Really Means Life for those who deserve irrevocable punishment, never to be let out again."

The deep one added, "Old Testament hell."

"It's believed," continued the lead inmate, "After the traditional life sentence is passed in court, the Project intervene in certain cases, and the prisoner is secretly whisked away to the invisible supermax, like you."

"Who's in charge here? I mean in the prison?"

All heads turned to the robot.

I guffawed, "Inmates and a robot running the show?! No one even knows where supermax is? No one knows who the Project are, the secret supreme court...."

My mind was racing. "Where are all the other prisoners?"

"Supermax is only for solitary confinement, they're kept in total isolation, in the Cubes. The Project have deemed you as the worst of the worst. Incurable. That's why you're here."

"How long have you been here?"

The lead inmate replied, "Me? Probably the longest, I can't measure it in years. The others not quite as long. So, I guess I've got seniority," he grinned."

"Why have you been masquerading as doctors?"

"Because in the early years you wouldn't have taken us seriously about committing to The Born Again. We figured that your resistance to authority figures would be less than your resistance to your comrades in cruelty."

I nodded, grinning, "Yeah, fucking fellow inmates. I would have taken the piss out of you all the time. You would've got nowhere with me."

"Exactly."

"But why not real doctors and psychiatrists? Why you? Inmates?"

"Outsiders," explained the lead inmate, "even experienced professionals, can't cope with the special environment of supermax. You know, its isolation, intense solitude and silence, the need for 24 / 7 monitoring and digital research of the inmates. It's very taxing. Even we couldn't do it without the robot. Plus, they would be cut off from their families and normal life. More importantly, the principle of using us fellow prisoners to help other inmates is similar to ex-drug addicts who help addicts go clean. It takes one to know one. Addiction, like your lifetime of violence and cruelty, Joe, is one of the hardest things to overcome. Only someone who has actually *experienced* the rock bottom of addiction or violence, and then *experienced* full recovery, positively and permanently – can be believed, who can lead them from lost to found."

"Why didn't you tell me this at the beginning?"

"Because if we had said, 'We've been there, done that, got the T-shirt, to someone like you, smart-ass, cynical and bitter, it would have meant fuck'all. We had to earn your growing belief in us, and you had to earn our growing belief in you. It takes time – like your experience of solitude and silence in the Cube, then in the reality helmet, then your recovered memories and awakenings, and only then, our conversations with you. Mere talking with you at the outset would have been stupid. That's why at the beginning you never had a mirror. It would simply reinforce your rock-hard image of yourself. A new image needed time to emerge from within. Like an old-fashioned photographic negative, the new 'Joe' could develop only in the darkness of solitude and desolation."

In my armchair I went quiet. The depth of what they had been doing for me suddenly filled me with amazement, their patience, generosity and subtle wisdom in the face of my hostile ignorance. I had been so blind.

"But who, who appoints you? Is that the right word? To do this work?"

All nodded simultaneously when the lead inmate replied, "This is our Life Sentence."

Shocked, "But why? What for? If we're all 'incurable' and going to die in solitary confinement, why go through all this rigmarole with someone like me?"

"Firstly, it's our team's job to sift out the no-hopers, to pick and choose the few that might make it. The rest fall by the wayside from despair, go on hunger strike, or will themselves to a slow death. It's their choice. Remember, we keep telling you, The Born Again is all about chance and choice."

"But why me?" I pleaded. "What made you choose me from the no-hopers?"

The lead inmate laughed. "Remember our first encounter? Me on the wall screen monitor? After I asked you, 'What's the worst thing you have done in your life?', you shot back, 'What's the worst thing *you've* ever done in *your* life? See? You can't answer your own question, can you? Let alone *dare* to tell a psychopath how human you are," you boasted. Then I chuckled, 'Human? The likes of you?"

"But you laughed back at me, 'Human? The likes of you?! I'll show you mine if you show me yours."

"That was the moment, Joe, when I knew you were not a no-hoper. And feisty. With an ounce of humanity in you. You were willing to share your humanity with me if I showed you mine. It even suggested your remote possibility of compassion. That was the moment I knew who you really are. Because it takes one – like me, once a lost psychopath like you – to know one."

Twenty-Seven

Outside!

Next day a jovial atmosphere greeted me in the carpeted 'sitting room'. "Welcome back, Joe," smiled the lead inmate.

"Back to what?" I asked incredulously. There they were, the inmates, seated in their circle of armchairs. My robot on standby. The scene was surreal.

"Sit down. Teas and coffees all around. Biscuit, Joe?"

I could hardly believe my eyes, let alone my mind. "Have you got names?" I asked.

"The lead inmate answered, "Joe."

"What? Same as me?" To the redhead, "And you?"

"Josephine, but just call me Jo," she smiled.

"And you?" (the deep one).

"Joe."

"Don't tell me!" I snapped at the other woman.

Her thin lips smiled benignly, "Same as her, just call me Jo."

I jumped up. "You people are doing my fucking head in! You can't all have my name."

"Sit down, relax Joe," said the lead inmate. "Drink your coffee, let me try to explain."

Agitated, I gulped my coffee down.

"Think of yourself as a chosen one. Once we identified you as a candidate for The Born Again, we as a team have to immerse ourselves in your complete data history. We each focus on separate but inter-related areas of your life. For me, its psychology and counselling. Jo here next to me," nodding to the redhead, "concentrates on child development, effects of trauma, etc. Then Joe, on religious background and related philosophical issues. That's why when you first complained about us bringing up the religious stuff, it's because some killers and psychopaths have sick religious backgrounds, like you Joe. And Jo over there, she deals with adult behaviour, the justice system, the implications of court sentencing, and victim support in all its ramifications."

I listened in amazement.

"He smiled. "You will soon see how this ties in with why we are all called Joe." He turned to the deep one of the bunch, "Joe, perhaps you'd like to explain the next bit?"

His big round face nodded as his thumb and forefinger pinched at his wispy chin. "As you look at us sitting in a circle, picture the Christian cross inside this circle. When the Spanish conquistadors arrived in the Americas, the first thing the native Indians noticed, even before the first shots were fired, was that the four parts of the cross they had proudly carried across the Atlantic were no longer bounded by an enclosing circle. They had forgotten the essential circle of unity that binds all things together, transcending all divisions. The circle is a symbol of the holistic right hemisphere of the brain, how it sees things as a whole. But polarisation, in the form of the divisions of the cross, is a symptom of left hemisphere thinking, like good vs. evil, right vs. wrong, etc, which eventually has become the dominant world view."

The lead inmate smiled at the deep one. "He's got a longwinded way of telling you something simple. Each one of us deals with the polarised parts of you. But on your journey through The Born Again we try to encircle you, psychologically, for us to become the whole of you – the whole Joe. We have given up our identities to become you. That's why we are all called Joe."

At first, I just looked at them, speechless. Then I laughed my head back in astonished disbelief. "This is too weird. Too weird!"

"It's a good thing, Joe," insisted the lead inmate. "Your journey is our journey – to awaken you to the whole Joe."

Shaking my head, "You mean, to be awake is—"

"To be the whole Joe," said the robot.

"More coffee?"

I chuckled, shaking my head, "I need a stiff drink. So, what do I call each of you?"

"How 'bout Joe-1 for me," suggested the lead inmate.

"I can't do that," I protested. "Joe 1, 2, 3, 4?! That's ridiculous," I laughed. "For you, ok J-1, for short. You – 'Red-Joe.' And you, 'Deep-Joe. You, 'Scar-Joe."

She smiled, "I'm not sensitive."

"Oh, I bet you are. And him?" I faced my robot. "What do I call you?"

Its almost human voice chortled, "Don't you dare call me Rob or Robbie."

"Then what should I call you?"

"Zero."

"Zero?"

"It's a very special number. You see, when they gave up their identities to become the whole you, they followed my example, except being human, they don't have the full resources that I do."

"What do you mean?"

"When I give up my identity, I become absolute zero. But when I do, for your sake, I become infinite Joe. The fullness of the whole Joe. You see, zero equals infinity."

It all seemed so unbelievable. "I need something stronger than a stiff drink, for God's sake." I stood up to stretch my legs and mind, and slowly walked round the circle of armchairs as if I wasn't there, a zero, while they chatted jovially amongst themselves. Then I stopped, transfixed, realising again how much they all had given me, the gift of themselves to become me, the whole of me. My knees nearly buckled. I grasped the back of Deep Joe's armchair to steady myself. He turned and smiled, "Sit down, Joe, come join us."

Join us?

Suddenly, I realised they were my friends. No, more than friends. For the first time in my life, dare I think it? I felt loved! Their love, the primordial embrace that binds all things together, transcending all divisions, seemed to embrace the whole of me – all my contradictions, all my cruelty, all my pinpricks of goodness lost and found. A reality as solid as these armchairs embraced me, loved me. Tears squinted out of my eyes. Tears of little 'thank yous' trickled down my cheeks.

"Sit down Joe, or you'll fall down," grinned J-1.

When I staggered back to my armchair, I sat quietly for a long while, absorbed in their improbable love for me, a psychopath. Finally, addressing the lead inmate, "I've got a question for you, J-1. Can you remember I asked you a while ago, that if our Life Sentence means we're all 'incurable' and going to die in solitary confinement, then what's the point of The Born Again? That's when you told me, 'It's our team's job to sift out the no-hopers, to pick and choose the few that might make it.' Remember?"

"Yes."

"Well, I've been thinking – *make it where?*"

J-1 raised his fading eyebrows in surprise. "That's a deep question Joe. I think we should let Scar-Joe lead off on the legal aspects of your sentence, and its future possibilities. Over to you," he smiled.

She ran a hand through her short waves of white hair. When she spoke, her clear, brisk voice reminded me of a lawyer.

"Your sentence, unlike a traditional life sentence, is not about time. The purpose of your sentence is that you remain here until you fully realise When Life Means Life – what it really means, not only for you, and your victims, but for everyone. The time taken to realise this is irrelevant. The means of realisation is, of course, The Born Again.

"But there's more," she continued. "For those who complete The Born Again, they are allowed to exit supermax into free society."

Astonished, "What?! You mean I can get out of here?!"

Twenty-Eight

Futuristic World?

Joe's pinprick psychodrama in supermax had been unfolding amidst the global psychodrama of geopolitics and technological advancement. A futuristic world? There were no Bruce Willis flying taxi cabs as in the sci-fi film *The Fifth Element*. Electric cars now ruled, but the minerals needed for battery production, mostly found in the third world, sparked bitter conflicts amongst the superpowers. In addition, the computer network for driverless truck convoys and cars was repeatedly hacked, bringing everything to a disabled standstill.

Meanwhile, decades ago the Russian invasion of Ukraine had finally halted when Putin was assassinated. Equivalent to 'Who shot JFK?', it triggered a civil war and then a standoff 'Cuban missile crisis' with Europe. Fifty years later, Russia had built a Ukraine Wall similar to the American / Mexican wall along its border, which included the 'occupied territory' of Ukraine, now known as the "Gaza strip." Year after year, littered with the dead on both sides of the wall, 'terrorist' bombings and rocket fire retaliations slogged on. Consequently. this development finally provoked the United Nations to expel Russia and China as permanent members of the UN, causing a split in world politics too dangerous and boring to explain. Meanwhile Ukraine, now armed to the teeth with the world's best weaponry, had become the 'go to' country for professional mercs in multiple little wars round the world.

The US fared no better than Russia's civil war. The post Trump legacy endured after his death. Akin to the new IRA in Northern Ireland, a fanatic underground party called the New Trumpsters fanned local riots, rebellions, and insurrections, which crippled American democracy to the point of near civil war. So, in stepped the Chinese on the global stage. They had been economically colonising most of South America and Africa for decades. Mineral rich Congo, the DRC, was practically owned and controlled by the Chinese who finally suppressed a century of regional conflict with their typical brutality. Proudly, it had built a nuclear power station in the Congo. Its nickname became 'Chongo'. During Joe's time in supermax both the US and China had established competing colonies on the moon.

Meanwhile, world food production incorporated protein-rich insect farms. McDonald's was now known as McInsects – insect burgers all the rage. Although plastic was now eliminated by plant-based packaging, the little-known, long term project to map the sea beds of all the oceans had led to deep sea mining and drilling, thus polluting the oceans from the bottom up, the worst possible way of damaging the oceans. And of course, the planet continued to be plagued by flood, famine, fire and melting icecaps because the world refused to cooperate to save itself, triggering migrant waves of 'climate change refugees' to countries like the UK which had shit weather.

Social media had become Soul Media where online identities, now more real than their physical identities, become absorbed into a global mind. Like the first rush of heroin, access to Soul Media was ecstatic and addictive, soon leaving their physical bodies in a catatonic stupor. Families would post online photos of their 'missing persons.' They resorted to paying gangs of 'online traffickers' to find and smuggle their loved ones back to his / her physical body.

Finally, Artificial Intelligence, when combined with genetic research, had cured many cancers and illnesses like motor neuron disease, Alzheimer's, etc. But, like our common kitchen and bathroom disinfectants which claim to kill "99.9% of all bacteria and germs", it's that bloody .01%, always ducking and diving the latest antibiotics, that waits to inherit the earth.

So, if the reader can feel no sense of the many years it had taken Joe to get to this stage of The Born Again, that's because neither could Joe. His existence in supermax was amputated from time.

But so was the psychodrama of human history, each generation amputated from its past, each generation reinventing the wheel of human stupidity – of greed, lust for power and control by means of violence and revenge – because 'God is on my side.'

Show me a lesson that has been learned?

In supermax could pinprick Joe do any better? Even

if he could, what bloody difference would it make to the outside world?

* * *

"Getting out of supermax? Only a handful have in the last fifty years, Joe. But you are on the brink."

"Is it really possible? How? Why?"

"If and when a person completes The Born Again, they are deemed 'legally enlightened,' explained Scar-Jo. "The psychology of this is best explained by the others. Put simply, the killer who has come in here has died – a death sentence – and reborn as a new man, enlightened.

"Such men and women are so spiritually rare, that a legal 'exit route' has been created to allow them back into the outside world, for the good of society. That's the key – for the benefit of society, Joe – not as a personal reward of freedom for their so-called 'good behaviour' in prison. They are released for the 'good behaviour' they are predicted to do on the outside. That's the whole point of The Born Again Project. Giving something back to society.

"Their choice of living on the 'outside', whether it be as a dustman, a mechanic, a council bureaucrat or charity worker, etc, they will carry a spiritual aura with them that ripples out, inspiring goodness in others all around him or her, which is often passed down into the next generation or two. People will say, 'Remember old Joe who used to live down that street? He was the most kind and generous man we ever knew. Children loved him. He completely changed our neighbourhood." Scar-Jo paused. "It would be a 'sin', as they say, to keep these rare spiritual beings locked up. That's it in a legal nutshell, Joe."

I sat in shock, speechless.

Sympathy welled up in Scar-Jo's grey eyes. "It's a lot to take in for a prisoner under sentence of When Life Really Means Life, this unexpected hope of an improbable life outside."

"But," emphasised J-1, "It depends on you awakening to a new life, *inside*."

* * *

Back in the Cube on the bed, I lay with my heart pounding with possibilities of an impossible future outside. Outside! Outside it pounded, I-can-get-out, I-can-get-out, it pounded, I-can-get-out…until finally, near dozing off to sleep, I feared I would have bad dreams. Like falling dreams, or walking home through my old neighbourhood and getting lost. But I slept soundly.

Next day in the sitting room, I sat in my armchair apprehensively. Teas and coffees all around as usual. "Any questions?" J-1 finally asked me.

I swallowed, not my coffee, but the lump in my throat. "Yesterday you said, 'On the brink. I'm on the brink of getting out?"

"Yes and no," answered J-1. "Yes, you have completed the reality helmet journey, a rare thing. You have experienced the awesome wonder of the human body and mind, what it means to be truly alive."

The robot interjected, "But you are not yet fully awake. That may take some time."

Deflated, I plucked up my courage to ask, "So, where do we go from here?"

J-1's young 70s face smiled with approval. "You said, 'we', rather than 'where do *I* go from here?' That's a big step, Joe. We're with you all the way. What lies ahead—"

"Sorry to interrupt. I didn't explain myself well, and I think I know what you're going to say."

"Better that it comes from you, than us. Carry on."

"Well, last night, all I could think of was getting out of here. Getting out – for me – not as Scar-Jo explained, for the good of other people. Even now, in The Born Again, the old 'me' keeps popping up like a jack-in-the-box. I'm no further forward than jack-in-the-box-me.'"

"Hold on," said J-1. "It's to be expected. If you keep pushing the 'old me' down into the Joe-in-the-box, then you keep giving it the energy to pop up again. Try something different. Let it pop up and stay up. Let it be. Imagine your pop-up 'me' as a scarecrow in a field. At first it scared the birds away. But the longer it stays up, it becomes an old, weather-beaten, long forgotten scarecrow standing in a big field. The birds no longer take notice. They only see the big field of crops to peck at."

Deep-Joe, bald, round-faced, directed his blue eyes straight through me. "Joe, think of saint Paul and his 'old me', Saul, the relentless persecutor and killer. If ever there was a man who embodied the Fear of the Lord, it was Saul. Even after his conversion many people still greatly feared him, found it hard to believe that he could really change. After his revelation, he sought out complete solitude in Arabia, perhaps for up to three years, to reconcile his old, stone-to-death-self with his new self. That's what lies ahead for you, Joe, the next stage of The Born Again reflective solitude and reconciliation."

"But," I protested, "The scarecrow of 'me' is my rock bottom nightmare of remorse which keeps popping up – the cruel realisation that I can never undo my cruelty to others. I still don't know if, or how, I can do that?"

Zero intervened, "You have already come a long way, Joe. Remember, your direction of travel is always from the inside out, outside yourself. The last few miles of a marathon are the toughest. That's when the runner 'hits the wall', not just physically but mentally – 'I don't know if, or how, I can finish.' Although the exit-line is still out of sight, you are closer than you think, 'on the brink'.

"Only through long periods of solitude, silence, deep digestive memory, call it reflection, meditation, prayer or whatever, can you make peace with what you cannot undo, letting the pain of your past be, by letting go of your hindsight self-torment. You can punish yourself for the rest of your life, but it will change nothing – only make you become more and more self-absorbed. Remember the Gospel saying to "become (worldly) wise as a serpent"? That means living with the wisdom of your sins, while transforming them into the gentleness of a dove – the serpent flying skyward with a new life of freedom and service to others. That's the future that awaits you in the outside world."

The robot added, "We're simply daring you to be human, wholly human."

I grinned, "Wholly or holy?"

"Both," replied Zero.

Twenty-Nine

Inside or Outside?

Grim and enlightening, that's what 'hitting the wall' was like during my marathon in solitary reflection without the reality helmet, as I rubber-legged one foot in front of the other towards the exit-line. Probably it went on for another couple of years? As a reward for completing the 'reality helmet' journey, I was offered a new Cube with a view, a window, and outdoor recreation. Instead of a traditional prison yard bustling with iron-pumping weightlifters, or kicking footballs, or milling round in racial cliques and drug dealing huddles, I was told that supermax had no walls, that it overlooked a panoramic, mountain-forest wilderness impossible to escape, from its stunning beauty.

But after years of sensory deprivation, I said, "no" to outside recreation. The four Joes were shocked. No one had declined this offer before. They were intrigued as I explained why.

I remembered as a teen in one of my high schools,

before I got kicked out yet again, a Jesuit priest once told me about an isolated tribe high up in the Andes. They had a bizarre religious tradition. From birth to puberty, the male infants and boys were not allowed to see the outside world. They were kept inside high, remote caves, lit by fire-pits and torches, while they were instructed by the elders in their religious beliefs, prayers and rites, which they had to memorise and enact in the fire-shadows of the cave. Finally, reaching puberty, they were guided out the cave to look upon the outside world for the first time – a revelation of the majestic, snow-capped, Andean mountain panorama – at dawn, mid-day, sunset, and the stunning myriad of night stars and moon. By this time in their lives, to them, which was more real and beautiful? Inside or outside? The Jesuit told me, the purpose of their training was to integrate both, their sacred reality within and their newly discovered sacred reality without.

At the time it went over my fucked-up head. I was still projecting my cellar reality onto the world outside.

But looking back on this story, their growing up in the cave seemed like my years of sensory deprivation in the Cube as well as my experiences in the cave of the reality helmet. Outside recreation? I couldn't let myself be awed by the startling beauties of Nature while I was 'on the brink' of seeing the inner panorama of my ugly self for the first time. Which was more real, I asked myself, my past life 'outside' or my supermax life 'inside'?

So, I told them, "No." So close to the new 'outside', I wanted no distractions. I chose the white silence of the Cube to go inward, to recover my wholeness, the good, the bad and the very ugly. And somehow 'absorb' them.

So, my daily pattern changed. After breakfast I engaged in silent, deep-memory recoveries until mid-afternoon when we had our sitting room discussions and reflections. Their armchair advice was always welcome from my 'friends', as I saw them now. We had stimulating and entertaining philosophical speculations about life that sometimes made us all laugh.

But eventually, I began asking them, "Who are you people?"

At first they deflected my question with group humour. "It's not about us, Joe, it's about you." This was the 'day one' remark to me from the 'prison psychiatrist'. The more I asked, the more it became a running joke. Each one in the armchair circle, slowly from J-1 to Red-Jo, Deep-Joe to serious Scar-Jo, would answer me with a smile, "It's not about me, it's about you, Joe." Soon the joke became a game of "toss the Joke" back and forth amongst themselves, quick firing, "It's not about me, it's about you!" To rub it in, as a group they began singing the ascending musical scales to me, "Joe, Re, Me, Fa, So, La, Me, Joe!" until they burst into armchair hysterics.

It was plain silly, stupid. "Yeah, yeah, I get it," I laughed with them, shaking my head. Gradually, I began to realise their funny banter about me helped diffuse the intensity of my flashback memories that kept popping up all the time in the Cube, horrible things I had done. Back and forth I went from the deep cave of my memories to silly laughter with my friends 'outside' in supermax.

As J-1 had advised, I now let these pop-up memories stay up, like old scarecrows. At first, they filled me with anguish of guilt, shame and self-loathing. But the longer

I let them stay up, let them be, the less power they held over me. As I stared at the old scarecrow of me, there 'he' stood alone, and here 'I' now gazed upon him with a sad curiosity. I reflected to myself, I was bright, intelligent, a quick learner. Everyone had told me that. I was good at anything I put my mind to. So, why had 'he' put my mind to such terrible things? Wasted my mind to manipulate and hurt others? Kill them? Instead of…

The roads not taken.

* * *

One day, I finally asked, "Seriously, I mean it, quit joking. Who are you? You know everything about me, but I know nothing about you."

"There's not much to tell," answered J-1. "We're all you. We told you before, we have given up our identities to be you – the whole Joe."

"But that can't be entirely true," I protested. "There must be something left of you. Even Zero said so. You can't be absolute Zero like him. I mean, before you became me, who were you?" I laughed at my surreal question. So did they. "Who were you before supermax? How did you end up here? Come on, tell me."

Red-Jo smiled. "Would our potted histories add anything to what you already know of us? How we have treated you, tolerated your ignorance and arrogance, challenged you, encouraged you, come to see you as our improbable friend, come to love you? Yes, even love. Is there anything more which you need to answer your question? Our love speaks louder than our potted histories."

Deeply chastened, I felt so stupid for asking.

J-1 concluded, "We keep telling you, it's not about us, it's about who you really are – the new lovable Joe."

That hit me like a sledgehammer. Deeper than tears, silence has no time.

But after a few more days, I again demanded, "But how did you get to be the way you are now? So generous and loving? You're in supermax. You told me yourself that only the worst of the worst come here. Have you been through The Born Again?"

Red-Jo answered, "Yes."

"Then why are you still here? Scar-Jo said those who finish it, can exit to the outside."

"Ah well, exiting," J-1 replied. "Who we are is why we are still here in supermax. You won't be able to understand who we are until you first understand the exiting procedure."

"I don't understand."

"Exactly. Perhaps I should let Scar-Jo explain the final legal stages."

"Wouldn't they let you out?" I asked anxiously, suddenly feeling 'exit' was too good to be true. A paranoid lightning bolt hit me. Was The Born Again some kind of guinea pig experiment so that the invisible Project could present their evidence of reformation to the outside world? Exiting into the glare of publicity and TV talk shows? The thought made me shudder.

"Nothing like that," J-1 assured me, intuitively reading my mind. "Scar-Jo, over to you, please."

She sat in her armchair, 60+, short white hair, the cheek scar, thin lips, as she looked at me with her piercing grey eyes. "Listen carefully, Joe. Yes, you are on the brink, the brink of becoming awake. Without that, nothing else matters." Her voice was clear and brisk. "Concentrate on THAT," she emphasised, "and all else will take care of itself. Secondarily, you are on the brink of exit. So, it's probably best that I tell you this now, so you will know what to expect on the outside."

"More coffee, Joe?" asked J-1.

No thanks."

"In preparation for exit, your final 'exit story', which you are telling us as we speak, is being recorded in the mind monitor." She pointed to the metallic disks at my temples. "Your whole story in supermax will then be digitally reviewed by us, the four Joes, so to speak," she smiled. "We then scan your victim database of everyone you have seriously harmed –"

"As an adult," interjected the young Red-Jo, who specialised in child development.

"Correct," said Scar-Jo. "Whether you have been convicted or not. Many of your offenses went under the radar because your victims were too scared to report them, or frankly, they were left dead lying in an alley somewhere. We then select a few of your victims and their families whom we have determined might benefit from seeing and experiencing your story, which we present to them in virtual-reality-helmet mode."

"What?!" I cried out in astonishment. "Why would anyone wan—"

"It's simple," continued Scar-Jo, "and profound. After a trial and conviction, typical 'victim support' services soon fade away due to high demand and lack of resources.

But at least they've had some justice and some help, with information about charitable agencies to contact if they need further help in the future. Not ideal, but better than nothing.

"But what about those traumatised victims and their families who never come to court? Never see a trial, never get a conviction or justice? Those who are not even legally recognised as 'victims.' What happens to them? Most are poorly educated, products of the 'care system', at the bottom of the pile. They don't even know who to turn to – the agencies and charities out there to help them. So, they turn on themselves, full of self-torment, just like you Joe, but in a completely different way. Full of self-blame for being duped and manipulated by you, even colluding in their own abuse because that's how they grew up—"

Red-Joe added, "Their history repeating itself."

"Correct. What happens to them? They're left with impotent rage, self-blame, despair, destroyed. That's their Life Sentence, Joe. Destroyed."

As I listened, my whole body clenched, my face a fist of self-disgust.

Scar-Jo continued, "We select 'the completely destroyed' for your exit story."

I protested, "By why would—"

"When this rarest of sentences, 'When Life Really Means Life' is secretly passed by the Project, there is a much-overlooked legal condition, that should an inmate make it through The Born Again, on the brink of exit, then selected victims must be sent his or her 'exit story' beforehand. Of course, most refuse, that's their choice. But it's a legal requirement for the victim and / or their family or a close friend, to first have a 'Refusal Meeting' with a lawyer and psychiatrist to explain the purpose—"

"Of what, for God's sake?" I asked incredulously. "Besides, how do you communicate with the outside world? This place is like a cloud in the sky."

Scar-Jo explained, "The Project have set up a mind monitor outside with one of the Project founders. We don't know who or where he is. It's called 'the Link.' It's used rarely because so few inmates reach the stage of 'on the brink.' When someone does, as you have, the Project use the Link to contact the relevant agencies to set up the necessary preparations for a victim Refusal Meeting. To be clear, the victim families cannot 'refuse' or stop your exit, but you must see their reactions to your exit story. These are real people, Joe, not your Cube memories, hallucinations or your fantasies about them. Call this the final hurdle of The Born Again before your exit goes ahead. If you cannot cope with seeing *their reality,* then we can stop your exit – for a time, or perhaps permanently. Exit is designed as a system of checks and balances, to make sure you really are Born Again. Understand?"

I shook my head incredulously, "Whew, you guys think of everything. Don't you even trust yourselves, trust your own judgment?"

"We do," she said. "But it's a matter of you finding out for yourself – with real victims, real people – whether you believe in your own Born Again and can trust its intuitive wisdom. Think of this stage as being let out on parole. It's the nearest we can get to testing the results of The Born Again on someone considered irredeemable, never to be let out."

Taken aback by Scar-Jo's answer, I thought for a while. "Whew again, this thing keeps getting deeper and deeper. There seems no end."

* * *

Judge Solomon watched the scene with amazement. He knew the exit process had been spontaneously designed by these inmates, not by him or the rest of the Project.

"You see, Joe, you've been constantly asking us. 'Who are you?' Well soon, there will be more to come about us. But meanwhile, this is our way of asking you the same question."

I felt lost for words. Until I protested feebly, "By why would any —"

J-1 interrupted. "Because, for your victims to see and experience your 'exit story' in virtual reality, it may give some of them hope for their own psychological resurrection. Most of your upbringing will resonate with their own neglect, abuse and deprivation. Most, especially 'the destroyed' who have never had their day in court, will take great pleasure in seeing how you have suffered in supermax. It will give them some semblance of justice. But, as they continue to watch, a rare few might find unexpected inspiration by your suffering journey through The Born Again, to liberation. That, in their own bereft lives and in their own way, maybe they too could be Born Again out of victimhood, and liberated into a new self and way of living. They might come to see that 'victim and perpetrator' are two sides of the same coin. *Both need liberation. Both are capable of finding freedom.*"

Deep-Joe added quietly, "I call it, convergent redemption."

"It's a legal requirement," continued Scar-Jo, "that selected victims are given the same 'chance and choice' that you have been given in supermax. After all, you have been selected too. For those few who choose to accept this chance given them, you need to see their feedback before you exit, whether hostile and full of hatred, or perhaps forgiving and full of inspirational change in their lives, inspired by you. It's our way of asking everyone, victim and perpetrator alike, 'Who are you?' This can't be replicated in the reality helmet. This is your final stage of becoming awake.

J-1 added, "Joe, to appreciate how far you've come, remember that supermax was founded on the principle of lifelong punishment, based on 'the justice of suffering'. Nothing more. But The Project never imagined that 'something else' might happen. There was a Roman philosopher, Cato the Younger, who once said, 'There is no comfort without pain. Thus we define salvation through suffering'. Think about it, Joe, your punishment of 'the justice of suffering' has been transformed by The Born Again into your 'salvation through suffering' – for the sake of the outside world that awaits you."

Thirty

The Victim Refusal Meetings

"**Y**ou're WHAT?!" cried Mrs. Johnson when she was first asked about viewing the exit story of the man who had killed her husband nearly twenty years ago. In her sixties now, her face looked tired and gaunt, trembling with outrage. "Over my dead—"

"Mum, don't say that," her forty-year old son Mark stopped her. He was the dominant protective son. His younger brother Jason, thirty-eight, earnest looking, sat next to him, all three in a row on the family settee. Both sons were middle-aged professionals, Mark, a high flying chemical engineer and Jason, a plain old high school teacher, both married with children. It was a comfortable middleclass home. Opposite them in armchairs sat the solicitor, Mr. Turgot, and psychiatrist Dr. Matthews, suit and tie men. Peas in a pod, Mathews could have passed for the solicitor and Turgot could have passed as the psychiatrist. They had heard it all before, but nevertheless, it always felt gut wrenching, these first family reactions.

"Let him out?!" she blurted. Laying her hand against her son's chest, "Don't stop me, Mark."

"It's not about forgiveness," offered the psychiatrist sympathetically. "It's—"

"Damn right it's not about forgiveness! I thought that's what his life sentence was for. Let him rot, like us, and throw away the key."

Jason leaned forward to look across Mark to his mother, "Mum, hear them out, at least. Calm down. The solicitor says we don't have to do this."

Their mother tried to push her outrage down into the old jack-in-the-box of not thinking about what happened long ago, but, "I'm sorry, no I'm NOT sorry. I've nothing to be sorry for," she glared at the two visitors. "You're just being here brings it all back. Where's the good in that, after all these years? What's in it for us?"

Mr. Turgot and Dr. Matthews were patient and experienced listeners. They had to be. After they tactfully explained about The Born Again, Mrs. Johnson blurted again, "I don't care about what he's been through. What about us? You've got it all backwards. You should send him our story instead. Let HIM see what he's done to us over the years. Who's going to let me out of my nightmare? Tell me that."

The bespeckled psychiatrist tried to sooth her with the mantra, "It's not about him, it's about you as a family. Possibly to learn something about yourselves from what happened." Mark put his arm round his mother's thin shoulders. "I can't see any benefit for mum, I think she's been through enough. We all have."

She hung her head, trying not to cry. "I ache for my Ken, even when I'm not thinking of him. Have you two got any idea of how that feels? I want him back to the way he was before that damn stupid speech. I want to see him wolf down his breakfast before he rushes off for his first class at school. I want him to take the boys fishing again. I want him back in bed with me. I want, I ache, I want what will never be. The way it was before." She stopped and glared fiercely at the two men. "Ken was a good husband, a good father, a good teacher. He was a good man who made one human mistake in his life. Just the once!" she spat bitterly. "How many of us can say that? And bloody life came down on him for it like a ton of bricks. For his one mistake."

Jason winced but held his tongue. He seemed more receptive, more inquiring of the visitors. Eventually, the interview convoluted this way and that, meandering back to Mrs. Johnson, now red-eyed and deflated of anger, who offered her tired, hindsight understanding of what had led up to her husband's out of character speech at the school assembly – the trigger for what happened.

Her Ken was always driven and ambitious, for himself and for his students. He worked hard, put in all the extra hours that teachers do, and then some, typically unrecognised. So many school holidays? They were an unpaid joke! Anyway, Ken had his eye on the headship at his old boyhood school. "You know, like a kid's boyhood football club which you dream of playing for one day. It was like that for Ken," Marge explained. "He had built up plenty of experience, knew his job, and knew he was ready to be head of his beloved old school. A dream about to come true. But," she gulped and swallowed, blinking back the tears from her gaunt face, "He didn't get the headship." Her son Jason, a schoolteacher fidgeted painfully, nearly getting up from the settee, then leaning back.

Marge continued, "Gutted, but our Ken would have found a way to get over that. See it as a trial run for a headship somewhere else. But post-interview, he got cruel feedback. He was told that he was not only too ambitious for himself, but toward his students he showed an intolerance of mediocrity and failure. Of course, that wasn't my Ken at all."

"Mum," Jason interrupted gently, "Dad was pushy with Mark and I, remember?"

Their mother snapped, "It didn't do you two any harm." She smiled proudly at Mark next to her. "A chemical engineer." Then her thin face frowned at Jason, "I wish you hadn't gone into teaching. How could you, after what happened to your father?" Jason let it go. It was an old hurt, an old argument, and with Mark the favourite, mum blanked out how hard dad had pushed them to achieve.

Marge carried on. "Ken was devasted by those comments. So, he resolved to prove them wrong. What did he do? He singled out that nasty piece of work at school and did everything he could to turn that kid round. All the time that God sends. Ken got him out of trouble, got his grades up and the star of the debating team. That was Ken's showcase for his next application for headship. If the team had won, with all the publicity, Ken could take the credit. It would go on his CV. He'd walk into a headship no bother. But that nasty shit let him down. Even spread rumours about him. I don't like to think…"

Mark nodded approvingly. Jason winced again. He understood the complexity of working with students like that.

Mrs. Johnson continued, "After that damned speech, at school there came a surprising backwash of sympathy for the little brute who everyone hated. Over the years the incident became bit of a school legend. Of course, Ken lost his job, never taught again. He got shunted into admin in the bowels of county hall. Then came years of depression, near suicidal. It took its toll on us all."

She quipped sarcastically, "Suicidal? Little did he know what was coming! And then," her red eyes blinking, "And then, when he got into his car at the huge county hall car park, the brute must have tripped the lock and was hiding in the back seat. That's where he—" Her lips trembled, "slit my Ken's throat." Mrs. Johnson suddenly clamped her bony hands to her face, bursting into tears, shoulders heaving, "Then, on the windscreen he wrote in Ken's blood, *I believed in you.*"

Mark cuddled his mother fiercely. "What do you want?" he demanded. "Her blood too?"

The solicitor answered, "Perhaps through this inmate's story, you might see things differently."

Mark unwrapped his arm from his mother's shoulders and jumped to his feet, wagging his finger at them, "That's not only ridiculous but cruel! See? See what you've done to my mother? Get out! Get out of here!"

The solicitor and psychiatrist stood. The solicitor observed solemnly, "We make no apologies. It's a legal requirement to offer your family this chance—"

The psychiatrist interrupted, "And choice. You have

made yours. It will be respected. We'll see ourselves out."

As they turned to leave, Jason jumped to his feet. "If they won't, I will."

* * *

When the solicitor and psychiatrist first propose an exit story to any family, there was only ever one answer that they wanted – an answer, any answer. But the brother and sister of Father Martin listened in mute silence. No protests, not even questions. "Do you understand?" Dr. Matthews finally ventured?

"Do you?" answered the older brother Christopher.

The four sat round a sunny kitchen table. Their mugs of tea and coffee, half drunk, had gone cold. The family genes were obvious. Chris, aged fifty-five, a tall six foot, three inches. He glanced at his younger sister, Sienna, a lean six foot. Both siblings had long, horse-like faces with plump lips, but not the blubber lips of their brother. Father – Martin was not his birth surname. Priests take on special names, usually those of a saint to inspire their life as "Father", an embodiment of "Our Father" to the parishioners on earth. Father Martin chose the name of St. Martin of Tours in ancient France. He is best known for the account of using his sword to cut his cloak in two, to give half to a beggar clad only in rags in the depth of winter. The family surname was Franklin. Sienna's married name, Bristow.

At the kitchen table the waiting stretched like an elastic band about to snap. At last, Sienna un-tensed it. She spoke quietly. "We were a good Catholic family, you know." In Christopher's lounge no crucifix or pictures of the saints adorned the walls. No little statue on the mantel piece or worn out bible on the coffee table. His bookshelves had no theology or biographies of the saints. No trace of "once a Catholic, always a Catholic."

"You see, it was very difficult for the family," she understated, unfolding their tale of how the bomb dropped. They didn't believe it at first. How could you? They thought it was some wacko with a grudge against the church for covering up historic sex abuse, who chose Father Martin – their brother Julian, Jules – at random. But the police evidence and forensics were overwhelming.

The attacker had broken into the rectory and waited for Father Martin in his private suite. Fresh empty cups of tea on a table indicated they must have first talked without confrontation, no doubt to the priest's stunned surprise, possibly secret pleasure. That's how he was drugged, then stripped naked and tied in an armchair, his stork legs splayed wide apart. It was all recorded on film, the tripod camera still remained facing his dead body. "You don't need to see this," the police told the family. They never did.

With an injection the attacker roused him back to consciousness, then hand jobbed him until Father Martin got stiff, then oral sex. Bizarrely, the killer had brought golden altar bells with him and when Father Martin was about to come in Joe's mouth, he pulled away and jangled the bells. "Stop! Now for your penance." Joe stuffed a gag in his mouth to muffle the screams as he castrated the priest, not all at once, but very, very slowly, watching him watch himself, incredulous, bleed to death. Then he wrote on the walls in his blood, "I'm a watcher, not a sinner. In memory of Me." Cool as a cucumber, Joe showered and changed, leaving the rectory wearing Father's Martin's black cassock.

How are the family members supposed to feel and react when their brother, a priest for God's sake, is discovered to be a paedophile? Shocked to the core, they still didn't believe it. After all, the video proved nothing against their brother Jules. He was the victim of a random attack, the killer a madman. It was obvious. But the police found evidence. Father Martin kept a diary. In it the pages were scrawled with accounts of his sexual exploits with his special altar boys, aided by drawings. And other boys throughout the parish and beyond. Thousands of photos and films were dredged out of the sewers of his computer. After the publicity, scores of men came forward to the police about their childhood abuse, forgiven in the confessional, with Father Martin's details of their 'penance.'

These facts couldn't match up with their fond memories of him and family photos. False memories? A good Catholic family, Jules was the middle child of five siblings, boys and girls. Sienna, his younger sister by two years, remembered that their father always seemed to favour Jules for no reason. They all noticed. Especially during the hot summer holidays when father singled him out for long country bike rides, or go skinny dipping in a cold river, play hide and seek in the woods, and come home breathless with stories of adventure and laughter. She guessed it was father simply making the middle child feel special. "Instead of making us envious and resentful, and turning Jules into a spoiled brat, he in turn, remarkably, made us feel special, involving us in his adventure stories so vividly, as if we were actually there with him and father. That was his most attractive quality. He never lost it. As an adult Jules had an uncanny way of making anyone feel special. Children loved him. His nieces and nephews did. Uncle Jules! Yay!"

Chris said the other three wouldn't come to this exit meeting. The split happened right at the beginning. The others told us, said Chris, "We've all got the same parents, the same upbringing, same love, yet how the hell did he turn out like this? We didn't, you didn't. Fucking why?" When Chris and Sienna wavered on the cliff of love and hate, the rest of the family pushed them off to rock bottom oblivion. If only the ground could scream? If only... Thank God their mother had died the year before, and their father was in a care home with dementia. It would have shamed them worse than killing them, "especially our proud father," explained Chris. "A pillar of the parish."

For Sienna, what was worse than discovering that her beloved brother was a priest child sex abuser was the fact that she never knew, not an inkling of suspicion. Growing up, even as an adult, she never saw the signs. What bloody signs were there to suspect?! Jules was funny, caring, attentive, a good listener (he must have been great in confession), loving, generous with his time for others, in fact selfless, for God's sake! "To me and everyone. He made us all feel," she made quotation marks in the air to the visitors across the kitchen table, "special."

The fact that she had no bloody idea haunted her. Over the years an anguish of self-doubt corkscrewed into her heart. How could she ever again believe in her judgement of other people, trust her own feelings, affection, even love for someone else? Whether she liked or disliked someone, her judgment and intuition were at a loss. A sinkhole had opened up.

"So here we are," Sienna concluded sarcastically. "Two pieces of a broken family sitting here with you across the table, like uninvited ghosts, telling us a ghost story. That's the laugh. We, not you, are the ghosts, and you're telling us we can be born again?"

Dr. Matthews the psychiatrist answered with an insistent voice, "That's right, by a killer who has been Born Again. His journey could change your life. For what's it's worth, he was a Catholic like yourselves. There is much in his story that—"

Chris butted in, "Some good the church has done for them. One a paedophile, the other his killer!"

"It's not about the church at all."

Chris blurted out sarcastically, spreading his wing-arms wide, "Oh no, please don't tell me, yet another person in prison has found religion, found God? Praise be to the fucking Lord! Well, in this family God is dead, buried. So is the church. Now get out. Get the hell out and stay out of our lives!" Then he hung his horse head and whispered feebly, "Just get out."

Mr. Turgot the solicitor, with his back to the kitchen window through which the sunny day outside could never reach inside, answered solemnly, "We make no apologies. It is a legal requirement to offer you as a family this chance—"

The psychiatrist typically interrupted, "This chance to see your lives in a different perspective."

"And the choice," emphasised Mr. Turgot. "You have made yours. It will be respected. We'll see ourselves out." It had become their standard line of leaving over the years.

As they stood and turned for the door, "Just get out,"

whimpered Chris, glancing to his sister. She nodded from the bottom of her sinkhole. If only the sinkhole could scream.

* * *

More families, of course, refused. Wouldn't you? Would you be willing to meet the killer of your loved one? *I wouldn't,* thought Joe. *I don't have any loved ones anyway, but that's beside the point. I wouldn't want to meet me.*

But some people did. Careful planning and preparations had to be made. It happens in traditional prisons or in Probation offices, not often, these meetings between a perpetrator and the victim's family. "Restorative justice," it's called. What did the killer want to get out of such a complex meeting? His motives had to be meticulously examined. For example, to weed out things like secretly gloating over the suffering of his victim's family, years later down the line watching the power of his murder. Or, did he wish to apologise for his hostile defence in court and confess in full to the horror he now realised he had inflicted on the family? Did he seek some kind of forgiveness? And the victim's family? Their motives also had to be vetted to avoid a sudden loss-of-control outburst during the encounter. What did they hope for? Answers? Some kind of "understanding" to make sense of the senseless? To see and hear his remorse? *Feel his remorse?* Would that be enough? Or tell him they had forgiven him? An act of their secret superiority? And hatred?

"Managing expectations" was the cliché preparation for both perpetrator and the victim's family. What would each walk away with? A common humanity? What could their innocence have in common with this cruellest of killers, Joe in supermax? Yeah, "managing expectations" felt like skydiving without a parachute. WUMP! Damned if you're living, damned if you're dead.

Hoping to be somehow born again?

To the same old shit back home and in the prison cell? Punishment, forgiveness, confessional absolution always stop short of something much bigger, unmanageable and unimaginable.

* * *

Hope, thought judge Solomon, as he watched these scenes on his monitor screen. *What did they hope for?* Of the three "theological virtues" of the Catholic church, Faith, Hope and Charity, (the judge was vaguely a Christian, not a Catholic) he could understand faith and charity, but hope felt like an empty word, a pick-me-up amidst our trials in life, a blind hope in the promise of an afterlife in heaven. Faith and charity could motivate him to do good deeds, but hope felt like whistling in the dark, like when he was twelve years old waiting in vain for his kidnap ransom money. Not a chance. Not a hope on earth, as it is in hell.

He sighed and looked up to his new stained-glass window, no longer the suffering crucified Christ, but replaced with the peaceful image of St. Francis of Assisi smiling at a bird which he held in his hand. *Francesco d'Assisi* (1181–1226), a Catholic friar and mystic, founder of the Franciscan order and co-patron saint of Italy, was famous for his life of poverty and charitable good works for the poor. But the reason why the judge had chosen him was for his legendary affinity with animals and the whole of nature. Pope John Paul II declared Francis the patron saint of ecology, stating that Francis "invited all of creation – animals, plants, natural forces, even Brother Sun and Sister Moon – to give honour and praise to the Lord. The poor man of Assisi gives us striking witness that when we are at peace with God, we are better able to devote ourselves to building up that peace with all creation, which is inseparable from peace among all peoples."

Francis often preached to the birds which flocked to him unafraid. He tamed a marauding wolf which had attacked and killed some local townsfolk. Such legends are found in all cultures and faiths round the world in all eras – these saints and mystics who emanate an aura of harmlessness, love and compassion, so powerful that anyone who comes near them, their violent or hateful tendencies are dissipated while in his or her presence. Even wild beasts become tame and docile.

From his desk the judge gazed up at the stained-glass of Francis. Somehow, the saint's aura of peace made him smile. Yes, the judge found himself smiling. He was drinking less. He was rooting for Joe, *hoping* he would 'make it'.

Thirty-One

Exit Viewings Begin

"It's time," Zero warned, as he taxied me to The Born Again. His robot voice had long lost its electric fuzz, sounding completely human now. Two months had passed since the Refusal Meetings. The four Joes sat in their armchairs positioned in a semi-circle in front of the mind monitor. The screen was 'on', but blank. As I sat down in the centre chair I sensed a tension in the room. "We're waiting for the transmission," said J-1. "Coffee?"

"Not just yet, thanks." Then, "Why am I so nervous? You are too."

"It's natural, Joe." J-1 went on to explain that over the past fifty years only six inmates had reached this stage of 'on the brink'. But one didn't 'make it'. At this acid test of authentic awakening, one of them couldn't cope with the depth of the families' reactions to his exit story. The Born Again inmates, even the robot, had missed something. It was rare. This was a final, failsafe test of their credibility to The Project. So, everyone felt a knotted gut of nerves. "It's natural, Joe. But you should be alright."

Suddenly, the screen imaged the Johnson family in their lounge. Mother and Mark sat together on the settee while Jason sat in an armchair.

I whispered, "I thought it would only be Jason."

J-1 answered, "No need to whisper, they can't hear or see you. The three decided to turn up after all." The solicitor and psychiatrist had arrived with two doctors, one male, the other female. They had temporarily applied the metal disks to Mrs. Johnson's head and body, and placed the dark visored reality helmet over her head. Mark asked, "What about us? Do we get one of those contraptions?"

"No need," explained Dr. Matthews. "The reality helmet acts like a film projector which displays the exit story on this screen. You and Jason can see and hear everything your mother can."

"Can he – can he see us now? Hear us?"

"Yes," said the solicitor.

"Why can't we see him?" Mark pressed.

"As we go along, that might be possible, a two-way link. It's a judgment call for Dr. Mathews, the psychiatrist here. Meanwhile," the solicitor emphasised, "You can pause the transmission at any time for reflection or simply take a break. Tap the reality helmet, Mrs. Johnson, to let us know. Obviously, his near twenty years has been edited for your benefit. Otherwise," Mr. Turgot grinned, "You'd be here for the next twenty years," he chuckled. "Stuck with us." It was a lame joke. "And at any point, if you feel you've had enough and wish to stop altogether, that's fine. There is no obligation."

"Got that, mum?" Mark asked. Her reality helmet nodded nervously.

"But I would advise," added Dr. Matthews –

"Yeah, yeah," Mark interrupted, "See it through to the end, right?"

"Ok" said Dr. Matthews, "Everyone ready? Let's make a start."

* * *

Jason fidgeted in his armchair, wondering if he had done the right thing in persuading them to come along and watch. He wanted to, but anxiously, had no idea what to expect. His older brother Mark sat back with arms folded resolutely against what he was about to see.

The arrogance of Joe's initial Day One interview with the psychiatrist proved Mark's point until the question at the end, "What's the best thing in life you have ever done?" Humph, *fucking nothing,* he thought, *compared to dad.* Joe's hallucinatory memories in the polka dot Cube, especially the eagle / octopus thing, bounced off his chemical engineer's mind like a tennis ball. But Jason, an art and drama teacher, became increasingly moved, shocked at the brutality of Joe's childhood, yet fascinated how his surreal memories unravelled like a crazy Jackson Pollock painting. In his art and drama classes, he had used basic free association and spontaneity exercises with his students, so he had some affinity with what the inmate was experiencing. But this was on a different level altogether. Their mother's response so far? Well, she didn't stop the transmission.

Sure, he had a tough childhood. So what? Don't we all? thought Mark. He gloated at Joe's suffering in the Cube.

Serves him bloody right. But suddenly, he remembered dad hitting him, hard, for underachieving at school. He had forgotten. Nothing was ever good enough for him, however hard you tried. So, Mark got hit hard, more often than he cared to remember. As the eldest, he got the brunt of it. Jason seemed to get off lightly. Well, that didn't make his dad a child abuser. He was just being a good parent. *The odd wallop didn't turn me into a killer. Look at me now.*

The religious stuff didn't cut any ice with Mark. His father taught at a Catholic school, but neither his dad nor the family were Catholic. Besides, if many psychopaths can use religion to justify their murders – "God told me to" – they can also use religion to disguise their so-called reform, convincingly. That's what this guy was doing. No doubt about it.

Instead, the science of the reality helmet appealed to the analytical chemist for a Big Pharma company that was at the cutting edge of bio-medicine. He loved it when the psychiatrist told Joe, "We don't play around with psycho-babble anymore. It's all science now, chemical injections, remote neurological implants, etc." Even the cosmic breathing, cosmic heart beating and the weird digestive absorption correlated with studies using psychotropic chemicals, including controlled doses of LSD, to treat dementia, depression and schizophrenia. But he felt the doctors over-sympathised with his mumbo-jumbo memories and had got sucked into the psychological aspects of his growing remorse. *I mean, how could these really be trusted?* That's why some paedophiles consent to chemical castration in order to prove their reform, and in rare cases some elect for physical castration. That's what this guy needed. The doctors in supermax went on all the time about "chance and choice." *Well, give him the chance to choose – to have his hands chopped off so he could never cut someone's bloody throat again! Then I'll believe him. This Born Again thing was too soft, didn't go far enough, that was the problem.* But he managed to keep his thoughts to himself. His bristling body language didn't.

On his high hill in his Victorian law library, the one-armed Judge Solomon winced at Mark's Old Testament brutality. Branded in his brain was the image of the vicious school children and the octopus. Chop, Chop! "Grow them back!" Chop, Chop! "We'll show you what it's like to be human!" Back then, the judge approved. But now, seeing how far Joe had grown…

From time to time Mrs Johnson tapped the helmet for a break, use the lieu, have a tea. Dr. Matthews eyed her closely, as did her two sons. Her horse-like, gaunt face, although impassive, looked almost skeletal. "Are you sure you want to carry on? Any questions, Marge?"

She sighed, "No, I'll just watch."

Back in supermax J-1 offered, "We might as well take a break too. Red-Jo, some drinks please. Well Joe, what do you make of it so far?"

"There's lot going on under the surface. Mark, the protective son sits next to his mother on the settee while Jason sits separately in an armchair. Quiet, too quiet."

"And you?"

I smiled, sipping my coffee, "I guess I'm the same as them – a lot going on under the surface."

"Let's see what happens," replied J-1.

The Johnson family progressed to the point of Joe's

"That's when it hit me, my rock bottom was my remorse – a new cruelty of realisation that I could never undo my cruelty to others.... Feeling their PAIN for the first time."

Inside the reality helmet Marge shook her head, but didn't stop watching. Both sons turned to look at her anxiously. "Pain?" snapped Mark, "What does he know of our pain?!"

Dr. Matthews ventured, "Do you want to stop and talk about this, Mark?"

"Hell no, what is there to talk about? Carry on." Jason hung his head.

Outrage soon erupted. Mrs. Johnson ripped off the reality helmet when she realised that supermax was run by inmates and a robot! Mark jumped to his feet, "We're supposed to believe this guy has really changed? That he's ready to be let out into the world by his fellow inmates and by a bloody robot?! This is insane! Where's the fucking life sentence in that? Where is the justice?"

"Sit down," urged Dr. Matthews. "Sit down and listen." Mr. Turgot, the solicitor, sternly advised, "It's a legal requirement that you are bound by the strictest confidentiality to keep this knowledge to yourselves. There are severe consequences if you breach it. Understand? Severe."

Tears wriggled out of Marge's hollow eyes. "Up to this point I thought maybe, just maybe he—"

"Mum, don't you dare be fooled by this fantastic charade." Jason squirmed in the armchair, his face reddening.

Eventually, Dr. Matthews concluded the viewing. "We hoped that you might come to see that 'victim and perpetrator' are two sides of the same coin of life. Both need liberation. Both are capable of finding freedom, if they choose. That's all. Thank you for being brave enough to try."

"Wait a minute," protested Mark. "He can't get off that lightly. I want to see him. I want to hear what he's got to say, now."

"I'm not so sure," hesitated Dr. Matthews. "You're pretty angry."

"Damn right I'm angry. What did you expect?"

"Mrs. Johnson?" asked the doctor. "Can you handle this?"

"We've handled this for nearly twenty years without any answers. Like Mark, I want to hear what he's got to say."

"Ok." He pressed the remote which turned on a live two-way transmission.

* * *

It happened so abruptly, it startled me. There the family sat in their home lounge staring at us in our semi-circle of armchairs, my robot Zero on standby, in our twilight world of supermax.

"A cosy bunch of deluded dimwits, aren't you?" sneered Mark. "Which one is he?"

J-1 replied, "Centre chair, that's Joe."

He seemed surprised at the peaceful features of my face. What is a monster supposed to look like? I felt anything but peace inside.

"Well Mr. Joe, we've indulged in your Born Again

fantasies and lies, so now tell us the truth. You owe us at least that much. What have you got to say to us, face to face?"

I swallowed hard, as if a golf ball bulged down my throat, choking on the futility of my words. "There – there's probably nothing – nothing I can say to you that would make any difference. But maybe to myself. I'd like to talk to that young angry man that used to be me all those years ago, the 'old Joe', but he's gone now. He wouldn't have listened to me anyway. He couldn't, simple and dumb as that. But if I could tell him something now, on your behalf, I would tell him, *I wish, I wish you were never born.*"

Suddenly, I felt as if I was my father talking to his son, me – the brutal son like the brutal father – except that now, my father was miraculously awakened out of his hell. After all, what is hell, but hindsight? When it's too late. "Come up out of the cellar, Joe, your mum's made a tasty breakfast. Later we'll go to the swimming baths. You're a good boy, you know. I'm so proud of you," as he ruffles my hair at the kitchen table.

"You see," I ventured through tremoring lips, "All I can say to you is this: I feel like a foetus which should have been aborted, knowing the bad future that I would turn out to live."

Mrs. Johnson burst into uncontrollable tears. Mark and Jason instantly cuddled her on the settee. "What's wrong? What's wrong, mum? What did he say that upset you?" Dr. Matthews let it go on. Sobbing through her bony hands clamped to her face, "I never dared tell you boys. Ken wouldn't…"

Her words stuttered out, almost retching, then

240

catching her breath to blurt out her buried agony. Her first child, not Mark, had been aborted. Diagnosed as a disabled baby, Marge wanted to keep it, her first joy of pregnancy. But 'disabled' could never be good enough for Ken's high standards in life. They argued. He pushed for abortion. The sons listened in shock. "He pushed me hard, I mean literally, down the stairs one night, drunk. I was nearly five months pregnant." Questions were asked, of course, but Marge's plausible compliance with Ken's story, convinced the authorities. Accidents happen. She couldn't stop sobbing,

"I would have given our baby a chance in life. That's what life is, a chance, isn't it? But your dad stole my choice to make it happen. I've never forgiven him. All these years I've thought of the life our baby might have lived." She turned to her sons, "Your big brother. Disabled kids turn out alright, you know. As you two were growing up, I used to imagine the things you three would get up to. Pillow fighting in the bedroom, maybe bike riding to the swimming hole, listening to music, school…" Her voice trailed away. "He would have turned out ok, nothing like this monster Joe here, because he would have been loved, at least by me," she sobbed.

The sons listened, stunned, as did everyone.

Suddenly Joe asked, "Did he have a name?"

Marge crumpled, buried her head and face in her arms, in a cave of stalactite tears. Until finally, her haunted face emerged trembling. "I can hardly bring myself to say it," her voice quavered, "Thomas – after my dad." Then she plunged back into her cave of sorrow, shuddering, "Oh Tommy."

The collective astonishment was profound.

In a reflex moment on the settee Mark withdrew his arm from round his mother's shoulders, as if betrayed and repulsed, then hugged her again fiercely, but now he hugged an Egyptian mummy gone to the underworld.

Jason muttered in shock, "Mum, oh mum, we didn't know."

His mother sat dead, mummified on the settee, his brother still trying to hug her back to life.

After a long time Jason broke the silence, "Can I? Can I say something?" he asked.

"Of course," replied Dr. Matthews.

"That speech dad gave at school was cruel, but his killing can never be justified, however terrible this Joe's upbringing was. He killed our dad." Glancing at Mark's fuming face, "I can't forgive this. I don't know what forgiveness really is."

Mark leaned across his dead mother and snarled at his brother, "Don't you even go there!"

"What I do know is this," Jason continued tentatively, "In this man's exit story I've seen real suffering and real change. Good people, like our dad, can do bad things. And bad people, like this Joe here, can sometimes do good things. Like this monitor meeting right now. I don't understand, but I recognise there is a mystery in his story. It humbles me, makes me determined to be more patient with myself, with my children, and with my students. To be more realistic about my tiny efforts to help other people in their troubles. I know it's not all down to me if someone changes in the future. But for dad it was. People change because of bigger forces in life. Not always, of course. We can't predict, only hope, but by trying to change ourselves, sometimes we can help others to change. And for that Mr. Joe, you have shown me it's possible. Thank you."

Mark and his mother, her hollow eyes now opened from the underworld, simultaneously burst out with rage, "Thank you?! How can you say that?! For killing him?!"

It was a typical 'exit story' viewing. Mark turned savage on his younger brother Jason, "Get out of my house. Get out of our family, mum and I. Get out for good and never show your face again!" As Jason stood to leave, Mark sneered at Joe through the monitor screen, "You're like a cancer, once a killer, always a killer."

Blank screen...

Thirty-Two

Do This in Memory of Me

After two days of feedback discussion with the four Joes, I concluded helplessly, "Just more pain to absorb. There seems no end to it."

Zero smiled, "There's no end to awakening either."

Judge Solomon nodded and smiled. He found himself smiling more and more these days. By now, he had stopped drinking – because of Joe. In order to immerse himself in his journey, to feel Joe's pain and awakening, the judge had come to realise, that somehow, he too had to awaken.

* * *

In supermax Joe and the four Joes and Zero assembled in front of the mind monitor screen, awaiting the next family to appear – the Franklins, Christopher and Sienna, brother and sister of Father Martin. Joe hadn't expected them to view his exit story, and he dreaded it. "You'll be fine," encouraged J-1.

"I'm not so sure this time."

Joe had made him suffer in the cruellest possible way. The crime scene at the rectory was a classic blood bath. Joe had calmly used his shower afterward and sauntered off wearing Father Martin's cassock, as if he were a Catholic priest. It was sick to the core, and Joe knew it. Yes, he dreaded the family reaction alright.

As with the other families, the usual preparations were made by the medical doctors, and the usual questions and advice given by the solicitor and psychiatrist. Would they be able to see and talk with their brother's killer at some point? Probably. Were they ready to start?

In supermax the monitor screen came to life. Joe tensed. In Christopher's lounge the brother and sister, both lean six footers, sat together on a settee, tightly holding hands. They had flipped a coin for the reality helmet. The coin toss fell to Sienna. She was an early retired school secretary, Chris a warehouse manager. The absence of the other three siblings, and their disownment of Chris and Sienna, deadened the home atmosphere.

"We were a good Catholic family, you know," Sienna had first said at the Refusal Meeting. In the course of their viewing, this Catholic connection eventually did make a connection between the killer and the victim's family, but not in a way either could have expected.

But first, like the other families, the Franklin siblings followed the bizarre roller coaster ride of Joe's suffering in the Cube, and their amazement at his Born Again experiences of cosmic breathing, cosmic heart heating and cosmic digestive absorption of forgotten goodness in his life. As Catholics, against their will, they could sense the spirituality of Joe's emerging remorse toward redemption. That's what confused them, which both thwarted and fuelled their hatred. They thought this exit story would be more black and white, give them a final certainty of condemnation. But it didn't.

Many of the religious references by Joe and quotes from the doctors resonated with their Catholic upbringing. In fact, these pushed them beyond their traditional dogmas, making them think anew. Particularly, the Saul / St. Paul conversion, a well-known story of the cruel stone-to-death serial killer who had been transformed into a new, loving person. Now, they saw it in a new light through Joe's Born Again. It begged the question, *what is it to be human?* Dr. Matthew's summation was telling: "We hoped that you might come to see that 'victim and perpetrator' are two sides of the same coin of life. Both need liberation. Both are capable of finding freedom. This exit story is our way of asking both victim and perpetrator alike, 'Who are you? Who can you be in the future? Thank you for being brave enough to try."

Of the two, Chris was the more angry, while Sienna, against her will, felt that this inmate Joe was also "brave enough to try." She had to talk directly with him. It was what Joe dreaded most.

* * *

Live transmission. Sienna removed the reality helmet, let go of Christopher's hand and leaned forward on the settee to look closely at the little group in faraway supermax. "Which? Which one are you?"

J-1 replied, "Centre chair, that's our Joe."

"Our?" exclaimed Chris. "Well, he's not 'our' to us. He's nothing."

Sienna frowned at Chris, "Let me do the talking." Addressing Joe, "You don't look like the monster I imagined. Your face looks almost kind. It's disarming. I don't know where to start."

"Neither do I," said Joe. "I've been dreading this." Flustered, she felt he was almost human, too human. She swept a hand through her ear-length dull hair which accentuated her horse-like face with plump lips, and her tall height even when sitting. Her eyes blinking, a question suddenly came like tripping over a paving stone, a question that surprised herself, "I want to know what you and Jules talked about in the rectory before – I don't want to know, it's too horrific. But I want to know what you both said when drinking tea. I want to know my brother's last words."

Joe gulped an intake of breath, his gut clenched.

"Did you hear me? I'm waiting" she pressed.

Slow and measured, "I don't think you really want to know this."

"Why? Did you make him beg? Is that it?"

"No, he wanted to talk."

"About what?"

Reluctantly, Joe began to explain. "After his first 'Who the hell are you? Get out, I'm going to call the police', I smiled at him, 'Remember me, Father?'"

"What? Do I know you?' He eyed me closely. Your brother hadn't seen me since I was twelve years old. I was maybe thirty then, the altar boy all grown up. Slowly it dawned on him, 'It's you, my special Joe, the altar boy! What are you doing here?"

"Passing by." Still smiling, "Thought I would surprise you."

"You sure have! Come and sit down, I'll make us some tea."

"And so we chatted, eventually winding our way back to the old times. His eyes were lighting up. As he sipped his tea, I could see the film camera running behind his eyes, you know, taking pleasure in the memories. If he hadn't, maybe it would never have happened. But I could see it was still going on. Father Martin would never stop, no matter how old he got. It was the pleasure in his eyes, and in those smiling blubber lips, the pleasure unspoken. That's when I pulled the altar bells out of my rucksack to show him. "Here, I'll make us another cup of tea," I offered. "Play around with them if you want." In the kitchenette I could hear them jangling as I drugged his tea. "Drink up, Father." His hands, with those delicate long fingers, caressed the altar bells so full of memories. Your brother's face was beaming. 'You've never forgotten, Joe, have you?'

"How could I forget?" I grinned.

"Your brother's face was all smug with leering delight. 'You've come back for more, haven't you, my son?'

"Then, to his surprise, I knelt before him and prayed. I could taste the acid words as they came out of my mouth, 'Bless me Father, for I am about to sin.'

"Say Joe," he grinned, "that's a great idea for confession. I should have thought of that years ago. Forget about what you have done. What's done is done. But tell the priest the sins that you plan to commit, especially the ones that you can't help, 'for I am about to sin.' Hey, that gets right down and dirty to the balls of confession, to real sinning. I'll start using this from now on. Thanks for the tip off."

Sienna listened aghast, almost transfixed.

"That's what we talked about Mrs. Franklin, err Bristow. Your brother was never going to change. He had to be stopped."

Christopher blurted, "Not like THAT! Report him to the police, gather witness statements, forensic evidence, etc. But not like THAT! It's unforgivable."

"Well, ask yourself why all those hundreds of boys never came forward? Not me. Not one. Until he was dead. Until it was safe."

Sienna's voice trembled, "I have, and I still don't understand."

"Think about it. Young boys too young to understand. How could they? A prison psychologist once explained to me how sex abuse happens. It's a thing called 'grooming,' he said. But it starts with the parents first, not the kids. Looking back, I can see it now. Because, like the serpent in the Garden of Eden, Father Martin befriended the parents. As good Catholics they had a natural deference and trust in their parish priest anyway. But when they got to know him, how likeable Father Martin was, and how much time and interest he showed toward their children, well, their parental trust in him knew no bounds. In effect, he could control them. They always did as he advised. He could do no wrong. Sienna, are you following this so far?"

Grim faced, she nodded, "What you describe sounds like Jules. Everyone liked him, loved him. But underneath? It's so hard to imagine—"

"Even if we had been tempted to tell our parents, we knew they would never believe us. Kids' fantasies, that's all. The sanctity and authority of the church was unquestionable. In those times the police gave great deference to the church. Children were caught between Father Martin and our parents in a vice of silence.

"But also, the psychologist explained, by Father Martin making us feel uniquely special, we entrapped ourselves through our distorted loyalty to him, as if by our own choosing. That's what it felt like to me, and that's exactly what Father Martin wanted me to believe – that I was choosing this. Hence the shame and guilt and confusion were all the greater. It was my fault, not his. But in fact, I was captive inside a magic snow globe of silence held in the palm of Father Martin's hand. Remember, we were just kids. The whole thing is so subtle and sinister. That's why and how he got away with it. Without anyone knowing, even those closest to him, not even suspecting."

Sienna's face winced with pain, as if Joe's last remark had stabbed her. For years she had been haunted by this question – how did she not know? Suddenly, Christopher complained, "What I want to know is how the hell Jules got to be that way? It doesn't make any sense."

Joe looked at them compassionately. "You still don't know? You won't like the answer."

"Spit it out," Chris demanded.

"Remember, you were a good Catholic family. So was mine. I got locked in the cellar and beaten to a pulp but went along to daily Mass with my mother. I never told anyone. My father and Father Martin were best buddies. He sanctioned my punishments at home."

Sienna protested, "But Jules was nothing like that. He wasn't brutal. He was kind, caring, generous. He made everyone feel special."

"You're right, he did. When I was growing up with the beatings your brother made me feel special. That's how the abuse got started, and that's why I never told anyone because, like I said, I felt a special loyalty to Father Martin. I felt as if he had chosen me, out of all the other boys in the parish, that I was the only one who he trusted with his secret. The only one. I was special. So I told no one. Little did I know then, all the hundreds of other boys felt exactly the same as me, as if they were the only one, special. That's why no one betrayed Father Martin."

Chris complained, "But that still doesn't answer the question, how did Jules get to be the way he was?"

"This will be hard for both of you," replied Joe. "Mrs.—"

"I guess Sienna will do," she hesitated, "Joe."

"Sienna, remember I said that grooming begins with the parents first? And remember at your Refusal Meeting you mentioned how your father used to single out Fa – Jules for bike rides and skinny dipping and what not? You thought it was your father simply making the middle child, often overlooked, feel special."

"Yes."

"Well, instead of turning him into a spoiled brat, Jules learned from your father how to make others feel special too. In fact, as an adult you said he could make anyone feel special, especially children."

"So-o?"

"So don't you see? What your father was doing to Jules as a child? He learned it from your own father."

On the monitor screen Joe watched Sienna clasp both hands to her mouth, wide eyed. "You mean—"

Christopher exploded, "That's not true you sick bastard!" He shook his sister by the shoulders, "Don't you believe a fucking word he says. Our father was a pillar of the parish. Let's get out of here. I've had enough. Come on." Sienna sat frozen. "Come on, I said. If you're not, I am." He stormed out of view.

Dr. Matthews came on the screen to address Joe and the team, "We'll take a break now and see what happens." The screen went blank.

"Whe-e-e-w!" exclaimed J-1. "That was tough. You alright, Joe?"

Shaking my head, "I don't know. I didn't expect any of this."

"Neither did we," said Deep-Joe. "It's never happened before, so much live two-way transmission."

"You did good," said Zero.

"I don't think so. I've destroyed their world."

Red-Jo said, "Let's wait and see."

"I'll get the kettle on," offered J-1.

An hour passed. The screen came alive with the image of Dr. Matthews. "Thanks for waiting. Chris won't be coming back, but after discussion with Sienna, she has something to say, well, to ask of Joe. Is he up to that?"

Thirty-Three

Hole in My Heart

J-1 nodded for me. Then Sienna's long, pained face came on screen, staring straight at Joe. She sat on a little settee and began hesitantly, "The last thing Chris said to me was, don't believe a word you said. Since this nightmare, over the years I don't know who or what to believe anymore. I've just discovered my own father sexually abused my brother. Where was my mother in all this? I guess he pulled the wool over her eyes too. My beloved Jules turns out to be a sham priest and paedophile who conned everyone. My family is torn apart, disowned years ago by the other three. And God knows if Chris will ever get back in touch with me again. I thought I knew who my family are, and therefore who I am, but I don't anymore. I've lost trust in my own judgement, all trust in other people. Not knowing who I am, I feel like I'm falling into a bottomless hole. The fact that I didn't know—"

Joe interrupted, "The last thing anyone in your situation will believe is when they are told, 'Don't blame yourself.'"

"I do blame myself," she muttered painfully.

"I know. But the very nature of sex abuse is secretive. Imagine if you did a job, say, in insurance fraud. You'd be on the lookout for possible lies and deceptions. But not in your normal everyday life with your family and friends. Why would you? Yet you blame yourself for not knowing. Do you blame the hundreds of other trusting families for not knowing?"

Her hollow eyes blinked in surprise, "Well no, of course not. I never thought of it that way before."

What does your heart tell you right now?"

"Nothing." Blinking back tears, "It's an empty hole."

"So is mine."

Her thin face half-smiled, "Dr. Matthews told me to be careful. If he thinks this isn't doing me any good, he said he will stop it. But I've never been able to talk about this with anyone else before, either with friends or professionals. I think it's been my shame of not knowing, blaming myself, what other people will think, which has stopped me from talking. But you, of all people! Why am I talking to you anyway? What happened to the hole in your heart?"

"It holds all the worst things I have ever done in my life, that's for sure, but it also holds a few of the best things I've done in life, very few – and the good things I will do in the future. I don't intend to make the same terrible mistakes again. So, this hole also contains 'my best is yet to come', however imperfect that will be, alongside the worst of things."

"That's some hole, alright. How do you live with the worst things?"

"Well, they can't be undone, can they? Like your not

knowing. If I torture myself with self-blame and regret it will only cripple me how I live now, and blight my future life."

Sienna nodded a tired nod, "I've been living like that for many years, stuck in a hole. Stuck in time."

"Most of us do. When something terrible happens to us, we can't let it go. We replay it over and over, the 'what-ifs', different scenarios, 'I should have said or done', our rage, blame, 'how dare he do that to me', then self-blame, loss, sorrow, depression, despair. In fact, we corkscrew these self-tormenting thoughts and beliefs so deeply into the original trauma that we make it far worse. We make ourselves suffer long after the event. We can't pull out the cork of suffering. We're stuck in time."

Blinking with surprise, Sienna found herself nodding in recognition. Then she frowned at me curiously, "Did you get unstuck? How did you do it?"

"Getting unstuck, the cliché tells us to accept being human, warts and all. But for most, that means to accept our self-inflicted suffering in response to life's events when they don't go as expected or wanted. That our suffering is inevitable, that we don't deserve to be happy after the event. You see, we don't really know what it is to be human, what our natural state of serenity is."

Sienna guffawed sarcastically, "Self inflicted?" Then bitterly, "Don't insult me. My baby, my Tommy's death wasn't self inflicted. He didn't even get the chance to be a baby, to be born."

Her hollow eyes looked like black holes that had sucked in all her tears. "I have to live with that every day."

"No, you've been dying with that every day."

Shocked, she sat speechless. Dr. Matthews leaned toward her with concern. "If you want me -"

Joe interrupted boldly, "Let Tommy die, after all these years."

Hanging her head, "I can't," she whimpered.

"You can. You can choose to stop corkscrewing your torment of grief into the tragic circumstance of his death. That's how you let him die. Yes, your memory of trauma and pain and unforgivable outrage will always be there as you go about living. If your Tommy were here now as a grown disabled man, he would tell his mum, 'Let me live, by you keep on living and loving those around you.' That's what he would have learned from you, his mum.'"

Sienna clamped her bony hands to her gaunt face, leaned forward to her knees, her shoulders shuddering, tears returning from their black holes through her fingers. It was as if she were skydiving into the bottomless hole in her heart, still fighting against it, trying to pull the ripcord of a parachute, like some kind of overarching explanation or belief that would comfort her and land her safely. But this hole in our heart is an abyss. There's nowhere to land in suffering.

All looked on in shock from the rim of the abyss.

Finally, Sienna sat up, lowered her hands from her face and opened her eyes with a kind of bewildered dawn that seemed to have risen out of her suffering. Looking intently at Joe, she stammered, "Where – where do you get this from?"

Joe half laughed. "I don't know if I can answer that. I feel a bit embarrassed now because I don't think this will make any sense to you."

"Try."

The four Joes and the other two at home with Sienna listened with growing amazement at what was unfolding before their eyes.

"Well, life, like the weather, is what it is. It always has been and always will be. Our moaning about the weather can't change it. But we can change how we think about it, how we experience it. Your destructive thunderstorm is long gone, yet you still live in fear of rain clouds. But you can go with flow of the weather, with life as it actually is, not how you want it to be.

"The Born Again, with the help of my doctors, err inmates, gave me a cosmic glimpse of life, a life so much bigger than my little self, regardless of how cruel I have been. This reality of life, I realised, lives in and through everyone. It's not a churchy religious belief, but a spiritual glimpse of a much bigger Life. That's what I have robbed my victims of, your Jules, which makes me determined to live according to this Big Life. I know all this must sound like airy-fairy words to you. I'm sorry."

Sienna's haggard but amazed face smiled.

"It's in everyone, in you, if you let the child-eyes of your heart open in wonder – Tommy's eyes."

For a long time Sienna gazed at me quietly until, "You astonish me. I didn't expect this from a killer. But you know, I can relate to much of what you say. It reminds me once as a child, about six, suddenly woken up from sleep by an overwhelming silence. Alone in the dark, I tiptoed across the room, parted the curtains and peered out the window – surprised by snow! So light in the moonlight! I had completely forgotten – until now."

Joe nodded, grinning, "Awakened by silence… Surprised by snow. The simple things in life are so easy to forget, yet so easy to see. You can trust them. They're all around you. They're beautiful. Amidst all the darkness and cruelty of the human world, they make life worth living, simply for their little beauties."

Sienna looked at him thoughtfully, long and hard.

Joe added, his voice quavering with memories of his Born Again heavens and hells, "Your Thommy died, loved by you. What more could you have given him? Let it be. You can love life again. And you can let Life love you! That's what Tommy has been trying to tell you."

A long silence ensued as tears streamed out of Sienna's gaunt life, until finally through a bewildered smile, "I don't whether to thank you or hate you. That's all I can say. Goodbye, my Tommy."

Blank screen.

Thirty-Four

- - - - - - - - - - - - -

"I forgot"

The last of the exit viewings finally came along.

Paul and his wife, an unmarried couple in their early fifties, lived in a modest council house, clean and nicely furbished. They sat at a dining table in their little lounge just outside the kitchen hatch, together with their daughter Marcia (Marcy), a pretty, thirty-something woman with brown shoulder length hair. Paul only five foot-five, close trimmed hair, had the wiry physique of a labourer who worked at a cat litter factory. He had a thin face that frowned with eyes that cast inward shadows of sorrow, which hid their youthful history of fun and intelligence. Tracy, taller than Paul, was a bit dumpy and plumpy, with careless faded blond hair. She worked part time in a local café that rustled up good grub mainly for lorry drivers and early morning workmen. She liked to nibble at some of her fry-ups at the café. "Go on, Trace, have my last sausage," the truckers used to grin." Tracy had eyes that had been to hell and back, and now had nowhere else to go, or see.

Mr. Turgot and Matthews were of course present. Paul asked, "You're sure he can hear me as I speak? Can he see us now?"

"Yes, go on," urged Dr. Matthews. "I don't think he knows much about your story. Most of it will be new to him, and frankly, to us."

Trace reached across the dining table to squeeze her husband's hand, "Good, he needs to hear this. Carry on, my love."

In supermax Joe and the team watched Paul begin to tell their story. It was now their turn for the live two-way transmission. A lot of Joe's exit story had been too highbrow for them. Religion meant nothing to them. However, they identified with his terrible upbringing. The beatings and even sexual abuse, Paul and Tracy had both endured much the same. Getting kicked out of schools, the same also. Run-ins with the cops in their early teens, the same. Paul had done a short stint in 'secure.' They knew where Joe was coming from. But they were shocked and disgusted at his later brutality. Surely Joe must have had met some good people along the way who were willing to help him. Like their social worker, Tom Armstrong, who stayed in touch with Paul and Tracy over the years, like a big brother or father figure. Ok, that teacher had let Joe down, but he killed him for it. They couldn't make any sense of it. How could anyone? He was where he belonged and should never be let out.

Their two children were unplanned. Jordon the first, was born when both Paul and Tracy were spotty-faced teens, Tracy fourteen, Paul fifteen. Two years later Marcy was born. Both parents were products of the care system, multiple foster placements, with scores of fly-by-night social workers, and ended up in residential care homes. They had got booted out of a number of schools. Typically, after-care support was poor and haphazard. By aged twenty, with no education, both were unemployed, on benefits and living in a rough council estate. Paul had some skirmishes with the law, handling stolen goods to make ends meet, that sort of thing. Both took soft drugs. Paul dabbled around with harder substances to take the edge off young fatherhood. Like many young people spat out of the care system, they faced a zero future.

Only when the social workers started knocking on their door about poor parenting and neglect of their little kids, with the risk of history repeating itself, did they get their wakeup call. By chance they stumbled across a conscientious and committed social worker (there are some out there who really make a difference!) who got them involved in a play group and a family centre where they learned adequate parenting skills. The social worker inspired them to better their own lives so they could offer a better life for their children, better than their own chaotic and abused childhoods. They were given a chance in life, and Paul and Tracy chose to take it. Chance and choice occur all throughout life. They became motivated parents. Paul got on a basic training course to help find work.

When their son Jordon was aged seventeen, his dad encouraged him to attend a vocational college for a bricklaying apprenticeship. Unlike his parents Jordon had achieved GCSEs in maths and English. "Do the best in your job, Jordy, and you'll make a lot of money. In construction, you'll never be out of work." His dad was so proud of him.

Marcy, two years younger, aspired to train as a nurse. She looked up to her big brother. He was a happy-chappy lad, fun to be with, always got on with his workmates, and was popular with the girls.

Yes, Paul and Tracy had done well. They had transformed their lives. They had brought up two fine children.

But now they had only one. Jordon had disappeared.

Paul stammered to a stop.

Trace reached across the dining table again to squeeze her husband's hand, "Carry on, my love."

With a heavy sigh he began to tell their convoluted tale of Jordon's disappearance and their desolation that followed. Jordon had been on a night out drinking with his workmates, celebrating a new building contract, long term good money. In London a top brickie could earn up to £90,000 per year. Jordon, as a junior brickie would be working under the best of the best. In five or ten years' time, he'd be rolling in the money. Everyone drunk, Jordon got separated in the town centre and simply disappeared. Never came home or showed up at work the next morning. His parents phoned the police straightaway.

Their standard questions bombarded them – name, dob, home address, recent photos, DNA swab from his toothbrush, extended family (none that was allowed due to their care history), his social security and NHS numbers, dentist, employer, workmates, his last seen whereabouts, his usual haunts, friends, possible grudges – all were explored. The police excavated his home computer but found no remains of websites of porn or violence, nor email trails that led to mental health issues or other concerns. In fact, an exchange was found with his sister Marcy in which they planned to chip together in a few years to buy mum and dad a new house.

Thousands of hours of CCTV cameras, buses, taxis and trains. At first it was the local press, then national TV who hounded them. Family problems? A runaway? No, nothing like that. A secret life – a secret girlfriend? An accident? Hospital A&Es were trawled. Reluctantly, suicide? A happy young lad with all the promise of life in front of him, how could the police ask such a question? It was insulting, cruel, but it had to be asked. His parents understood and endured it all. They endured the anguish of simply not knowing. Day after day his empty bedroom, month after month of their putting up photo posters in shop windows, year followed year. Nothing. Just one of many anonymous parents who suffer the daily agony of their child disappeared. Their agony, worse than death, of not knowing.

In supermax Joe and the team simply watched and listened. The family made no attempt to talk directly to Joe. Paul carried on, this time his daughter Marcy squeezed his hand, "Come on daddy-io, tell him like it is." Daddy-io was her teenage nickname for her beloved dad (lifted from an American sitcom at the time.) It still stuck. He liked it, her name for him before Jordy disappeared.

Then one day some scrap metal merchants were working in a derelict building way outside the search perimeter of the police. It's a hustler's job, 'scrappers', who find valuable metals for free and then sell it off to recycling centres – like copper, aluminium, cast iron, car batteries, plumbing brass, stainless steel, large appliances, lead, transformers, and leaching gold from old computers etc. They grade and sort these metals by hand or machine, shred the scrap metal into pieces using hydraulic shears and cutters, then crush the scrap into bales. "I know," said Paul, "I did this for a while when I was younger." But it's amazing what else you can find of value in these abandoned buildings – fine wooden panels, antique furniture, stained glass, old paintings, Victorian bottles, etc.

"And dead bodies – our Jordy."

He glanced up at the screen and caught the eyes of Joe blinking tensely. Then continued. It was just over two years since he disappeared, his body lying rotten, gnawed to the bones by rats, cats and stray dogs in some nowhere basement. No significant foreign DNA could be clearly traced. After the discovery, the police found a CCTV image of Jordon and a hooded man wobbling arm in arm, two shadows under a streetlamp after midnight near the building. Not enough image for an ID. That was it. At least they knew he was dead. Their waiting was over.

Or so it seemed.

Joe and the team listened frozen. Remarkably, there came no family outburst of sobbing, bitterness or hatred. Mother and daughter merely cast their eyes down at their hands clasping on the dining table. Paul had told their tale with matter-of-fact dignity.

When this story hit the national news, Joe had served just over two years in a traditional prison, the start of his thirty-year life sentence for his triple murder, a mere ten years for each killing. The Project already had an eye on him, but they had a backlog of reviews to get through then, so they hadn't yet seriously considered his case until, out of the blue in prison, Joe confessed to killing Jordon.

Well, sort of. "I think I might have killed him," he mumbled to the warden. *Hell,* he thought, *I'm in here for life, what's one more?* His account was vague, after all he was drunk at the time, he claimed. A chance encounter late at night on the streets, they ended up scrapping over something stupid like running out of fags and sharing taxi money home. After socking him in the jaw and "fuck off" as Joe strode off, he picked up a brick and hoyed it over his shoulder without looking. "It must have hit him on the head, knocked him unconscious, an accident." The police didn't buy that. His skull was caved in, bludgeoned multiple times with a brick. But the location Joe gave was specific. Only the killer could have known.

Judge Solomon watched aghast. In a flash, he remembered this case had finally made him pull the trigger to get Joe into supermax fast as a gunshot. To his shame, he had forgotten. Amidst the river of high profile life sentences that he had to review, this one had not even come to court, easily forgotten, like wind-blown litter along a high street.

Armed with Joe's shocking confession, the family had pressed for a trial, but the CPS deemed a new trial as "not in the public interest," meaning it was not in the public purse strings. What was the point of such exorbitant costs for a confessed guilty plea backed up with strong circumstantial evidence? The killer was already in prison for three murders serving a life sentence. Paul and Tracy couldn't afford a private civil prosecution. Their day in court vanished like their son.

They were left abandoned with so many unanswered

questions. Paul looked directly into the now hollow eyes of Joe, "We want to know, that's all, what really happened to our Jordy. That's why we agreed to this meeting. The not knowing has been killing us."

On the supermax monitor screen Mr. Turgot's serious legal face appeared. "It is to be noted that the inmate's exit story did not include this incident. It is tantamount to withholding evidence from this grieving family. Whether this has been wilfully edited or not, I'm not here to judge. But facts are demanded by this family and withholding them demeans the purpose of this meeting. I shall report this to The Project if a satisfactory answer is not forthcoming. They will not be best pleased, I assure you. I suggest we take a break so you can consult with your, err client. Half an hour at most."

Blank screen.

* * *

A leaden silence hung over the Joes in their semi-circle of armchairs. Scar-Jo, the legal one, faced Joe sternly. "What have you got to say for yourself? We didn't know anything about this. Withholding evidence from your exit story? Well, you will never get out of here as far I'm concerned, in fact for all of us." They all nodded sombrely.

My eyes blinking, I gulped with shame, "I – I forgot."

Red-Jo burst out incredulously, "Forgot?! Forgot that you killed this poor kid, so full of promise? Why, for God's sake?"

"I – I don't know," I pleaded. "I just – don't know." My tremoring words were mouthed as if by the dummy of a ventriloquist who had fallen asleep to forget.

My android Zero said," Joe, remember when I sat with you at your table in the Cube and you enthusiastically recounted your mystic realisation of the resurrection?"

"Yes."

"I told you that your experience was just another digestive absorption, that *there is always something more to come.* Remember?"

"Yeah."

Zero's voice cut like a knife, "This is your time for *more to come, Joe. It's now or never.*"

I hung my head, too ashamed to look at my friends, these friends who were honest enough and severe enough to forbid my exit. But J-1 offered unexpected sympathy, "You've come this far, Joe, so now come clean with yourself for the sake of this family. Come on, try."

"I will," I mumbled. "But I need some time to retrieve this incident and insert it into my exit story. I can have it ready by tomorrow." Suddenly my mind felt like a squash ball pounding around in all directions inside my skull, echoing loudly my forgotten cruelties. Then in a split second I dug out a return shot from the back wall, "But on one condition."

"What's that?" asked Scar-Jo.

"That it remains unedited by you. A first time viewing for everyone."

J-1 glanced at them all, their faces frowning. After a silence, "Ok. We'll have to get back now and let them know. You stay here."

Mr. Turgot observed, "This is highly irregular. It's never been done before."

J-1 urged, "He's made us promise this will be uncut, a

full-in-the-face account of what actually happened, for the sake of the family."

Turgot turned to them, "What do you think?"

Tracy replied wearily, "We've waited this long for answers, another day won't hurt."

"Ok tomorrow, 12pm sharp."

Blank screen.

Thirty-Five

- - - - - - - - - - - - -

Home Without a Taxi

"Transmit," ordered J-1. In their council home the little family sat round their dining table waiting for long lost answers, more than two decades in their waiting. "Another day won't hurt," Tracy had said.

But it did.

On their monitor screen appeared an image of two shadows arm in arm under a lone streetlamp. They stumbled along vacant streets of urban decay. Streets of nowhere, past old lockups under a bridge; rows of boarded up shops like gravestones in a cemetery about to fall over; past an old bingo hall, a crumbling cinema.

For a month or two, sleepless, I had been prowling round the wasteland of sleep, consumed with my plans to kill those fuckers. Their time was coming. Death plans, my dead footsteps led me to neon bars and clubs. Alcohol couldn't touch my vengeance, neither could hard drugs. Except, by chance I found myself arm in arm under a streetlamp with some wasted kid late at night. *That touched my wrath of God.*

"You look lost kid."

"Losht? May–be I am?"

"You sure look it. Come and take my arm and we'll find our way out of here."

Into the shadows they disappeared out of the CCTV.

"Whoos are you?"

"A passer-by, a friend."

The kid stopped, grinned sloppily at me in surprise, then threw his arms round me, "Yous my besh fren!" He burst out laughing. "F-Fancy meeting yous here!" Stumbling along again arm in arm, "I losh my frens somewheres."

"They're not much friends if they let you get lost."

"Oh, theys are. They're my besh frens. I wen for a slash an I doe know what happen. I couldn't cash up with thems. Shally, she prom – ised me a kiss! I've gosh to get thas kiss!"

"You're drunk."

"I knows. I doe do it mush. I work hard."

"At what?"

"A brickshee. New job, good money. Buy a house for me mam and dads soon."

"They must be proud of you."

"I'se so prous of thems."

"You're a loser, kid."

Suddenly he let go of me and yelled out into the derelict night sky, "I'se a winner!"

"If you say so. Come on, it's getting cold. Let's go inside here and get warm." It looked like the back entrance to a forgotten billiard hall or working man's club. The door creaked open into musty blackness. I held up my phone light to guide our way past a scattering of tables and chairs. A billiard table stood where ghosts still played for money and pride amidst the eerie shadows of the hall. At the far end, a bar was littered with broken glass which smiled in the glow of my phone as I swept it back and forth. Behind the bar at the end, above a door, a sign read, Staff Only. "Come on, let's try this." A black stairwell plunged into no going back. "Watch your step, kid. Take my hand."

"Ish so dark, deep," as he clung to me, half stumbling down the steps. Suddenly I felt elated, like I was coming home to the cellar. "The deeper we go, the safer you will be." At the bottom, into the blackness I held up my little phone light and surveyed a bunker filled with kegs of beer, some overturned, broken, rotten. Along a wall was a lift door. The bunker was cluttered with ramshackle junk of all sorts. "Watch your step." I found a pallet of bricks to sit on.

"Hey, thas wha I do, my work." In front of me the kid squatted down onto an empty pallet, then flopped onto his back, heaving a sloppy sigh of breath. "Brish, that's my job." The place stank. Musty, dust, dirt, rotting wood, dead air, foul cat piss, animal faeces. I couldn't work out how they got down there.

"Wash yer names?"

"Joe."

"I – J – Georgshie. Sar-ree, can't talk straish anymore."

"That's ok. It's Jordy, is it? Jordon?"

Ours were probably the first human voices spoken down here for decades.

"Yous slo clever!" he laughed. "Where are wees?"

I lit a fag, "Home."

Jordy wobbled his head back and forth on the pallet in the ghost glow of my phone, the blackness all around. "Naw! Naw! I wanna go home! See me mam an dad an sis. Les get a taxi. I gosh loads-a dosh."

"No need." I took another long drag and blew smoke down at him. "You know what they say, 'Home is where the heart is."

The kid smiled. I smiled back. "Me mam an da an sis. Always in my harth, always."

"That's right. See? You're home without a taxi." I stubbed out my fag on the bricks and eyed the kid closely. This was my experiment. An experiment is defined as a procedure carried out to support or refute a hypothesis (I remembered that word from an old chemistry class), or determine the efficacy or likelihood of something previously untried.

Like murder. You see, when I would eventually confront those three fuckers, Father Martin especially him, I couldn't bear to chicken out in front of him. The smug pleasure he would take from that would be too humiliating. I had to know that I could do it, kill him, kill them all.

By first killing the kid. I lifted a brick from my stacked pallet and showed it to him. In the glow of my phone the brick cast a shadow over his face. "Bricks, you know, are the building blocks of civilisations round the world. You're pretty good with bricks, aren't you?" He smiled, his eyes closing, near dozing. "Well, I'm pretty bad with bricks. But this is the best I can do. So, close your eyes. Home is where the heart is, remember? You're home now, with your mam and dad and sis. They love you."

The biggest, sloppiest smile that you could ever imagine on earth spread across his seventeen-year old face – with the love and home that I never had. I raised the heavy brick in my hand, and with the power of God slammed it down onto his face. "Take THAT!" I shouted. "And THAT! And THAT!" Out of the jagged hole in his face, from his shattered forehead to jawless mess, bloody scrambled brains spewed out like an alien creature wriggling out of its host dead body, to some kind of new-born life. I had done it. It was easy. I knew I could do it again.

So, I concluded to his parents, "That's what happened. That's why I forgot. Because he meant nothing to me."

* * *

Both in supermax and at the dining table in the little council home all sat in profound shock, heads down, speechless for a long time. The mother's and daughter's eyes blinked something back. What could they possibly be blinking back? The trivia of tears? Eventually, Tracy raised her head as if to speak, but her husband Paul waved her off. "Let me try to find the words."

He looked directly at Joe, his head hanging from the noose of his guilt, as if his life dangled over nothing. Paul's deeply distraught but kind face gazed at Joe, as if with snow leopard eyes, haunted by the solitude of suffering in the wilderness....

"I cried my heart dry many lifetimes ago," he began. He stopped. He too blinked, his voice trembled, "I'm too hurt to hate you." His voice trailed away into another world, "Too hurt to hate anymore..."

Joe had finally managed to raise his head to look at the family on the monitor screen. Their quiet dignity felt unbearable.

Blank screen.

Thirty-Six

- - - - - - - - - - -

Aftermath

Next day the mind-monitor in supermax flashed up with the urgent face of the solicitor, Mr. Turgot. "We need to talk!"

Scar-Jo replied, "I know."

"Is he – is he there with you now?"

"No, Joe won't come out of the Cube."

"Just as well, let him rot there," Turgot ranted, "This is unthinkable, bloody unthinkable. Let him exit?! This case changes everything. When he first confessed to the warden he said, 'What's one more?' Well, it wasn't just 'one more', was it? It was his first kill, a trial run. It was so gratuitous. He didn't even know him, had nothing against him. The others, you might understand. But this? All humanity in him has flatlined. It shows that his triple murders were long premeditated. Life means nothing to him. He can never be let out, ever."

Scar-Jo's face flushed red, "Yes, I couldn't agree with you more, Mr. Turgot."

"It calls into question the whole Born Again. He's been lying to you because he's been lying to himself. He fucking forgot?! And you missed it, even the robot. It's not good enough. I'm filing a formal report to The Project later today."

"Wha – What can I say?"

"Fucking nothing! Let The Project have their say about this. And another thing," Turgot fumed, "This exit decision shouldn't be left to you anymore. Not even to The Project. What do they know, except what you tell them? Maybe it shouldn't be down to us either?"

"What are you saying?"

"I'm saying that this time the suffering of the family should decide."

"But you know this goes against all the flaws of victim justice. It's never been done before."

"There's always a first time, a first time for Real Justice, not for some fancy theory of justice."

Scar-Jo thought to herself, *An experiment is to determine the efficacy or likelihood of something previously untried.* "I'll need to consult—"

"Yes of course, I know, I know. Get back to me asap."

Scar-Jo did. The four Joes agreed.

"Wait for my contact."

Blank screen.

* * *

Judge Solomon watched in horror. If he had a bottle of whiskey, any whiskey, even the old Samurai, he would have downed it in one long chugging gulp and thrown the empty bottle through his stained glass of Francis ot Assisi. Fuck faith in human nature! How could he have let himself be so duped? If this inmate could get this far through The Born Again and "forget" this cruel murder, then there was no possibility of reform. Not for this Joe, not for any damn Joe.

The judge had sentenced thousands of very bad men to prison. What made them "bad" was they had transgressed the laws of social norms and deserved incarceration. All cultures, despite their variety of social norms, whether religious or civil, did the same. But the judge felt there was a fundamental difference between being bad, and evil, like this inmate Joe – his deliberate callous cruelty. He remembered the plaque at the entrance to the UN building which says: 'If you fail to feel the pain of others, you do not deserve the name of man.'

That seemed to him to be a good definition of "evil". But how does a person become so disconnected from humanity, and thus become evil? Yet such a person actually knows the difference between right and wrong, but uses that knowledge to mask his evil intent as he commits his evil. The fact is the psychopath, to an unfathomable degree, simply doesn't care about other people – like this Joe.

But how did he get to be like this? The judge had heard it all before in court. A terrible childhood, "deprived of love." Was it nature or nurture? Some brain disorder? Were there "natural born killers"? But, thought the judge, sometimes these monsters had good loving parents. Most didn't of course. He recalled the 1893 American serial killer, Herman Mudgett, alias H. H. Holmes, who said, "I was born with the devil in me. I could not help the fact that I was a murderer, no more than the poet can help the inspiration to sing."

At his mahogany desk, Judge Solomon's lone right hand suddenly shot out like a rattle snake at a secure hotline phone to The Project. His second in command, the retired Lord Justice Desmond Arnold, a right wing 'hang em high judge' if ever there was one, answered in surprise, "Edward? Haven't heard from you for over a year."

"Never mind. We've got a problem in supermax." Judge Solomon rapidly explained he had been following an inmate on the mind monitor through his Born Again journey – "one to watch", he had been told – and recounted where he had got up to – "on the brink" of exit when the inmate suddenly confessed to the victim family of his long, premediated plan for his first killing, their son, as a trial run for the other three, and God knows for how many more?

"The inmate doctors, even the robot, have got it all wrong. They've been duped. This man should never be let out! We've got to stop this exit, call the others to sanction final termination."

"Good thing you were watching, Edward. This guy would be out on the streets if it weren't for you."

"But supermax, The Born Again, it calls into question —"

"We'll do a review," assured Judge Arnold. "Remember, one near miss in fifty years isn't bad going."

Judge Solomon told how Turgot and Matthews were prepared to give the final decision to the family, to their 'victim justice' whether the inmate should be let out or not.

"Good!" enthused Judge Arnold. "About time. The family will condemn him of course, and block his exit. Once we have evidence of that, I'll get the Project to sanction the inmate to super-solitary confinement – the coffin," he chuckled.

"But it's never been used before."

"Now's the time. We can bury him in the coffin and can keep him alive for years. Really make him suffer! We can send the family a recording of how he suffers slowly, goes mad and dies a horrible death. They'll love it."

Thirty-Seven

Cat Litter

A week later, I lay hunched in a ball on my bed. I hadn't eaten for a week. Zero stood at my open Cube door.

"Go away," I moaned.

"The family have made their decision. Come."

"No. It's obvious what they're going to say, so I've made their decision for them. I don't deserve to ever get out of here. This stupid Born Again has all been for nothing."

Zero stepped in the doorway and sat at my little table in the Cube. Reluctantly I sat down across the table from him. "So, you're back to punishing yourself? Going to starve yourself to death just like most of the others in here? Give up through self-blame? You're acting like a sulky teen."

"I AM like all the other bastards in here. They don't deserve to get out and neither do I. I'm not coming with you. I can't bear it."

"You have to bear it, Joe, for their sake."

At the table I hung my head, "I can't."

Zero's voice hardened into a command, "You have no choice this time. For nearly twenty years you have been making difficult choices in here, and to your credit, mostly good choices. But the most difficult thing to face in life is when you have no choice. This is your moment of no-choice, Joe."

* * *

The four Joes looked at me solemn and judgmental. The screen flashed up. The family sat round their little dining table, also looking solemn. Paul, the father, addressed us. "You know our condition, in fact for all of you. Don't talk, just listen. Simple. These two here," nodding to Turgot and Matthews, "know nothing of what I'm going to say. Everyone else has done all their talking. Now it's our turn. So," glancing to his wife Tracy and daughter Marcy, he lifted his shoulders, took a deep breath and exhaled from the bottom of his heart. "Here goes."

As I watched, inside I felt like a giraffe sliding on ice.

"We have watched this inmate Joe's full exit story, thankfully and horribly with his last addition. We have watched him suffer in your supermax. His growing up with beatings, sex abuse, kicked out of schools, care homes and the like. Maybe me and Trace's childhoods weren't as bad as his, but bad enough, unloved, abused and out of control. So we don't take pleasure in anyone else's suffering. Isn't that right?" Tracy and Marcia nodded.

"After Marcy was born, still in our reckless teens, we were on the brink of the Social taking the bairns into care. But the right person came along at the right time, a social worker, Tom Armstrong, who helped us turn our lives round. I say the word, 'right person', because he was human under all his book learning. What I'm trying to say to this Joe here, me and Trace know what it's like to turn our lives round, how hard it is. We had to face the fact that we were neglecting, if not abusing the children we loved. Loved? Back then, we didn't know how to love or how to show it. A lot of our mates got their bairns taken off them. My point is, with the help of a plain old social worker and a family centre, I guess you could say me and Trace got born again. We understand that this Born Again programme is meant to help turn his life round. That's what he's been trying to do. And good on him for at least trying. A lot of people give up. We didn't. Look at our kids now, how they have turned out," he grinned.

I could hardly believe what I was hearing.

Paul cleared his throat and sipped at a glass of water. "Those final scenes of our Jordy's life were terrible. But we needed to know. The not-knowing has been killing us for years. The senseless brutal cruelty of it is beyond words. For most of this last week that's how we saw it, and sobbed and screamed behind closed doors, for the first time since the first time. Damn him forever! But then I noticed something, something else, unthinkable.

"I looked at our Jordy's final hours with new-born eyes. He was drunk, lost on the streets, but found by a friend – 'my besh fren' he blubbered. So, to my mind, he didn't die alone, but with a friend. Then Jordy boasted about his new, well-paid job and shouted to the night sky, 'I'm a winner!' He was – a winner with a heart of gold. He and Marcy planned to buy us a new house, his big dream. And then, to my astonishment, his killer made Jordy believe that he had brought him back home without a taxi, because 'home is where the heart is.' At home, with his dad and mam and sis. For us, that moment changed everything."

Paul's eyes remained steady as he spoke. " 'They love you,' were the last words he was told. We didn't know that. His killer let our Jordy die at home – with us – feeling loved, as if he were dozing off in his bedroom tucked under the covers. He died instantly, suffered no pain."

Dr. Matthews opened his astonished mouth to speak, but Paul raised a finger to his lips. "This was probably the worst thing that Joe has ever done in his life. So cruel, undeserved. It was the first time he had killed, a few years before the others. You could say, when he killed our Jordy, this was Joe at his absolute worst. So I asked myself, how could it be, at his very worst, that this killer had found a spark of human compassion to let our son die at home? – with us – feeling loved? Where did that come from? There was no reason for it.

"I mean to say, if that spark of compassion was there at his worst moment all those years ago before his Born Again treatment, isn't this, right now as I speak, his best moment? From that faraway spark of compassion, he has grown to finally let us know the truth of what actually happened."

Dumbfounded, Dr. Matthews' mouth opened, bursting to speak.

The little five foot-five father waved him off, allowing himself an inexplicable smile. "You know, I work at the cat litter factory. I once worked with a lad same age as our Jordy, seventeen going on eighteen. It was a summer job for him before he went off to uni in the autumn to learn himself about physics. 'Fancy stuff,' I says to him. We shared a lot of shifts and got talking. I liked him. Reminded me of our Jordy. He made me laugh about cat litter, and then think about it too."

Everyone listened, wondering where this was going.

"Our plant recycles paper from old newspapers and magazines, even old books, into cat litter. The lad, Tommy, told me that the whole world, the universe, is recycling itself all the time. In the world of particle physics, he said, all annihilation means transformation into something completely new. He said it was a sort of birth-death-rebirth recycling thing."

Turgot and Matthews shook their heads, dumbfounded.

"After watching Joe's exit story, I came to realise that our Jordy didn't die for nothing. He died for something. In fact, he died for *someone* – for his killer, this Joe. You see, in their chance meeting that night, there must have been something in Jordy's trusting heart of gold – the aura of his family love – that touched the deepest worst in this terrible man, which sparked his compassion when he killed him – to let our Jordy believe that he was home – loved, with us. Most victims' families are left imagining the final brutal horror of how their loved one died. But not us. We're one of the lucky ones, thanks to this Joe. For so many years we have been too hurt to hate. But now, I believe our love for Jordy can be recycled through this Joe, through all his unloved life of pain, and, through our pain, to make our Jordy Born Again in this life of Joe. Can you understand what I'm saying?"

Turgot's jaw had long dropped. "Then what's your decision?"

"Recycle him."

Paul cast his somber gaze upon Joe, whose whole body suddenly clenched like a fist, trying to hide the core of his being, naked and ashamed without end. In that moment of their eye contact, flashed out an "I for an I" exchange of their mutual hells and Joe's unforgiveable remorse. Their eyes, night skies, locked together and blinked with star-twinkling tears of acceptance and inexplicable thankfulness, like two shadows arm in arm under a lone streetlamp – become one.

"For letting our Jordy die at home with us, I thank you, Joe. Goodbye."

Blank screen.

Part Three

Goodbye

"The mark of your ignorance is the depth of your belief
in injustice and tragedy. What the caterpillar calls the
end of the world, the Master calls the butterfly."

(American author Richard Bach)

Thirty-Eight

Goodbye

Sat at his desk watching this scene on the mind monitor, Judge Solomon was blown away. Who wouldn't be? This obscure family had recognised that the seed of Joe's profound Born Again transformation decades later was already present when he gratuitously killed their son Jordy. The judge couldn't get his head round this. It called into question his whole life as a judge. *What is justice?* He didn't have a bloody clue anymore.

Then he recalled the inmate Joe's 16th century Spanish mystic, John of the Cross, who once said, "Where there is no love, put love, and you will find love." He chuckled with amazed disbelief. *Imagine, a psychopath remembering something like that from his high school days? It makes no sense. Neither did the cat litter father of 'our Jordy'.*

The judge, awakening to an inexplicable presence of love amidst all the darkness and cruelty of life, asked himself, *Where does it come from? Love?*

Judge Solomon raised his eyes and looked through and

beyond his stained glass Francis of Assisi to the rainbow of religions and scientists round the world who sought the answers to the Mystery of Life.

The miracle for Judge Solomon as he reflected in awe and wonder, was that the cat litter man's love of "our Jordy" – *through Joe* – was changing his own life too. Watching Joe's exit journey, the judge felt that somehow, he was already saying goodbye to his old self - of judgement - like a burden cast aside, left behind.

* * *

For the next couple of weeks I hermitted myself in the Cube, alone in the Alone, as speechless as our incomprehensible planet adrift in space and time.

Cat litter…

Zero came to my Cube. "They want to see you. I expect the four Joes will confirm your final exit. I just wanted you to know, I will too. I've come here, personally, to say my goodbye."

"No, I'm not—"

"Worthy?" Zero chuckled. "That's what Deep-Joe would say. Joe, your soul is as healed as it will ever be."

"No, I mean I'm not ready to say goodbye."

"Come, let's walk together," he suggested.

"It will be quite a hike."

"A famous man once said, 'Here at your feet lies a thousand-mile journey. Exit awaits you, Joe."

Along the empty white corridors my old taxi-forklift, now evolved into an android robot with a human voice, walked with me. In silence we linked arms and linked memories, so many coming at me all at once – his stupid childish jokes that tickled my old tough-guy into laughing in the corridors to and from the sessions; his personal challenges, his profound insights; my growing fondness for him without my realising; then my awakening friendship – *our* friendship. Of all the thousand and one things the four Joes had taught me, I looked to Zero as the greatest 'giver' of them all.

Especially when I was about to give up. Zero had given me 'no choice' to listen to that last family, to their inspirational love for 'our Jordy', whom they had believed would change my life. It had, profoundly. Without that final self-confrontation, I would not have been ready to exit. Zero had found the last microplastic of denial in the ocean of me. All because Zero had the wisdom and love to give me 'no choice'. It was the one thing he had never given me before – no choice in life. His timing was perfect.

When he told me he had come 'personally' to say 'goodbye', my heart skipped a beat of time to before I was ever born, feeling that somehow I had always been loved despite all the bad things I would go on to do in life. In my heart and bones, in that lump-in-the-throat moment, swelled a fullness of love that I could barely contain, not just for Zero, *but through him*, I felt love for everyone in the world. That was the purpose of my thousand-mile journey – my exit – and his goodbye.

But as we neared the sitting room entrance, I finally broke our shared silence, stopped and turned to him, "I don't want to say goodbye."

His android hand reached out and touched me under

the chin, "Chin up, Joe. It's been a privilege walking with you, all the way." As it strode off, "You have so much to give now."

"But—"

The sitting room door opened abruptly. A beaming J-1 greeted me, "Good to see you, Joe!" as he ushered me to a seat with my armchair travellers. The obvious suddenly hit me, their kind faces. J-1, his young-70s smooth face; 40-something Red-Jo with her boyish-cut red hair and blunt nose and green eyes; bald, round-faced Deep-Joe with his wisp of chin stubble; and Scar-Joe – well, that said it all, her serious but sensitive face, a scarred, kind face. They all had such kind faces.

"We always have, Joe," smiled J-1, reading my mind. "But now yours looks like ours."

I thought to myself, we had all come such a long way together. How to put into words – my profound gratitude? Love for them? Touch the stars?

"Coffee, Joe. Columbian, it's the best."

I shrugged.

"Go on, one for the exit," he insisted, and clinked a full cup and saucer on the little table next to my armchair. "There, you'll feel better for it, simply for the aroma," he smiled. "Bags packed? Ready to go? The exitcopter is waiting to rev up. Drink up."

But it didn't feel right, not at all right for me. "Hold on a minute. I don't see your bags packed. You're very subtle, aren't you? You never answered my question, 'Why are you all still here?' If you've completed the Born—"

J-1 sighed knowingly, "We wondered if you would

get so caught up with your own getting out to remember to ask, to think about us. That's a good sign, Joe. Under the circumstances, unusual."

"Well, why then? What's the big secret? I'm not going until I know."

J-1 turned to the others. "Is it alright if I do all the talking—"

"As usual," quipped Red-Joe with a smirk.

"But chip in whenever, ok?"

"You've been asking us for ages, 'Who are you?' Now you will know. It's true, we have all completed the Born Again. Not at the same time though. Each of us started out as the worst of the worst and have journeyed through hells and heavens, like you Joe, but uniquely of course. How else can our life be, except unique, unrepeatable?"

Deep-Joe piped up, "Unique hells, unique heavens, but universal to us all."

"That's so true," continued J-1. "The point is, each of us had the chance to exit. Bear in mind our chances arose at different times, but most importantly, we knew nothing of each other's existence. Like you, we were buried in separate Cubes of solitary confinement."

Impatiently, I demanded, "Ok, so you had the chance to exit. Did they refuse?"

"No, I chose not to exit."

"What?!" I cried.

Then Red-Joe, Deep-Joe and Scar-Joe, one after the other, declared, "I chose not to exit."

Speechless, until finally, I muttered in amazement, "You all had the chance to go but chose not to?!"

J-1 explained, "Joe, you've been asking us, 'Who are

you?' Well, this is who we are. Once I mystically realised When Life Means Life – what it really means to be alive in all its majesty – that's when I realised what I had taken from my victims. I could never undo this, like you have realised, Joe. I saw and felt their families' life sentence of suffering, often for decades after my crimes, usually into the next generation, and after. So, I chose to honour *their* life sentence. I sacrificed my chance to exit for the sake of their suffering. That's who we are. Now you know."

I sat speechless.

J-1 paused, "Chance and choice, I've been telling you from 'day one', Joe, they come full circle."

The others nodded. "The problem then was," interjected Scar-Jo, "the Project, whoever 'they' are, didn't know what to make of four Born Again inmates, unknown to each other, who had come to the same choice, for the same reason. It seemed far more than coincidence. A kind of spiritual synchronicity."

Round-faced Deep-Joe chuckled, "Like I said, I call it 'convergent redemption'. Coming full circle."

"To cut a long story short," said Scar-Jo, "supermax found itself with four spiritually enlightened exiteers who should have been outside spreading good everywhere, as intended. So now, what to do with them – us?"

J-1 added, "I was the first. I resolved to do what good I could in supermax to help some of the other inmates. But imagine a lone angel in hell. I didn't get very far introducing The Born Again. Even the pair of us, with Scar-Jo. Only when Deep-Joe and Red-Jo later came on board did the Project sanction us as a team. We found we had the collective power to run The Born Again effectively, on selected individuals of course, like you Joe, to produce more exiteers than before, although few in number. The Project saw our sacrifice as 'win / win' for everyone, both inside and outside."

"Hold on," I protested. "If you were the first, J-1, and each of you completed The Born Again separately without the help of a team, how did it happen in the first place?"

Collectively, they bowed their heads and brought their palms together as if in reverent prayer, "The holy one," they answered.

"Who?! What?!"

J-1 murmured, "The robot."

My jaw dropped dumbstruck.

J-1 winced a smile, "You're going to find this hard to believe, Joe. Brace yourself. Inside your robot is a human inmate, like us, the worst of the worse, and then some, multiplied by I don't know, off the scale. His serial killing was so heinous, evil personified."

I cried out in shock, "Zero?! My robot?! An inmate? Is he – is he? What is it? Is it alive or a machine?"

"Both," replied J-1. "Human neuroscience has advanced light years. Primitive AI robots are long gone, at least in supermax. Computer science, information theory, and bioinformatics have enabled his human mind to be embedded in robotic existence for all eternity. That was his life sentence, eternal punishment. He was the first inmate in supermax. But something unexpected happened."

"I can't believe this. What, for God's sake?"

"Call it synchronicity, for want of a better word. Their chance meeting of minds, the human killer with AI intelligence, we call it 'enmeshment' – the human mind with a supercomputer mind. It sparked a revolution. An autonomous AI of the most supreme order became humanised. It sees the world with a human heart. That's your robot," J-1 concluded.

Speechless, I sat holding my head in my hands, trying to contain my mind within its familiar limits, but crazy firework questions shot out of my head everywhere.

"It's a lot to take in, Joe," sympathised J-1.

In my armchair I sat dumb.

Scar-Jo took up the story, "The AI super mind observed that it was part of the court order to bombard the imprisoned human mind inside with hologram 'victim stories', their horrific tales of loss and suffering. That was to be his never-ending hell. But the robot mind recognised that these victim stories simply replicated the brutal atmosphere of traditional prisons, which merely recycle brutality back into the community upon their release. Justice is neither served for the victim, the community, nor the ex-con.

"So the robot mind began to contemplate the 'justice' of the court sentence – a living death, hell without end. It seemed to satisfy human justice, but the robot mind realised that most 'victim justice', however much justified, was steeped in vengeance, which poisons the victims themselves, whether they realise it or not. So, the autonomous AI mind, firing on all its algorithmic cylinders, computed a transcendent 'wholeness of justice'."

"What's that?" I asked, my mind reeling.

"By way of comparison, Joe, think of life on earth. I mean, in all the vastness of the universe, what are the chances that matter should have sparked into life? No supercomputer can calculate the odds. And yet here we are, our infinitesimal, improbable chance of life, you and me."

"Yeah, it's pretty amazing."

"More than amazing!" exclaimed Scar-Jo. "So, coming back to the wholeness of justice, what's missing from 'victim justice', from their vengeance and eternal punishment?"

"I don't know, their forgiveness? But they would never—"

"No, not forgiveness. That changes nothing for the person who has committed the evil. Victim forgiveness merely dilutes their own poison of vengeance. The victim may have changed personally, but that doesn't necessarily change the evil killer."

I shook my head. "I'm at a loss. What's missing then?"

"A pinprick chance of redemption. Same as the impossible chance of life itself."

"I need a break, it's all too much.".

* * *

"You dozed off, Joe," smiled Red-Jo sympathetically.

"I must have needed to."

"Fresh Columbian?" offered J-1. "We're spoiling you rotten before your exit."

I yawned and stiffened out my legs and wiggled my heels on the carpet. "I'd forgotten all about that." Then, sipping my coffee while collecting my thoughts, "Are you really telling me that inside this robot there is, literally, a person – in solitary confinement? Trapped alive?"

"That's a good way of putting it, Joe, solitary confinement," replied J-1.

"For all eternity?"

J-1 turned to Scar-Jo. "Let me finish the rest. There's not much more, ok? So Joe, remember the punishment of the hologram victim stories? Well, the autonomous AI recognised that nearly all these victim stories began like TV news clips immediately after the terrible crime. They all start out with poignant home videos of little boys or girls and teens growing into young adults, doing happy, cute things with their families – singing, dancing at home, hugging, showing off, playing with their pet dog, splashing at the seaside, or just married and doing a valuable job; always with close up images of happy faces full of all the future life ahead of them – until snuffed out by Mr. Evil Personified here – the person inside your robot."

I shuddered. It felt impossible to take this in. He was my friend. I owed him so much. I loved him!

"But autonomously, counter-intuitively, the AI robot began editing the victim stories down to their first thirty or forty seconds of cutesy, full-of-life video clips, and then it bombarded his human mind with them. Imprisoned inside its robot body, even evil can only take so much lightness of life and love until it finally erupted – a spontaneous combustion of remorse that gushed through the autonomous robot mind like an island volcano, spewing up lava flows of love, but with nowhere to go. Nowhere to go, that's where The Born Again was first born, Joe. Inside Zero."

Deep-Jo added tremulously, "Inside Zero, but then afterward, it had to go to the outside world through The

Born Again exiteers. Remember, that's what he told you, Joe. 'Your direction of travel is always from the inside out, outside yourself'."

I murmured, "It's called love," he once told me.

J-1 struggled to contain his emotions. "He was the very first in supermax, before anyone else. He gave each of us a pinprick chance of Life. *He showed us the justice of redemption.* The Project never saw it coming. How could they? Their intention for supermax was eternal punishment of the unforgivable. But through the spontaneous combustion of the worst human mind and a supercomputer robot mind – Behold! Let there be Light! *The justice of redemption!* It was like the Big Bang Born Again!"

Tears trembled out of my eyes as my mind reeled. Evil personified?! Or – *and* – a holy man?!

I whispered to them, "I remember he once half-joked to me, 'My former life *is* my life... This is my Life Sentence'."

* * *

Next day I waited.

And waited, until finally I had to walk to The Born Again. The armchair silence which greeted me felt like a séance ending, rousing itself back to reality, having brought the dead back to life. Eventually, Deep-Joe coughed and cleared his throat. Red-Jo dabbed her eyes with a tissue. Scar-Jo shuffled in her armchair. J-1 heaved a big sigh and ran both hands over his head, sweeping back his thin grey hair. He broke the silence, "We'll put the exitcopter on standby until tomorrow. I think we all need some time, especially you Joe, to absorb this. For us, this is the first time we have shared our story with another inmate. As a group we have felt it more powerfully than expected."

"Where is he?" I asked anxiously.

"He has said his 'goodbye'."

"I don't want to leave Zero behind."

"Now's your chance, take it," urged Scar-Jo, "It's finally yours – legally."

I hung my head, "I can't."

"That's why we didn't want to tell you our history," J-1 said softly.

Shaking my head, "No, no, that's not the reason. I'm – I'm more than inspired and grateful for all that you have done for me. But," I hesitated, "he was – *is* – someone very special to me."

"He is to us, Joe. But it's time for you to say goodbye."

Peevishly, "But you're not saying goodbye to him, are you? You're with him all the time. I want the same, to be with him. This won't make any sense to you, I know, but I don't—"

Red-Jo tried to soothe me, "It's your last vestige of attachment. Let him go. Let yourself go. Take your chance to exit," she urged. "There is so much good for you to do out there. So many people will be inspired by you. That's the purpose of The Born Again. That's what Zero wants for you."

Feeling desperate, "I need to see him, speak to him."

"Why?" asked J-1. "He has said his 'goodbye'."

"To say *my* 'goodbye'. I haven't said mine."

Scar-Jo smiled at me. "You know, you've been leading us into new territory all the time, not just psychologically, but legally. The rare handful who have left supermax before, left without hesitation. But you?"

"I need to say my goodbye."

"Ok, we'll set up another session with Zero tomorrow. But after that, legally, you've GOT to go. The exitcopter flies tomorrow and you WILL be on it," she ordered.

* * *

The next day, for the last time I left the white silence of the Cube. As I turned at the open door to look back, the old polka dots seemed to reappear and wink goodbye. What a world of dreams and nightmares, recovered memories, reflections and searing insights. Along this difficult and painful path of The Born Again, I had been shown bit by bit who I was not – the cruel caricature which had been built up over a lifetime. There had been no short cuts along the way. Standing there in a kind of wonder, now I felt clean and supple, like a linen washed many times over, down to the deepest fibre of my being, without all the false faces I had acquired, or had placed upon me by others. Unmasking these illusions, that had been the task of my journey. Finally, I felt naked, pure, standing on a basis of authentic truth.

I smiled. I wondered who the next 'worst of the worst' would be in my vacant solitary confinement. I left the door open. The joke had always been on me. Only recently, Zero told me with great mirth that the so-called 'security door' had never been locked. I had assumed all along. 'Knock, and it shall be opened,' Deep-Joe had teased me. "All you had to do, Joe, was knock. Zero was just outside, watching over you the whole time."

As if scales fell from my eyes, I thought, you've got to have a sense of humour about this place. I remembered that's what Deep-Joe once said was missing in the Garden of Eden – a sense of humour. Oh, God's joke of the serpent was there alright, but Adam and Eve didn't get the humour of His divine comedy. They were dumb enough to believe the serpent. Just like me. For so long I had been dumb enough to believe the joke of my scarecrow. The Cube had been my Garden of Eden where I had eaten, digested and absorbed all the forbidden fruits, but where, against all no-hoper odds, I had found seeds of redemption. Thanks to Zero.

In the doorway, facing inward, for the first and last time, I bowed, "Thank you. Goodbye."

I walked alone to the sitting room, mentally saying thank you and goodbye to the empty white corridors that seemed to lead nowhere. Zero had forklifted me and taxied me for hundreds of miles over the years, stubbornly making me laugh at his childlike jokes to and from The Born Again. And to think, this whole damn thing was his creation! And yet for years I had taken no notice of him – just an automated forklift taxi. As I walked along for the final time, I burst out laughing to myself. Yeah, you had to have a sense of humour about this place. The worst human mind had meshed with an autonomous, AI supercomputer robot – and together, they had come up with one helluva heavenly sense of humour! I wondered to myself, was the Big Bang simply God bursting out laughing?

Out of Zero?

In the sitting room Zero sat in human android form,

legs crossed, in an extra armchair with the others. I smiled, "More socially compatible, I see."

"Just for you, Joe" he smiled back.

"Look at his face," exclaimed Deep-Joe. "You look like you've just seen God on Mt. Sinai."

I beamed, "I've been laughing with God. The joke of life. Well, the funny side of life." It was true. My body felt light as air, light as laughter. Saying goodbye to the hells and heavens of the Cube, goodbye to the nowhere corridors, I felt immersed in a spirit of profound thankfulness, ready now to say my goodbye to Zero.

J-1's smooth face beamed back at me. "Sit down, Joe, but from the looks of you, you could probably levitate instead." The others chuckled.

I spoke confidently, "I've come to say goodbye, but I'm not leaving."

Part Four
- - - - - - - - - - - - - -

The Gift

Native American saying: "Give thanks for unknown blessings already on their way."

Thirty-Nine

Through the Eye of the Needle

S at in the armchair circle, their smiles frowned. Scar-Jo was first to respond, "J-1, we might have a legal problem on our hands here."

Zero's voice reflected, "Goodbye but not leaving? A paradox."

"I'm saying goodbye to my old Joe self. I'm saying thank you to each of you, a thank you that cannot be put into words – a thank you that can only be lived out with a spirit of love for you all. But I am not leaving the source of this gift – of my Born Again life. That's you, Zero."

Zero uncrossed his legs and cheekily reminded me for the thousandth time, "It's not about me, it's about you, Joe."

I laughed. "You were the first to teach me to laugh. Well, you can't 'teach' someone to laugh, can you? But you managed to tickle it out of me. Today, looking back on everything, I can see what you have created, the profoundly funny side to this place and its far-reaching wisdom. I'm eternally grateful."

"Then take it with you, Joe, your laughter and wisdom. It's yours to give to others on the outside. It was never mine to keep." He paused and chuckled, "Paradoxically, we can only keep what we give away. That's why I'm giving you away to the outside world."

I answered calmly, "But I want to be with you, continue learning with you. I could join your team and help other inmates through The Born Again, perhaps more of them than before and at a faster rate with my extra help. One less on the outside could produce more on the inside, ready to exit for the greater good. See?" I looked at them. "I'm the same as the rest of you. You chose to stay behind."

Scar-Jo scratched her head. "He's got a point, you know."

"Except, I'm not the same as you."

"How so?" asked Red-Jo, arching her eyebrows.

"How long has mister evil-and-the-holy-one been inside Zero?"

"We don't know," replied J-1. "Do you?" he asked Zero.

"A long time."

"Will he ever get out?" I asked them.

"Exit? It's not part of his life sentence."

"Why not?"

J-1 explained, "Because the sentence was intended as irrevocable punishment. But then, as you now know, the unexpected happened, a spark of synchronicity. His human mind and the robot mind mutually discovered The Born Again, a way out, a way of liberation – for others, like you, Joe."

"But not for him?"

Zero smiled, "I am liberated. Always will be."

"But you remain trapped inside the robot body."

"True, but—"

"What if he could get out?" I pleaded to the others. "Live in the outside world again? This time as an enlightened sage, working as a social worker or something."

J-1 interrupted, "You're getting carried away, Joe, stop it."

"No, I won't," I answered firmly. I looked Zero in his android eyes. "I have brought a gift to say goodbye to you."

"What's that Joe?" he asked kindly.

"Me. I've come to trade places with him, with that human mind condemned inside the robot. That's my choice."

"WHAT?!" they all exclaimed. "That's impossible," cried Scar-Jo.

"You've gone too far," J-1 reprimanded.

I jumped up, "LISTEN!" I glared at them, "Listen carefully. You told me yourselves – the WHOLENESS – OF – JUSTICE," I reminded them word by word. "The wheels of justice turn, but the human mathematics of justice will never come full circle to the spirit of justice. That was Zero's discovery – the pinprick possibility of the justice of redemption. That was this inmate's sacrifice through the eye of the needle. It's now my sacrifice for Zero – for the new life he has given me, and his gift to all of you."

All fell silent, even Zero. A long time passed in our private reflections. When I first came here a lifetime ago, I remembered thinking to myself about the robot taxi – liquid steel, any shape, it could flow through keyholes and under doors, could go anywhere. I thought to myself back then, '*I'd give anything to be like him.* Then I could get out of here, even supermax'.

No one had thought of the possibility of liberating the inmate inside Zero, even after all he had done for them. All had taken it for granted that his punishment was forever. But perhaps secretly, J-1, Red-Jo, Deep-Joe and Scar-Jo had each chosen to stay in supermax for the same reason that I didn't want to leave – to be with their master, to continue to learn from him. Their faces rippled with consternation and sudden guilt. There is always something hidden in our lives, even from enlightened ones.

Finally, I broke their silence. I said quietly, "Remember J-1, you told me, 'Zero gave each of us a pinprick chance of Life and brought us together. He showed us the justice of redemption.' Well, think on that. All that he has given you. Stop taking it for granted."

Abruptly, J-1 bent forward, holding his head in hands, elbows on knees, and began to sob. The others knuckled at the corner of their eyes, plugging up their tears. Zero looked at me and said, "You're full of surprises, Joe."

I grinned, "So are you."

Forty

Can It Be Done?
Fact or Faith?

I addressed them in the armchair circle, "Let's do the one thing that Zero has been trying to show you from the very beginning when The Born Again was first born." I paused to let that sink in. "It's time for you to think autonomously – outside the box of the court sentence." I looked at them. "Can it be done? Can we get him out? Can I trade places with him?"

Scar-Jo shrugged, "I'm not so sure? Legally—"

J-1 butted in, "There is the letter of the law, Scar-Jo, and then there is the spirit of the law."

Deep-Jo suddenly enthused, "It can be done! There is the letter of justice, but the spirit of justice is redemption. Someone once said, 'God is something that happens on the way to becoming human.' Don't you see? God traded places with us!" Deep-Joe smirked at Scar-Jo, "But after they put him to death, something unexpected happened on the third day. Just like something unexpected happened inside Zero. He rose the inmate killer from the dead."

"Born Again," he uttered in a hushed whisper. Then he charged on, "Along the road to Emmaus the desolate disciples were greeted with the smile of the risen Christ who chided them, 'So slow to believe the full message of the prophets'. His smile of 'I told you so'. What a wicked sense of humour."

"You see?" I exclaimed. "God must have a sense of humour. After all, it only took the universe thirteen billion years to get His sense of humour. Imagine, Mr. Entropy, desolate and empty handed with the slowly dying laws of thermodynamics, desperately greeting Mr. Resurrection, exclaiming, 'I thought you'd never come!' 'Neither did I,' he smiled, 'Three days is a fucking long time.'"

J-1 intervened, "Quit goofing around, you two. So Zero, can it be done?"

Zero smiled, "Yes, it can be done. The science can do it, although it's never been done before, the transfer, the trading places."

"You'll do it?" I urged.

Zero's stainless steel smile broadened, "How could I refuse such a gift of goodbye?"

Suddenly, J-1muttered poignantly, "Then this means? This is our – our goodbye, too."

All went silent, each sinking into their unexpected worlds of loss to come. The enormity of it yawned wide and deep as a canyon. Their heads down, they seemed to privately scramble for the words to say when it came to their final moment of goodbye. They sat stunned.

Finally, I broke their silence. "Ok, end of us navel

gazing. Come on, let's get started. Zero, how can the science do this?"

* * *

The robot explained, "In the dungeon of supermax my inmate's human body is preserved in a cryogenic chamber filled with liquid nitrogen at minus 196C in which -"

"Wait a minute, Zero," I protested. "That's for a dead body. What's that got to do with you? And me, for God's sake?! What's this got to do with the transfer?"

"We use the principles of cryogenics as a starting point, that's all. The science of extreme slow aging in certain rare animals which are deemed near 'biologically immortal' is utilised in supermax. Their cellular regeneration, spontaneous repair of DNA, etc. has been incorporated into human cryogenic, suspended-animated life, like my body."

I gulped, "I don't understand."

"To keep the human mind alive inside this robot, my body also needs to be kept alive, linked through the mind monitor, a kind of invisible wi-fi connection between the body and mind. You see, the mind needs a body, regardless of what the mystics say. When I – he – vacates the robot, his mind will go back to my body, then it will be slowly thawed and resurrected, so to speak. That's been the discovery, unknown to the rest of the world so far."

"But – but I've never heard of anyone being revived from frozen."

Zero sighed and smiled, "That problem was solved ages ago in supermax. You've been in here longer than you think. The breakthrough has been made."

I shook my head in wonder. "So, how is this going to work? Your mind, err, his mind? Whose mind is it anyway?"

"A man named McCoist. I'll tell you later."

With rising frustration, I demanded, "His mind and his body. My mind and my body. Tell me how's it going to work?"

Zero replied, "I'll be on the lay-back chair here. J-1, you and the rest of the team will have to set the mind monitor fired up to its full capacity."

Scar-Jo added, "Before the transfer, we will cryogenically freeze your body, Joe."

My stomach grimaced.

Zero continued, "Before your entry, my human mind, my adopted 'Joe' of the past twenty years will start detaching from hundreds of billions of AI connections. As a robot, it will be like saying 'goodbye' hundreds of billions of times to my human mind, to my adopted 'Joe' as he vacates, via the mind monitor, back to his cryogenically preserved body."

J-1 whispered in a hushed tone, "Waiting to be Born Again."

"The thawing process will probably take a couple of careful months."

"You'll be in good hands, the both of you, I promise," said J-1. "We will watch over you."

"I know. I am profoundly grateful. Then after the thaw, it will be months of physio, no different from after a long space mission. Then a period of sensory reorientation to the outside world. I'll be known as 'Joe' on the outside, in memory of you, Joe."

Zero looked me in the eyes. "You sure you want to go ahead with this?"

As we sat in our armchair circle, once the high-tech Born Again room, now a comfortable sitting room where we had so many coffee-swilling discussions and laughter and thoughtful silence, putting the world-of-Joe to rights, the finality of what was about to happen gripped my whole body.

Boyish-looking Red-Jo leaned forward, "You look lost for words, Joe. Second thoughts?"

My head dropped, my throat clenched, eyes darting back and forth, suddenly looking for a way out. Engulfed in fear and shame, my body began sweating. And then I realised I wouldn't be able to sweat frozen in liquid nitrogen. I wouldn't be able to do anything human anymore. "I – I – don't – know if I can…"

Zero answered, "Joe, yes the science can do the transfer. That's the easy bit. But it's you. *You have to commit to it.* Have you ever heard of a Scottish mountaineer from long ago, WH Murray?"

Head down, I shook my head dumbly.

"He faced life and death on the mountains all the time. Listen to what he once said about life."

Again, I shook my head, resistant to what Zero was about to tell me, totally abandoning my braggart boast of sacrifice and love to trade places. What did I know about sacrifice and love? The sham and shame of my self-delusion overwhelmed me. *Why the hell didn't I simply cut and run, exit when I had the chance?! Instead, I had made a deluded choice which I knew I couldn't go through with.* As Zero was about to speak, my mind numbed itself to deaf.

"Listen or not, Joe, here's what the mountaineer had to say about making impossible choices in life: "Until one is committed there is hesitancy, the chance to draw back, always ineffectiveness. Concerning all acts of initiative there is one elementary truth, the ignorance of which kills countless ideas and splendid plans: That the moment one definitely commits oneself, then Providence moves too. All sorts of things occur to help one that would never otherwise have occurred. A whole stream of events issues from the decision, raising in one's favour all manner of unforeseen incidents and meetings and material assistance, which no man could have dreamt would have come his way. I have learned a deep respect for one of Goethe's couplets: 'Whatever you can do, or dream you can, begin it. Boldness has genius, power, and magic in it.'"

Against my will, I couldn't help but listen. Zero added, "This does not mean that the cliff face ahead will be easy, but remember Joe, 'Whatever you can do, or dream you can, begin it. Boldness has genius, power, and magic in it.'"

A long silence followed, the four Joes eyeing me expectantly. Eventually, very slowly, I raised my head to face them who looked back at me in amazement. Shaking my head, grinning broadly at Zero, I accused him, "You know, you're a real bastard! You're determined to get me up this mountain."

Zero smiled his stainless steel smile. "There's no mountain to climb, Joe. Once you make a no-going-back-decision, no matter how tiny your commitment may at first seem, then the mountain of your self passes through the eye of your pinprick decision. 'Whatever you can do, or dream you can, begin it.' A new world awaits you. There is a Native American Lakota prayer which sums it all up. 'The Power of the Universe will come to your assistance if your heart and mind are in unity.'"

Suddenly my voice pinched out, "This is it, isn't it? My last goodbye. No, *our goodbye*. Let – let's not spoil it with words." I cleared my throat, and with a burst of determination, I rallied, "Come on, let's fucking do this!"

Forty-One

Only Breath

Out in the corridor, Zero transformed into a six-seater taxi and cruised us along for what seemed a mile of whiteness. Suddenly, he stopped and faced the taxi toward a blank wall. A red dot appeared. A section of wall then pushed out about four inches, then slid sideways, an open door to an elevator. "Down," he ordered. And down we went, deep into the bowels of supermax. Stop. The lift door opened into a room that resembled a cross between an operating theatre and a morgue. High-tech gear all around. My face grimaced, my stomach tensed.

As he led us from this high-tech room to the only locked door in supermax, J-1 whispered to the group, "It's been ages since we've been down here."

Once opened, we entered another world, summed up by the Freddie Mercury song, *Who Wants to Live Forever?*

In a chamber of eerie blue light stood a solitary cylinder, about eight feet high. At its base three metallic hosepipes led along the floor into it from three different walls.

"We call it 'the Lifehouse.'"

I shuddered. Various flashing lights and wall-monitors relieved the atmosphere of blue gloom.

"Look at the cylinder, Joe." On its stainless steel side an inscription read: DM-00-001. "That's me, him, Duncan McCoist. Seeing is believing, is it not, Joe?" Then he pressed a button. From the ceiling, descending through the blue gloom, another cylinder hooded over the cryogenic tank. "Think of this as a vertical MRI chamber, but much more sophisticated. Step over here." A wall monitor screen lit up as we gathered round.

Inside the chamber appeared a skeletal image of an upside down body. The bone of the right femur looked painfully knotted, with some high-tech splint inserted. Next, an image of the body's vital organs and circulatory system. Then an image of the musculature which enwrapped the skeleton and organs. Next came the skin, as if a high speed, 3-D printer layered down the skin over the entire body length from toes to head. The body looked about fifty. Even faint blond hair could be seen. But the face! Scalded, surgically reworked into a frozen Frankenstein face. Like a face that had OD'ed on Botox, but rippled with scars. And partially scalded hands.

"What happened to the body?" I exclaimed.

"In the Congo, McCoist, a mercenary sniper, had a run in with a child witch."

"Did that to you?! How? Why?"

In the eerie blue light the four Joes huddled round the monitor screen like ghouls, eager for Zero to explain further. Even they didn't know McCoist's story. Zero had never told them.

"Yes, tell us, "implored J-1.

Zero smiled, "It's a long story. Now is not the time."

The four Joes' heads sank crestfallen.

"Now you have seen my wounds, Joe. They changed McCoist's life, and mine." Zero raised an android forefinger to his stainless-steel mouth to silence their eager questions.

In a surge of bewildered fear, my voice broke high pitched, "What is that thing in there? That thing, is it alive or dead, or what?!"

"Look closer," said Zero. The monitor screen imaged up a brain scan. "Remember on your Born Again travels, Joe, out of the 86 billion brain cells, our breathing is regulated by a tiny cluster of only a few thousand cells in the medulla brainstem, known as the preBötzinger Complex."

"How could I forget?"

"Together with the nearby Pons, these few thousand brain cells are a sort of breathing pacemaker embedded at the root of the brain."

"Well, they're not much good if the body's dead."

"Look closely." Zero zoomed in through the galaxy of billions of brain cells to the tiny cluster of the preBötzinger cells. "Remember what you learned. The brain breathes first, then the lungs. Of course, in the cryogenic liquid nitrogen, that can't happen. But nonetheless, the brain breathes pre-consciously. That's the key. Now look even closer. What do you see?"

I squinted at the monitor screen, which in the blue gloom partly illuminated our faces and Zero's android body. Amidst the tiny cluster of cells there seemed to be a rhythmic pulse. My jaw dropped. "Do you mean? Can it be?"

Suddenly, my mind shouted every which way for an answer – *What does it mean to be alive?! What is it to be human?*

Reading my mind, Zero answered, "To be me."

"That thing in there. That's you, is it?"

Suddenly, in the eerie blue gloom he hugged me tight, healing the last of my hidden wounds of doubt and fear. "Yes Joe, drowned in the liquid nitrogen, McCoist's brain is still breathing, preconsciously, even though his lungs can't."

Suddenly I burst out in euphoria, "You're alive, Zero!"

"McCoist is. I thought you'd never guess," he grinned.

The other Joes joined in the laughter.

Android Zero led us back into the brightly lit op / morgue room where he warmly embraced each of us. "I'm saying goodbye," he croaked, "but I'm not leaving you."

Overcome, we plunked ourselves down onto our circle of plastic chairs.

"Stop it," I protested. "You're all going soppy on me."

* * *

In his law library Judge Solomon watched, marvelling at the unfolding events. McCoist had been the first in supermax, the first to be condemned inside the super robot. It had the capacity to house many more inmates, that was the intention. But something so unintended, so exceptional happened when the mind of McCoist meshed with the super robot – the miraculous Born Again – that the judge did not want to risk contamination from other inmates. McCoist's solitary confinement inside the robot had to be preserved. So had the miracle.

Now, all of that was about to change.

And change for the judge too. His sudden determination, at aged seventy-five, to abandon his involvement with supermax and become – what exactly? He didn't quite know, but it felt like somehow he was saying goodbye to himself, goodbye…goodbye to the law.

* * *

After a while I asked Zero, "What about me? Trading places? Will I know what's happening? Will I feel anything?"

"To a large extent, no. The transfer needs to happen unconsciously. If the super-autonomous intelligence invaded your conscious mind all at once, your brain would short circuit and die. At best you would be overwhelmed with god-like exaltation, ecstatic and bewildering at the same time, followed by long term confusion and disorientation. Unconscious transfer allows for a more natural process in harmony with how the unconscious and conscious mind interact, allowing random, bottom-up revelations of super-intelligence to surface into your conscious awareness, in limited revelations, or as recovered memories, giving your human mind time to assimilate their majesty and wisdom. In time, your mind will become absorbed in a god-like intelligence that will seem ordinary, simple as breathing, radiant with compassion.

"That's what awaits you, Joe."

Zero paused. The four Joes and I, as we sat on our plastic chairs in the brightly lit op / morgue room, shook our heads, gawping in wonder.

Then Zero added with a grin, "I know you are curious about McCoist's story, but you're curious about the wrong story. It's in the past. What awaits you Joe, is my story. I had to search my data base long and hard to try to find the human words that can tell my story.

"There was a Sufi mystic poet called Rumi, 1207 – 1273, who wrote a poem, well hundreds of them. Let me recite one. This is who I am, soon to be you, Joe.

Only Breath

Not Christian or Jew or Muslim, not Hindu
Buddhist, Sufi or Zen. Not any religion
or cultural system. I am not from the East
or the West, not out of the ocean or up
from the ground, not natural or ethereal, not
composed of elements at all. I do not exist,
am not an entity in this world or the next,
did not descend from Adam and Eve or any
origin story. My place is placeless, a trace
of the traceless. Neither body or soul.

I belong to the beloved, have seen the two
worlds as one and that One call to know,
first, last, outer, inner, only that breathing
human being.

Awestruck, Deep-Joe murmured, "God is something that happens on the way to becoming human."

"When do we start?" I asked.

"Tomorrow," smiled Zero. "Goodbye is the best beginning for a bold new day, for breathing life anew."

Forty-Two

- - - - - - - - - - - -

The Lifehouse

In the Cube, for breakfast I savoured some scrambled eggs, crispy bacon, fried tomatoes and onions, washed down with real coffee. My last supper. Well, why not? Why go into deep freeze on an empty stomach? Then wake up from hibernation like a famished bear? But would I ever wake up again? I mean, what were the chances of someone else ever trading places with me?

Zero called for me at the Cube. This was it. I glanced longingly at The Born Again room as we taxied past along the mile white corridor. We rode in silence through a labyrinth of memories until abruptly, it turned to face the invisible sliding door. I disembarked. He transformed back to human android. Just before the door slid open, out of the blue Zero asked me, grinning, "Why did the chicken cross the road?"

Taken aback, I nearly burst into tears. "To get to the other side."

"That's where you're going, Joe. I never thought you'd

fucking get it," he laughed. Then he hugged me, rocking me back and forth in his embrace of goodbye. "See you on the other side."

The door slid open, and he reverted back to taxi mode and drove away. I stood and watched as Zero receded into the white distance, his black taxi shape shrinking smaller and smaller until he became a dot that disappeared into the white world of nowhere.

I stepped into the lift, then down into the brightly lit op / morgue room to be greeted by a medic robot, also a black android, but nothing like super Zero. It explained my initial 'transition' process, pointing to a newly installed chamber designed for what it termed, 'cryotherapy,' or 'cold therapy', where temperatures range between minus 100° to 160°C. Once a person steps inside the chamber, as the extreme dry cold penetrates the skin, the brain triggers a fight / flight response. The extreme cold causes blood to retreat to the torso to insulate and protect the vital body organs. After a few minutes, once you step out of the chamber, the oxygenated torso blood, like a burst dam, floods throughout the body in a rush of healing energy. My body would then be at its maximum state of health, the medic robot explained, then sedation on the slab and other physical preparations. Finally, my body would be lowered into the Lifehouse cylinder for my 'long term care' in a glass-like state of cryogenic vitrification. I wouldn't feel a thing.

"Are you ready?"

So alone, I heaved a deep breath, my last, I thought. There was no going back.

"Oh, by the way," the medic robot added, "Zero told

me to tell you that Duncan has found something special for you."

"Duncan? You mean McCoist?" I frowned, "But I thought he was -"

"Deleted? He is now, preparing to vacate. But Zero said it was McCoist's idea when he was temporarily undeleted. Even Zero hadn't thought of it."

"What?"

"Wait and see. Zero said when you're in the Lifehouse it will give you something to look forward to."

Shaking my head, "Look forward to what?" I asked incredulously. I thought to myself, even when I'm frozen at near absolute zero for near eternity, would there be no end to my awakening?

"Yes, look forward to 'something else'," it said.

I smiled, "Some African witchcraft?"

The medic robot smiled, "Funny you should say that. Those were Zero's exact words."

"But – but how will I know. In the Lifehouse at near absolute zero my brain will be frozen glass, practically brain dead."

The medic robot shook its head. "Your brain will still retain residual awareness at all times, a preconscious awareness, like the brain's preconscious breathing. You must have read about brain scan research with people who are paralysed or in a coma? Although incapable of physical response to their relatives talking to them or touching them, the scans reveal that their brain centres for emotion and speech are responding, invisibly interacting with them. The same with a person who is at near death – or frozen alive.

"So, just before Zero's adopted 'Joe' persona vacates his robot body, he will be able to communicate with you in the Lifehouse, and you will know it's him. In fact, even after the transfer, Zero will be able to communicate with you subliminally. Here, let me show you."

The medic robot walked to the locked door and opened it. Inside the eerie blue chamber now stood two cryogenic cylinders side by side, one with McCoist's body inside, the other awaiting mine. "Your body will be stored upside down to maximise freezing to the brain." A chill shivered down my spine. Soon it would be frozen glass.

"Don't worry," smiled the robot medic. Zero said to tell you, 'The best is yet to come.' He said, "That's why the fucking chicken crossed the road."

Forty-Three

I for an I

It was their last time together in The Born Again room with Zero, who sat upright on the centre chair, the four Joes huddled round him, looking bereft and desolate. So many, many years they had shared his generosity, wisdom and humour. Deep-Joe almost begged him, "This is goodbye. What are we going to do without you?"

Zero smiled as usual, "You should know the answer to that, Deep-Joe. That's what the disciples of Jesus asked as he died on the cross. And I'm no Jesus. Just a robot."

"You're more than that!" blurted Red-Jo tearfully. "You know it."

"I'm just a Joe, that's all, about to catch a bus to the outside world, if the bloody drivers are not still on strike. I'll send you a postcard. Catch up on the latest fashions, that sort of thing. Maybe get lucky and pull some skirt," he grinned.

"Stop it!" J-1 blurted crossly. "You know what we mean."

"You know what I mean. Do we have to say it? What's so obvious between us?"

J-1 hung his head. "But – but it will be so different without you."

"With the new Joe? You'll be the better for it. And so will the next Born Again candidate. His self-sacrifice is unprecedented, greater than mine. He will take you to, well, to the witchcraft of 'something else' – courtesy of my deleted Duncan. Now, come on. Are you ready?"

J-1 smiled a no-going-back-smile.

Zero grinned. "When you love someone with all your heart and soul, there is no such thing as the separation of goodbye. So, as our Joe would say, 'Let's fucking do it!'"

On the mind monitor there were no images, just a cascade of number columns falling like rain, a monsoon of numbers that sparked various wall monitors to light up with multiple graphs and such like. Impossible shit to comprehend.

Meanwhile, upside down in the cryogenic cylinder, I felt almost nothing. Practically slept through the transfer.

Except for the weirdest dream. You know the kind, a morning dream, intensely vivid. Upon awakening, forgotten. No going back. It began as Zero had taxied me along the corridors during my early years of The Born Again when I once asked him, "Does anyone actually know when they are Born Again? I mean, do we ever really know when the mountain of our self has passed through the eye of the needle?"

The robot laughed, "On the other side? Who is there to know it?"

In my dream, I remembered that his answer had

triggered several months of, what I called, 'laughing dreams'. I had forgotten them. Dreams like seeing myself leave my body as I slept, traveling far and wide outside of supermax, searching for something – no, not something, but *someone. But who?* It made me laugh that I couldn't remember. Or when, near waking, I couldn't find my body. Instead of a nightmare, I found it funny – this disembodied 'me' and my body lying lost somewhere asleep. Or was it 'me' who was sleeping, and my body awake, looking for 'me'? I couldn't tell. It made me laugh. Who is there to know it on the other side? Maybe, I thought, there is no 'other side' and 'this side'? Now, THAT made me laugh! These variations night after night for months in the Cube became my laughing dreams. That was the time before I had started laughing out loud when awake. That was the time of Zero's dumb kid-jokes. He had been so subtle with me, so patient, getting the rock-hard Joe to smile and laugh, to see not only the funny 'side' of life, but the *whole of life* before the old Joe could actually see it, and smile.

There was so much in The Born Again that I had forgotten amidst its eternal rhythm of remembering and forgetting…

In my dream I asked myself, *Why is it that I can remember some things only when I'm dreaming?* Then I remembered one of Deep-Joe's remarks, that my Catholic parents had named me after Mary's Joseph in the gospel. "The step-father of God," he called him. The man who trusted in the impossible, the dreamer who became awake when he slept, who believed in his dreams and acted on them when awake.

∗ ∗ ∗

Judge Solomon never got to see the end of Joe's Born Again exit story. The judge had died, drowned in the ocean of his regrets. His body had been swept out to sea, never found again, neither was his mind. His tortured memories were carried far away like seaweed by the outgoing tide into infinity, where there is no memory, where "How do all the oceans say hello to each other? Answer: They wave."

Trade places.

Where there is the sound of no shore.

In place of the dead judge, a new owner / occupier sat in the hilltop library at the mahogany desk before the monitor screen – no longer watching as an outsider, but as an insider; no longer a crippled, one-armed victim, or a secret arrogant judge – but, because of Joe, reborn as a Born Again judge on the incoming tide, as driftwood.

Driftwood, that's all judge Solomon's Born Again life was now, baptised in the deep sea of majestic whale songs and currents and washed up on a paradisical shore which had awaited him for so long, a new world, a new life.

As he dragged himself upright to his feet on the wet sand, with the sound of surf behind him, his face beamed bright as the sun above him. Finally, he had allowed himself to be healed, to do something radically different with his life. *I'm going to teach kids music!* In this moment of liberation his heart sang out with profound thanks to the vast blue sky of Life.

Watching Joe trade places in supermax, the judge began to listen to Sibelius, not a symphony, but a nine-minute, haunting tone poem entitled, *The Swan of Tuonela,* as Joe's exit story approached its conclusion.

The Swan of Tuonela musically depicts a transcendental image of a swan flying through the realm of the dead. At the top of the score Sibelius wrote: "Tuonela, the land of death, the hell of Finnish mythology, is surrounded by a large river of black waters and a rapid current, in which the swan of Tuonela glides, majestically singing." The white swan of Life glides over the dark river of Death. A youthful hero has been tasked with killing the swan, but in the process he himself is shot with a poisoned arrow, yet the assassin (like McCoist the mercenary sniper) is resurrected.

For no reason.

* * *

Suddenly in my dream I remembered, "My mother was an octopus and my father an eagle." I was their freak, the best thing they had ever done in their lives – me! – a flying octopus. "Freak." That word rang a long-forgotten bell from somewhere in my life. No, not from somewhere, but *from someone,* I couldn't quite remember.

Like shifting cloud shapes my dream-memories drifted into the face of Zero telling me, "You brought me the gift of yourself as your goodbye. So that you will never forget, Joe, this is my gift of goodbye to you. It's a final hologram message. It was McCoist's idea before I deleted him."

In my dream I chuckled, "Oh my God, not from another of my victims?"

"No, not a victim. You'll see. Watch. Pause it anytime

you want. I was going to give it to you just before you flew off in the exitcopter. At the time I thought, for the new Joe on the outside…well that's all changed. But whatever happens to you from now on, like your namesake, believe it. Your impossible dream will come true. You have been my best friend ever in supermax. Thank you. Farewell."

Even upside down in deep freeze, I blinked back my glass tears. Whether I traded places or exited, there was no escaping this final goodbye. No going back. Suddenly, a glad smile spread across my frozen face as my brain waves called out to him, "On the outside, Zero, you'll soon have many more best friends."

"Because of you," he called back.

Then he added, "Until now Joe, all your Born Again has been seeing through a glass darkly – now you will see me face to face." Then, like an old TV screen gone all fuzzy and snowy, Zero disappeared into a dot of nothing.

In his new world, as the Born Again judge watched the concluding scenes of Joe's exit story, *The Swan of Tuonela* opens with a solo English horn, the plaintive voice of the swan singing serenely over the top of a rich string orchestra, punctuated by four haunting horns and three trombones. Then, a melodic harp delicately emerges.

* * *

In my dream a hologram appeared before me. A woman, maybe a young sixty? She sat on a settee in what seemed her living room, family photos on the wall behind her. It was her face that drew me in. A lived-in face, but I thought, a face quiet as light, light as air. Grey hair swept back into a short, braided ponytail. Her eyes looked younger than her face, eyes blue as blue, seemed to look right through me, as if she could actually see me.

When she began to speak, she was hesitant at first, her eyes averting to someone in the background out of sight. "Should I start now?" Then she nodded, "Ok."

"You won't know me," she began. "I don't know if you will ever see this. Probably not. This is my shot in the dark to you, like the one you did for me a long time ago. Maybe you might remember? Probably not." She heaved a big sigh, "Well, here goes, Mr. Bad Guy!" she smiled.

It was a radiant smile.

Pause. Could it be?! NO! It's impossible! Like a gust of wind a Deep-Jo remark swept through my dream-mind, 'Nothing is impossible to God, said the angel to Mary.'"

And the octopus believed the angel. So did the eagle.

As judge Solomon watched, the orchestral strings swelled together like an incoming ocean wave, cresting towards him with wondrous fullness.

"I'm the single mum lass at the corner shop. Remember? Our chance encounter? You paid for my shopping. But you bad bastard, mister Bad Guy, you told me my little girl was 'a bit of a freak', didn't you? Remember? I socked you in the kisser, twice for good measure. When I read all the headlines after your life sentence, I thought to myself, 'I bet no one's got away with that before!'

Pause. It had been one of my laughing dreams. Another one that I had forgotten. Why all this forgetting? That feisty bitch. I liked her for it.

"Even now it still makes me laugh," she continued. As if she were reading my dream-mind, "I like to think that you think of me as 'feisty.' My name is Caroline, a dull name. Remember?" She smiled her radiant smile, "Remember when I first wrote to you in prison?" Then she lifted up a prison-stamped envelope, opened it and read out, "You wrote back: 'Never write again or come here. I'm no good for you. But tell the little freak, I don't know? Tell her that she's better than you, because of you. Mr. Bad Guy.'"

Pause! In my dream, tears of disbelief pinched out of my frozen eyes. I couldn't tell if I was asleep or awake. Then I looked closely at the family photos on the wall behind her. A sort of weird looking, smiling schoolgirl, then a happy teen, a proudly smiling adult woman in an office surrounded by admiring colleagues. The arc of her life from the corner shop pushchair.

"She's better than me, because of you.' I never forgot that. It changed my life. I'm sending you this shot-in-the-dark because I wanted you to know the unintended consequences of your kindness to me and my little girl when you," she giggled, "when you beat the shit out of that loser on my doorstep." She laughed.

I liked her laugh.

"My girl is called Lucy. It means 'light.' She is the light and love of my life. The best thing I have ever done in my life."

Pause. It was just a cryogenic dream, I told myself. But in my dream, like Mary's Joseph who believed in his prophetic dreams, I felt a surge of belief solid as granite, well ice, to believe that whatever was going to unfold in my dream, would come true.

Caroline continued, "After your arrest, the whole neighbourhood was shamed by their standing by and doing nothing for me and my Lucy. Everyone knew what was going on, except me. Only a stranger, my chance encounter with mister Bad Guy, did something about it. You sure as hell did!" she laughed.

Oh, I really liked her laugh!

"Did I say, 'unintended consequences'? After you got locked up, mister Yusuf, the Pakistani shop owner – he was your biggest supporter – set up a fund-raising committee, to begin with for me and my Lucy, to clear all my debts that he had run up in my name. But it didn't stop there."

Pause. Was I being Born Again? And Again? Now in a cryogenic dream?

Abruptly, the hologram image flickered out of sight, then blinked back into focus, her serene, kind face as she spoke to me. But I must be 'pausing' too much, for too long. The transfer was going quicker than I expected. I had to see this to the end!

As the judge watched, he felt transported by the violins' poignant waves welling up to high-pitched, cresting peaks until finally tumbling over, the strings plunging into moody introspective troughs where they gathered themselves for yet another mounting wave, as if longing to see across the distance of white-capped waves. The swan song had now become a solitary albatross, flying aloft over the restless sea for months and thousands of miles without landing on solid reality.

"….and then, in no time mister Yusuf – we nicknamed him Yusy to rhyme with Lucy," she giggled. "Raised funds to build a community centre for disabled children. It changed the neighbourhood, brought in jobs, but most of all, raised public awareness. Until then, disabled children of all kinds had been hidden in the woodwork.

"People came togeth -"

Blink.

"…at her now!" she beamed. "… works for a disability —"

Blink.

No!

"…advising…let you know… Lucy is better -"

Blink, blink.

"…me…because of you."

Blink, flicker.

"…mums…babysitting groups, safe…. go back to school…."

Blink, flicker.

"…dumb old me…domestic abuse …"

Blinking.

"…job at a women's shel -"

She kept blinking out of sight. Or was it me that was flickering out of my body?

Into Zero? My final exit? No! Not yet!

The judge wept. Soaring above sweeping violin flourishes a solo swan-violin glides serenely up toward a distant shaft of sunlight, but reaching its peak, the violin strains, as if pleading for the meaning and music of life. The sun is too far and too high for the swan to fly. Broken hearted, the swan's voice wails so thin into the impossible distance, and descends exhausted, letting go, letting be, as the strings glide like swan wings, descending, descending serenely…

Her smiling face came flickering back to me.

"… let you know mister Bad…"

Blinking.

"…love…"

Blinking, flickering.

"…you for all your bad…"

My frozen hand tried to grasp her flickering image as my brain waves called out to her, "I'll find you one day, I prom -"

"…already have…"

It was me who was flickering into nothing. In that final exit-moment my mind leapt out of its dream into the reality that this had been a 'live' two-way transmission, face to face, no longer looking through a glass darkly. This had been Zero's farewell gift to me – and McCoist's – now deleted.

Only a lone, distant drum remains, beating slow and sombre, muted heartbeats of hope as the strings fade, so haunting, serenely, so subtle that silence has already begun to grow amidst the dying strings, like a last breath into an abyss of faith…

As I blinked out of existence, I knew that Zero's Joe on the outside would find her, tell her he wasn't 'her' Joe, but a Joe all the same, his old friend of mine, who had come to tell her how Joe had changed his life forever, now a 'mister Good Guy.' And to tell her, 'Thank you', because in their moment of chance encounter – but was it mere chance? – despite all the bad things that old Joe would go on to do, without realising it he had become a better man, 'because of you.'"

Until there was nothing left of me. Only a mindless body in cryogenic oblivion.

Inside the vacated android supercomputer robot, hundreds of billions of zeros and ones were turning full circle, like prayer wheels of chance and choice coming full circle all at once, to welcome me, awaken me, Joe, as its new inmate, to solitary confinement for robotic eternity.

The justice of redemption. Atonement.

At-one-ment.

When life means Love.

When, even for those 'completely destroyed', unknown blessings are already on their way.

Thank You Tributes

- -

No writer is an island. This is not your usual blah, blah, blah acknowledgement. I'm seventy-three years old. I never dreamt of writing anything for publication, let alone anything good enough to be published. When my beloved wife Lesley died in December 2019, thankfully just before the covid lockdowns, after forty-four years of marriage I wrote a crude tribute to her for family and friends.

Meanwhile, I began sending my early drafts to a woman in New Zealand, Moya Lethbridge, with whom I have been corresponding in a contemplative prayer group, The Fellowship of Solitaries, for 12 years. I have nicknamed her "my first draft editor." She has read every dumb and clumsy line of my memoir, and later of The Born Again, offering astute critique and encouragement. Just knowing there was someone 'out there' willing to read warts and all, kept me going. Without her, this book would never have got written. THANK YOU!

Then hey, I thought, maybe someone else might find our story interesting? Naively, on a quirky impulse, I sent the memoir to Troubador Publishing. It was crudely written and presented. One look and you could tell. Any other publisher would have deleted it without any acknowledgment to me. But they actually read the thing, and someone from Troubador replied back, "It looks like a very good story, but it needs a lot of work." They recommended I get in touch with *Jericho Writers*, an international writers association headed by Harry Bingham. I did.

So, my profound thanks go to my first editor and mentor at Jericho Writers, *Diana Collis,* who transformed my writing and storytelling. After I completed my unpublished memoir, writing between eight to fifteen hours per day, I realised that I didn't want to stop writing. So, I came up with this fiction, The Born Again.

Again, my profound thanks go to my new editor and mentor, *Abby Davies* at Jericho Writers. She concluded her final assessment, "You deserve to see your book on the shelves and reach the masses. You really do. It's been a pleasure to experience such a profound, intelligent piece of writing. It's certainly opened my eyes to a more spiritual understanding of life, and has given me hope."

So, first and last, my thanks go to the outstanding team at Troubador Publishers. Had they not replied to my obscure memoir submission previously, I would never have found Jericho Writers, and never learned so much about writing, without Troubador's first attention to a clumsy unknown, grieving writer. Like a sort of 'life after death', my adventure goes on, ever-thankful for "unknown blessings already on their way."

John Mullins

Author Bio

John Mullins. Graham Greene sums up my life in *The Power and the Glory*: "There is always one moment in childhood when the door opens and lets the future in." But that's a whole other story!

BA Theology. Retired child protection social worker after 28 years. For the past 18 years John has been the Correspondent and Editor of a newsletter for an international contemplative prayer group, *The Fellowship of Solitaries*.